Adventures of a Mystic Warrior

ROCCO ROBERT D'ORDINE

ISBN 978-0-9967549-0-3 (Paperback)
ISBN 978-0-9967549-2-7 (Hardcover)
ISBN 978-0-9967549-1-0 (eBook)

Written by Rocco Robert D'Ordine
Illustrations by Bryce Widom

First Printing Edition 2020

WWW.ADVENTURESOFAMYSTICWARRIOR.COM

WWW.ROCCOROBERTDORDINE.COM

WWW.DAYDREAMINGWITHANGELS.COM

I & Thou, my beloved

Choose to follow a path.

Trust your heart.

Trust your wits.

Trust your training.

Know yourself before trusting yourself.

THE GREAT BLUE SNAIL

THE BEGINNING

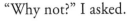

"OU CANNOT DO THIS in a conscious state," he said.

"Why not?" I asked.

"You are not ready."

I left it at that. How could I argue the point? He was a master mystic warrior. I was not.

I set about readying myself for what, lacking any better term, I called 'daydreaming.' Sometimes, I sat on the sofa in my living room to do this. At other times, I would lie down in a hammock in the backyard or sit on a camping chair in a grassy meadow in the mountains. Today, I was by Lake Isabelle, investigating a waterfall that had set off my mystic intuition. Nevertheless, it was all daydreaming to me. Theo, my mentor, had said it would be this way for many years as I trained.

"When will it change?" I asked.

"When you realize you are wide awake, maybe for the first time."

Readying myself was about following the protocols Theo had set down. I had a relationship with the Dream Talker – the angel who guides my nighttime excursions, a fair amount of practice exploring the invisible landscape, and hours of corrective POEM therapy. 'POEM' stood for 'Processing the Obstructions of the Everyday Mind,' an acronym I created after discovering how clearing my thinking filled my head with poetic thoughts pulsing between moments of quiet.

Once in an optimum state, I proceeded through the basic steps, floating through them like a butterfly dancing from flower to flower. Soon, I was in the deep well of forgetting, leaving an empty space for daydreaming to occur.

"Mystic daydreaming is different than what we know as everyday fantasizing," Theo told me. "It is not appropriate for fragile minds. Most importantly, mystic daydreaming is a necessary tool for encounters on the invisible landscape."

"Can I use it to win the lottery?" I asked flippantly.

"You are welcome to try, but you will find the cost is too dear, the sacrifice too great, the trade-off dire."

He didn't elaborate further, but it was a safe bet that his idea of 'dire' consequences was much worse than I could imagine.

Silence came quickly. Emptiness was right behind. Fully immersed, I reached total vacuity. That was when it all changed. It wasn't that the physical world disappeared; it was that it was overlaid by another world, one just as real. It was one of many levels of reality, and my years of preparation had given me a unique body with which to traverse it. I stood, leaving my 'physical' body behind, and tried to remember the Dream Talker's exact instructions.

"Travel along the trail leading past the Lake of the Lady. Follow the path until you reach Lake Isabelle. There, find a place of comfort and safety before transcending your physical form. Once you're ready, walk along the falls. When you get to the opposite side, climb down onto the ledge flanking the falls. Jump to the rock face. You will see two large boulders. Drop down to them. They are the twin angels of cosmic imagination assigned to guard the entrance. Step between them repeating, 'Stillness washes muddy waters' three times. Speak with a clear mind, a pure heart, and a strong will. A cave will become visible. It is magical. Do not be distracted by what you encounter. Its contents exist outside of normal time and space. Enter respectfully. Once your eyes adjust to the darkness, search for a small snail. If your timing is precise, he will appear by the entrance. His iridescent blue glow will guide you. As predicted, he returns every 100 years, just before the great flood. Follow him. Be patient. This will take as much time as you fear, and as little time as can be calculated. He will lead you to an ornate wooden box, impeccably carved. Open it. Inside, you will find a scroll with an ancient prophecy. It was written by the first, approved by the last, and followed by all mystic warriors in between."

The instructions worked as intended. I became slightly worried following the snail. It seemed to take a long time. I was aware that any errant concepts or feelings could express themselves as physical realities in my current state, so finding my way was as much a matter of attitude as the literal path I was taking.

Sure enough, the snail led me to the scroll. As I read it, my mind spoke to me as a character in the middle of an unknown story, far removed from my daily walks in the foothills of Boulder Valley.

The great flood is due, so it returns
To meet the fire cycle's burn.
Every 100 years, prophecy speaks
Of the land rebirthing the life it seeks.

How must this at last occur?
Find the Water Dragon's lair.
A mystic warrior it must be,
To search, to find, to set her free.

Comes in a dream, the request of old
'Find the cave' states the scroll.
'Follow the snail a mysterious blue
To hidden words that so hold true.'

Many an adventure will the hero brave,
If to prove worthy he dost crave.
The way of doubt, he must face;
The visionary landscape will set the pace.

Confidence in the mysteries must grow,
Enlisting companions is the way to go;
Togetherness will prove sincere
For, in others, faith holds life dear.

Freeing the dragon acknowledges the turn;
The land will remember and no longer burn.
When a seer is born in the land of light
Angels of Earth will complete his sight.

The prophecy was true. There could be no doubt. But was this *really* proof? Was it what I had been expecting to find? How had this scroll ended up buried deep inside a cave behind a waterfall? More questions wanted to sprint across my mind. I had to stop them.

I rolled up the scroll as gently as possible, not wishing to tear the paper. It was delicate and felt silky in my hands. Was it made from husks of corn? Perhaps, but it was softer and more pliable.

I looked closer. There was something about the lettering that wasn't quite right. It didn't resemble the writing of any culture I'd seen in museums. It was more stylized, like the work of Tibetan scribes. And what about the strange glyphs drawn around the edges? Those symbols looked ancient; any word warrior worth his salt would know that. I grabbed my camera and took a few pictures, making sure I captured the whole of the document.

Everything unfolded exactly as the Dream Talker had described.

I put my camera away and looked around for the snail. He was gone. I retraced my footsteps by following his slimy trail back to the main entrance.

My analyzer – that part of me that couldn't resist assessing and examining the logic of any situation – became obsessed with the scroll. Why was I being instructed to do something unheard of? Something unimaginable? As soon as I asked the question, a shadow of hidden fear cast doubt across my mind.

"This is preposterous," I said.

I pulled my camera out of my backpack and flipped through the pictures again. There they were, straightforward directions: Find and free the Water Dragon.

I couldn't believe it. I didn't want to. Dozens more questions flooded my mind, creating a log jam. I had to stop these thoughts from piling up, or my mind would burst.

Was I really considering following these instructions? I took a deep breath, repressing a shiver. Why me? Was this the next test in my training? Why wasn't it given to me by my mentor, Theo? He must know about this prophecy. After years of training, it should have come up at least once.

On my way down the mountain, I came up with ten good reasons *not* to accept this assignment. All ten were met with silence. I expected my wisdom guides to chime in, but they were absent. Why aren't they more attentive? Unlike my ceaseless chitter-chatter mind, or my exceedingly direct analyzer, the mysterious voices of my wisdom guides spoke little and replied less. When they did, it came out like a cryptogram, taking hours, sometimes days, to decipher. Why didn't they have something to say about my predicament?

"Where are you?" I pleaded. "I need your advice."

Nothing.

I wasn't overflowing with certainty by the time I made it home. I was exhausted from the mental gymnastics of the pros and cons battling it out in the thought arena of my mind.

"Dealing with internal disparities must come later in my training," I grumbled.

Since my wisdom guides were still a no-show, I tried to silence my mind. But Fear made another attempt to torture me. I would have none of it. I chased him away by using his vanity and pride against him. How? I conjured up a cartoonish image of a bleating, devilish goat, then I asked, "What is that, last century's Halloween costume?"

He skulked back into the shadow world on my backside where I couldn't see him, and he avoided me. Temporarily. A mutually agreed upon safety zone. For both of us.

"That was easy."

What does Theo say about Fear again?

"What a character, this being called 'Fear.' Don't buy into his intimidation tactics. Stay neutral. Become invisible by using the blind-eye trick."

"The blind-eye trick?"

"See Fear as you want to see him, not as he presents himself. Magicians use sleight of hand; mystics use sleight of eye. Use this technique and Fear departs. Let him locate the numerous compatriots who believe in his nonsense."

When I made it home, I performed my qigong movements until I felt like cool water in a slow-moving stream. Thoroughly liquefied, I ate some popcorn and read a bit of Marcus Aurelius' *Meditations*. After zipping through the day's events, I fell asleep as the pictures of the scroll became sheep grazing in the peaceful meadow where I go to meet my Dream Talker.

CHAPTER ONE

THE DELL OF FAERIES

HEO AND I WERE standing by the manmade canal along Niwot Trail. My quest was to walk until I found my way to the front door of the Dell of Faeries, but I didn't have to do it alone.

"You can ask the gnomes for help," Theo suggested.

"I don't know any gnomes."

"Ah, but you do," Theo responded.

I painted my face with the best look of confusion I could muster.

"Everybody knows gnomes. You remember how we met? My note on the golf course?"

"Of course," I said.

"Well, you didn't find that note on your own, did you?"

"I…" I paused, realizing the truth. "No. Someone moved my golf ball. *Three times!* A gnome did that?"

"You may not see them straight away, but gnomes are always here. They are attracted to mystic warriors. Once you acknowledge a gnome's presence, he becomes visible to your eyes of light. When you begin to see something with your eyes of light, your inside eyes, you will see more than ever before. Think of it this way. You see visible light. You take that for granted. You do not see ultraviolet or infrared light. But they always radiate. Apply the same analogy. What you see anew is always here; it's just that your vision becomes more…" he paused, closing his eyes for a moment as he searched for the right word. "Inclusive."

"How do I see gnomes with my inside eyes?"

"Empty your mind. Focus. Breathe rhythmically. Go to your center. Ground yourself. Then, wait for a gnome to appear," Theo explained.

"That's it?" I asked.

"That's it," he responded, closing his eyes again.

It took time to work through my usual setup ritual. I extended my awareness with eyes half-closed. Invisible cords stretched out from my torso, burrowing to the center of the Earth – grounding me in place. A gentle clarity gathered in my mind. My seeing became more fluid. Niwot Trail still ran alongside the canal, but my softened gaze acted like waves washing over a still picture. Images slowed, stopped momentarily, then were reanimated by more waves of perception. I waited, expecting nothing to happen.

Another wave crashed. Suddenly I saw him. He was archetypical. A genuine fairytale gnome; a squat, rotund figure wearing a red felt hat, gold-threaded vest, rope suspenders, woolen pants, and shoes that sparkled with gold dust. He walked toward me, stopped, and smiled shyly.

I smiled back. He was compact, but his presence was undeniable; a little like Theo. Theo could easily have had gnome heritage in his blood. Maybe a first cousin on his mother's side?

Theo's voice interrupted my whimsical speculation.

"Ask him his name, but don't say it out loud," he warned.

"His name is a password. A private calling card only to be spoken by you."

"What is your name?" I asked.

"This is my...Now, where did I put it?" the gnome said, feeling around in the pockets of his vest and pants. "Oh, I remember."

He lifted his blue hat (hadn't it been red a moment ago?) to reveal a silver badge. A Nordic-looking word was stamped across the badge in gold. It was twelve letters long and contained only two vowels: the third letter was an 'e,' the eighth letter was an 'a.'

"I am not sure I can pronounce that word. Your name, I mean."

"I am not sure I can pronounce it either," he echoed.

"I have to call you something," I replied, and thought for a moment. "Okay, how about...Bobby?"

"I like Bobby. I like that very much!"

"Bobby," I said again.

An enchanting delight traveled down my spine into the ground. It quickly spread, attaching to gold and silver veins inside the Earth. With my inside eyes, I could see massive, hexagonal crystals and deposits of exquisite stones extending across the underground landscape.

"Wow. Theo, gnomes are connected to underground treasures through a network of tunnels!" I said excitedly.

"Ask your gnome friend to lead you to the Dell of Faeries but be specific. Gnomes can be mischievous; unless you are precise, they will lead you on a merry chase all over the countryside. A journey that should take thirty minutes could easily turn into three hours. Say 'please lead me directly to the front door of the Dell of Faeries.'"

BOBBY THE GNOME

I repeated Theo's words to Bobby, "Please lead me directly to the front door of the Dell of Faeries."

With no hesitation, Bobby answered, "Yes, of course!"

He pulled a crystal from the pocket of the vest he wore atop his wooly shirt, reached for his belt that was crammed with miniature tools, and detached a small hammer. He struck the crystal and raced toward the top of a nearby knoll. After stopping for a moment to scan the horizon, he walked over to a nearby stone and patted it three times.

Unexpectedly, a riot of activity began moving in our direction. Twelve gnomes appeared in a cloud of dust, tripping over each other as they moved. I giggled out loud at the spectacle. Theo, unable to see my personal gnomes, gave me a quizzical look. I explained what was happening.

"Typical," he replied.

The gnomes abruptly stopped just before flattening Bobby.

Not disturbed by the gnomes' frenzied arrival, Bobby said, "This is the Keystone Clan."

I smiled at the group of disheveled gnomes as Bobby spoke to them. Most of them listened, but a few kept busy preening themselves, straightening their clothes or brushing themselves off, paying little attention to Bobby. When he finished speaking, they took off quickly, a few stragglers scrambling to catch up.

Bobby began moving again and I followed, informing Theo it was time to go. The clan was already thirty yards ahead of us.

Five minutes into the adventure, the path split in two. The wider path along the manmade canal continued to my left while a smaller path, which led between a tree and some shrubs, curved to the right.

"Show me a direct path to the front door of the Dell of Faeries," I repeated to Bobby.

The clan took the right path. Bobby followed.

I stopped, turned to Theo and said, "To the right," with a slight doubt in my voice.

The trail began to wind to the east, north, east again, then north. At times, we would go off the trail, only to find ourselves on another branch of it. I couldn't distinguish the pattern from the ground.

"A mystic's path is a mosaic of minute details, scripted on the land. Psychic elevation helps a warrior avoid danger," Theo explained. "It is all about perspective."

My wisdom guides suggested, "See it from above."

"Why not?" I replied.

Rising above my body and looking down, the landscape stretched out, extending to the base of Haystack Mountain. There it was, the Dell of Faeries! I returned to my body and saw the clan make a left turn around a small knoll and disappear. By the time Bobby, Theo, and I arrived at that spot, they were gone. There was a small stream in front of us, easy enough to cross. With a short jump I landed solidly and looked around. There was no indication of which direction to go.

I turned to Bobby and asked, "Where did the clan go?"

"Gnome tunnel shortcut," he replied, proudly hooking his thumbs through his suspenders.

"Which way do we go now?" Theo asked.

I looked back and forth between the two of them. Neither one said a word.

During my training I learned a good leader makes a confident, calculated decision then continues on his journey. One can occasionally bridge the gap between the seen and unseen worlds through self-reliance.

Waiting for someone to respond was getting me nowhere, so I guessed.

"That way," I said, pointing.

I pushed my way through a briar patch, climbed over a fallen tree, and barely missed falling into a soupy puddle.

"This has to be it," I said proudly, turning to face Bobby and Theo while standing at the edge of an exposed clearing.

"Next time, you might save yourself some trouble," Theo said, pointing at his clean shoes.

I looked down; mine were splattered with mud. Sighing, I wiped them off with a clean rag from my backpack.

"Congratulations! You found it in record time."

To my surprise, we were standing at the front door of the Dell of Faeries.

"Should we go in?" I asked.

"Not today," said Theo. "This was enough of a test. Besides, dells can be dangerous places. You will need more preparation before facing what awaits you there. Need I remind you of what happened to Rip Van Winkle?"

CHAPTER TWO

FIRST ENCOUNTER

HEN I RETURNED FROM the Dell of Faeries, my mind was buzzing. I had a gnome buddy and the clan to call on in times of need. It was a revelation. The incident at the golf course now made sense, but I wanted a deeper understanding of the sequence of events that took place. I believed I was still missing valuable clues. But what were they? I needed to find out. With my warrior attention dialed in, I focused on summoning the memory of that day.

My awareness traveled directly to the recollection archives. They were located beyond the physical plane, stored in the Life Stream Temple just north of Estes Park. I'd traveled there many times to review occurrences from my past.

The temple had steep spiraling stairs like many of the majestic temples strategically place throughout the Rocky Mountains. It was multileveled and run by a past-life character whose name was Achilles. It was his job to maintain the film archives. Achilles was a direct report to Edmond, my records keeper who resides on the far side of the mountain range in the library of the Mystic Castle. I was thankful to have these two managing my multiple existences.

All lifetimes were available on etheric video film. Active ones were in living color, while processed, copied, and resolved slices of life were reverted to black and white movies, to be used as reference material for a personal records keeper to store in the archives. Each reel was sent to the viewing room by Achilles' twin brother, Aesop.

To access a film, I filled out a short form in triplicate (using carbon copies that somehow stained the hands of my astral body). A copyboy ran the form to the records room where Aesop found the materials I requested and packed them in a container. A few minutes later, they arrived in the viewing room through a vacuum tube where Achilles mounted the contents on a replica ALOS reader. Once the segment of microfilm was chosen, it was sent off to a print station to make a copy for review.

Sure, it was a lengthy process, but there was no better way to learn than from my own experiences. Once everything had been prepared, I settled down in front of the screen and watched my memory play out.

I finished playing the fourth hole at Haystack Golf Course. As I crossed the bridge over to the fifth tee, I stopped to look down at the fast-flowing water, listen to its roar, and breathe deeply. The river wasn't cresting, but it was close, with the water a few inches below its banks. The extra moisture fed plentiful flowers and the meadowlarks sang. Winter's domi-nance was diminished in the face of spring's approach.

A gust of wind caught my attention by nearly lifting the hat off my head. Leaves swirled around at the far end of the bridge, imitating a dust devil. Two eagles called as they rode the air currents over the open space next to the course. They made a sudden dive above a settlement of prairie dogs whose warnings grew incessant before they escaped into their network of tunnels. No unfortunates for the eagles today.

As I feasted on the impressions of the symphony of river, birds, and prairie dogs, a crumpled piece of paper grazed my cheek, startling me. It continued on its journey, performing a gravity-defying dance before plummeting straight down onto the wooden slats of the bridge, tumbling twice, and landing by my right shoe. When I bent down to pick it up, a still photograph of me and my friend Maria, standing arm in arm by the water's edge, popped into my mind. I engage the picture, pulling it closer for inspection. As soon as I did, it turned into a warmhearted movie.

Maria lived on the other side of a small stream that lazily meandered between our houses during our childhood years in the Italian Alps. It flowed year-round, partially freezing during the winter. In the summer months, we would imitate industrious beavers, piling up rocks and branches on a stretch of the stream, creating a makeshift dam to form a swimming hole.

I watched my nine-year-old self tie a note to a small stone with kite string and toss it across the stream. The wicker basket on the opposite shore, borrowed from my mom's picnic collection, held the note until Maria retrieved it. She was an expert marksman. I cringed when I watched my younger self miss the target, ending the tradition for good when an errant shot crashed through Maria's basement window. Soon after, we received walkie-talkies, upgrading our communications and reviving our cross-river play. From then on, we directed our stone throwing at the stream, sans the notes and baskets.

I embraced the memory, reaffirmed its feel-good sensation and 'smiled down' as my qigong teacher instructed me to do on such occasions.

"When good memories return, share them with your house of internal organs," was the official instruction.

Theo's take on it was, "Give your inner star a twinkle."

My hand that was holding the wad of paper dipped. The paper was suddenly wrapped around something heavy. But how? This was not inside when it danced on the wind and brushed my cheek. Where did it come from?

I opened the paper, fingering the white stone inside before tossing it over the railing of the bridge into the river. There was writing on the paper.

Wanted: Trainee.
Must be willing to re-engage freedom.
Pre-existent desire mandatory.
If interested, meet at the library on Tuesday.

The note was beautifully written, with a small smudge of ink on the upper right-hand corner.

"Who wrote this?" I asked aloud.

Somewhat frightened, I looked around, hoping to see someone. Few golfers brave the frosty temperatures this early in the season.

I stuck the note into my pocket, grabbed hold of the handle on my golf caddy, and moved on to the next tee. I intended to toss the note in the trash along with the assortment of discarded objects I'd already collected.

My next drive off the tee took off like a cannonball, flew toward the bend on the dogleg left, turned the corner, and disappeared.

'My best drive yet!' I wrote in my golf journal.

When I found the ball, it was in the middle of the fairway, just fifty yards from the green. I couldn't believe I hit a ball that far! My short-lived exhilaration was interrupted by a rustling in the woods. Someone, something was skipping across dead leaves. It continued for a while then stopped.

"Who's there?" I shouted, tightly gripping the shaft of my club and holding it up in a threatening manner. I was fearful and uncharacteristically angry.

My golf club would be useless if it was a mountain lion or a bear. Any fear and anger would cancel out a rational response, forcing me to run away and return for my golf clubs when the perceived danger was gone. But the rustling stopped.

The silence reassured me. I turned back toward the fairway, but...

"That is impossible!"

My ball sat twenty-five yards closer to the green. But how?

The crunching started again. Cautiously, I moved toward the tree line with my club raised. This time I heard giggling.

So, it *was* just some kids having fun at my expense. Determined to sound amused by the pranksters, I laughed out loud.

"All right, that was pretty funny, but it's time to move on. I don't need to report you to the management for trespassing, do I?"

I paused and listened. It became completely quiet. Maybe they had taken me seriously and left. I turned back to address my ball. Now it was at the edge of the green.

"Very funny," I shouted.

I walked toward the ball with my head still turned toward the trees. When I looked down to address the ball again, it was gone. I looked back to where it had first landed, but it wasn't there either. It was back at the fifty-yard mark, a full wedge shot from the green.

"What?"

Behind me, I heard a golf ball strike a tree trunk. Did the next player catch up with me?

"They're going to be teed off at how they teed off," I said under my breath, seeking an internal laugh to alleviate my fear and anger.

I stepped up to my ball and hurried my wedge shot. It popped up, landed on the green and rolled three feet, stopping right next to the flag. I made the putt without hesitation and headed to the next tee box, still confused by the whole episode.

Every other stroke I hit on the nine-hole course was close to perfect. I parred the rest of the holes confident my bogey days were over. Not quite; though uninvited, the bogey ghost returned the next day.

I thought about the strange note each time I rode past the library. For the next six weeks, I was too busy to investigate, and was starting to grow skeptical about its veracity. How could it have anything to do with me? It was just a note flying around the golf course on a windy day.

One morning I reached into my pocket for my keys and found a piece of paper instead.

It was the note from the golf course.

"How did this get here? These aren't my golf pants."

I read the note again.

"What does it mean?" I asked, half expecting my wisdom guides to answer.

Coincidentally, it was Tuesday, and I had the day off. I planned to visit an exhibit about a local hero, Chief Niwot, at the campus museum. It was a trip that would take me right by the library. The museum exhibit was open until seven – more than enough time to visit some old memories and a vintage book or two. Was my logical mind giving me permission? My curiosity strings were tugging away. They were already on board.

I loved the library. My younger self discovered so many magical stories there. I was thrilled when my sister asked me to tag along. I would run around the house singing, "Books! Books! Books!" until we walked out the door. It drove my sister crazy. When I was older, she waited in the foyer of the library by the front door. In those private hours, I was on my own. I felt quite grown up with this new-found freedom. Later, I discovered my sister was having a secret rendezvous. I wrote a poem about it for my third-grade class:

> *Sister Joy's tryst has been found out.*
> *Boy did she get in trouble for that!*
> *Yes, it was discussed at the dinner table.*
> *When my dad filled his plate and sat.*
> *Did that mean she had boy trouble?*
> *She was not very buoyant after that.*

The other kids laughed, but the teacher reported back to my mom. My sister was doubly embarrassed, and I still tease her about it to this day.

Books were everywhere in our house. I had a few on my bed, some on my dresser and floor, a stack in the bathroom. One corner of our family library was filled with books I could organize in any way I chose.

The books in the library, like the ones in my home, spoke to me as I walked up and down the aisles. But their voices were different, and I wondered why. Was it because they didn't have a permanent owner to hold, caress, and love them?

"Are the books in the library lonely?" I once asked my sister.

"Why do you think that?"

"Because they want me to pick them up and take them home."

My sister wasn't surprised, and I wondered if it happened to her, too. Did hearing books speak run in the family? She never said.

My library experience had always been a magical adventure of pictures, words, and voices.

"You should read me next year," one book would say from down on a low shelf.

Another would shout from a higher shelf, "Read *me* today!"

Sometimes, when I heard a book prompting me, I ran over to Ted the librarian and ask for help. He shadowed me until I pointed at a book, which was frequently on a shelf too high for me to see the title. At first, this puzzled him, but after a dozen times, Ted just smiled, chalking it up to my vivid imagination. Eventually he accepted my peculiar ways, but still inspected each book, making sure it was appropriate.

If a book seemed beyond my years, he'd ask, "Are you sure you want this one?"

I would pause, close my eyes, then name the chapter or pages that wanted to be read, saying, for example, "The Book Fairy suggests I read chapters three through five," or, "The Book Fairy says start on page nine and stop on page twenty-three."

Ted would verify the chapter or pages and hand me the book, usually saying, "Tell the Book Fairy I like her choice."

These memories filled my head on the ride to the library. I was there within the hour. I placed my bicycle on the rack and sharpened my focus. I walked through the door on high alert. Today I wasn't looking for the perfect book; I was here to find a stranger who wrote the unusual note. And what of the Book Fairy? Would she know about this? Would any books cry out to me?

I walked up and down the aisles. The library was mostly empty, and the few people I encountered were immersed in reading or ignoring my presence. Even when I approached someone, they would look up for a moment, wonder who was invading their space, then turn back to their books. It didn't take long to get through both floors, scanning the stacks of books and every person. No stranger. No Book Fairy reunion. No Ted, who'd long since left the library.

I sat down in a high-backed wooden chair, breathing in the silence. Sunlight streamed in through the stained glass window, casting pastels across the floor that danced in time with the windswept trees. The chair had been in the library since those first days, somehow set in a difference place each night. Who could have been responsible for moving it around for all those years? I closed my eyes, remembering *The Magic Chair and the Restless Ghost*, a short story I'd written to explain the phenomenon. I even devised a plan to hide out in the library and catch whatever spirit was at work. I never actually stayed overnight, but my young imagination had enjoyed giving voice to the story.

"Back then, you read books," intoned a voice. "From now on, you will read the invisible landscape."

My eyes snapped open.

"Who said that?"

"Come outside," the voice replied.

The comfortable feeling of the library, of the familiar chair, was being invaded by a voice resounding inside my head. What's more, it was a voice I'd heard somewhere before.

I rose from the chair and made my way to the front door, trying to fit small pieces of insight into some bigger picture. The note at the golf course was part of it, and so was this voice. Could I be imagining it? Was there a ghost in the library after all? It didn't make sense, but while I knew I should leave, I was certain something important was taking shape. I tried to gain more perspective, but my probing thoughts were interrupted again.

"Meet me on the bench by the creek," ordered the voice.

What choice did I have?

I exited through the library's oval entrance and moved along its east side. My path lay in the shadow of the building's second story, which extended over the creek. This was a long passageway to a smaller wing mostly occupied by a single auditorium. It was used for movies, lectures, meetings, and Saturday afternoon plays for children.

The voice mentioned a bench, but there were three: one on this side of the creek and two on the other side, accessible by a small stone bridge. They were all empty.

"Choose wisely," said the voice as I analyzed the setting.

The creek was loud this time of year, with runoff from the mountains racing down the canyon and filling it to its banks, but I could still hear the voice clearly.

"It's more like a river than a creek," I said under my breath.

"Yes, it is," the voice agreed, still sounding inside my head.

Three benches, and I am to 'choose wisely.' Is that an instruction or a clue? My analyzer was taking over. Choose the bench that a wise person would sit on. Is that the closest one? Or would the south-facing bench on the other side of the creek be the warmer, wiser choice? The bench closest to me was under a large oak tree. Could that be a factor to consider?

"Your mundane sleuthing skills will not help you here."

The voice was really getting on my nerves.

"That's it, I'm not playing this game any longer!" I barked, sitting on the closest bench.

When I did, I glanced up into the tree. A snowy owl with

pure-white feathers was perched on a branch just above my head. If I reached out, I could almost touch him. I looked closer at the vibrant feathers around his eyes. Connecting their spots in my mind, he looked like he was wearing large, wire-rimmed glasses.

I laughed. 'Choose wisely?' Of *course*, it meant under a tree with an owl wearing spectacles!

"I see you found my advertisement," a man said, sitting down beside me. The way he spoke was slightly stilted, with the faintest trace of an accent; perhaps Italian, perhaps French. Whatever the accent was, this was the voice I'd heard in my head.

"So," he continued, "you are interested in the position, yes? You have come for the interview?"

"So, it *is* a job?"

"Well, yes and no."

"It can't be both a job *and* not a job!"

"Do you have the note on you?"

"Yes."

"Good. Let me see it."

I pulled it out of my pocket and handed it to him.

He looked at it and read it out loud. Too loud. Almost shouting. Embarrassed by his performance, I looked around to see if anyone was nearby, listening. The area was oddly deserted for a weekday afternoon.

"Wanted: trainee. Must be willing to re-engage freedom. Pre-existent desire mandatory. If interested, meet at the library on Tuesday."

Seized by a peculiar visual sensation out of the corner of my eye, I looked across the creek. He was sitting on the bench, reading the note.

"Well, that *is* a pretty obscure note," he exclaimed.

Startled, I jumped up. He was sitting next to me. I looked at him, on the other bench and then back at him again.

"Do you want the position?" he asked, ignoring my confusion.

I was incapable of answering. For a few seconds, I was inside a blue bubble whirling around a vortex hovering above the creek. The spinning stopped abruptly, tossing me back onto the bench exactly where I was seated a few moments ago.

I straightened the halfcocked glasses on my face and soberly peered at the stranger, recognizing that I was uncharacteristically calm.

"What *is* the position?" I finally asked.

"Isn't it obvious?"

"Well, no. You never said what it was."

"It is spelled out quite clearly in the note. See?" he asked as he held it up.

Under the last line was written: 'Duties include cataloguing books in a private library in exchange for training.'

I'd seen that line before, but not on the note. Not even on the same piece of paper; it came from a book I read in the library as a child.

Achilles volunteered to provide a movie to support my memory. Aesop was more than willing to set up a screen to play it on.

As usual my sister led me through the front door and sat down in the foyer while I went inside. I waved my library card, hanging from a lanyard around my neck, at the person staffing the front desk and raced down the first aisle of books. It was another magical day. I was beside myself with glee.

"Book, book where are you?
I've come to find you,
I am no fool.
Do not hide,
It is in vain;
The Book Fairy knows your name
And I will know your claim to fame."

Ted shushed me for being too loud as I sped by him, so I sang the words under my breath.

The last aisle, past the staircase that led to the second floor, was a dead end. The shelves were classic brown stained wood. These books were the oldest in the library. Most were vintage multi-volume sets with green-bound covers.

When my singing turned to humming, I slowed my pace, glancing first at groups of books, then individual volumes. Titles weren't the object of my attention; I was waiting for a book to light up. It was a game the Book Fairy and I played together: spot the book first. Could I see a rainbow shining on a book before the Book Fairy recommended it? I was getting good at this new game. I'd beaten her the last three times.

There it was: a book lit up by the primary colors of the rainbow and their companion shades of translucent pastels. Fourteen colors in all, flashing unabashedly.

"That one," I said as I pointed to a shelf just above my head, feeling proud of my accomplishment.

"Not quite," the Book Fairy responded. "But you are close."

"How could that be? It lit up. That one, right there," I said, pointing.

"Call Ted over and ask him to take the book down *and* the two books on either side of it."

I was puzzled, but I did as the Book Fairy suggested.

"Would you mind helping me?" I asked Ted politely.

"Of course not. Did your Book Fairy find a book for you today?" he asked. Before I could answer, he stood up and stepped out from behind his desk, saying, "Show me where it is."

I raced in front of him, zigzagging like a cat leading the way to its food bowl. When we reached the shelf, I stopped in front of the group of books.

Ted stopped behind me and asked, "Which book shall I help you with today?"

"The Book Fairy said to take down those five books."

"Why those five books? They're not even a set," he asked, puzzled by my request.

"I don't know," I responded, shrugging.

Ted looked at me for more information. When I offered none, he looked around, half-expecting the Book Fairy to supply the answer. He reached up and pulled the books down onto a rolling tray table.

"There you go, but that's a lot of reading, even for you," he said as he turned to go.

"Excuse me, the Book Fairy is still pointing at the shelf," I insisted.

"What?"

"I said the Book Fairy is still pointing at the shelf."

"I don't understand," Ted replied, standing in the same spot as the Book Fairy and looking toward the empty section of shelving. He squinted hard through his glasses, reached his hand in, and pulled out a small book that was laying on its side. It was covered with dust.

"It must have fallen over and slid behind the other books," he surmised as he picked up a small cloth from the cart and wiped the book clean. "I wonder how long it was back there."

Dust particles flew off the book. They sparkled in the sunlight streaming in from the window. The heavier particles floated down onto his shoulders and shoes. I looked over at the Book Fairy to see if she was responsible. She winked. Ted handed the book to me.

"Thank you for discovering the lost book," he said, addressing the invisible fairy. "Maybe we should hire you to find the other missing titles from our catalog."

Ted smiled and went back to his desk.

After he was gone, I ran over to a chair and plopped down at the small, round table by the stained glass window. The light sprinkled down on the book in my hands. I pretended each color was a friend.

I closed my eyes, stopped my thinking, and silenced my breathing. Then, I opened the book to a random page. The Book Fairy taught me this when I first met her.

She said, "This is the best way to get to the vital part of the book. You can decide to read more later."

How she knew I would open the book in the right place was a mystery, but it worked. When I opened the book, I read:

Wanted: Trainee.
Must be willing to re-engage freedom.
Pre-existent desire mandatory.
If interested, meet at the library on Tuesday.
Duties include cataloguing books in a private library in exchange
for training.

My imagination soared.

"Are there really jobs out there like this? Wouldn't that be grand?"

To oversee a library, a whole room full of books to spend

my days in! Organizing, reading, listing, reading some more! I imagined myself in a large room stuffed with books in every corner, stacked in towering piles that needed someone to organize them.

"It's time to go," I heard someone say, which brought me out of my daydreaming state.

It was my sister. Apparently, our visit was over. All I could think about was the job. 'Duties include cataloguing books in a private library.'

"Thanks, Aesop," I said as the screen was dismantled.

"Achilles, I'm finished for now."

I was beginning to get a headache. Rubbing the bridge of my nose, I turned back to the stranger next to me.

"Well," said the man on the bench, "do you want the job?"

I was reeling; I'd completely forgotten my first encounter with the note until this moment. I needed to come up with an answer fast, but I wanted more time to decide.

"What kind of training?"

"That is a good question," a voice inside my head answered.

"That *is* a good question," the man agreed in the same voice. "Mystic warrior training, partly, in addition to intuitive training, in conjunction with geo-mythic landscape training, combined with solar meditation practice and, of course, invisible—"

"Wait a minute, wait a minute!" I said, interrupting him. "I don't understand."

"Apparently, there is a lot you do not know, so let's get started. Meet me on the east side of Haystack Mountain," he said as he got up to leave.

"When?" I asked.

"When you realize it is your only course of action."

THE MENTOR

That was not something I wanted to hear. It didn't sound like a choice; it sounded pre-determined, like destiny. Even if I never met him at Haystack Mountain, I thought I should know who he was.

"Who are you? What is your name?"

"I am a mystic warrior. You may call me Theo."

I wasn't sure what I was getting into with this strange character, but a sense of calm came over me. I knew in my heart that I didn't have a choice.

Haystack Mountain was big; there were houses, farms, cottages, a lot of open space. "How will I find you?"

"You won't be able to miss me. My place has the smallest entrance but is the biggest of all. It is cleverly hidden, no one can see it unless I invite them in, but then it is as plain as the laces on your shoes."

I looked down at my laces automatically, wondering how to decipher the directions I'd just received.

"Can you be more specifi…"

My words trailed off as I looked up. Theo was gone. He couldn't have just disappeared. I looked around. Not a trace.

Should I really interact with this strange character again? And what about that job description? I hadn't a clue what it meant. Would I have time for all that training? Those questions and more bounced around inside my head as I ambled back to the bike rack and rode off to the museum.

Chapter Three

Seeking Advice

FTER TWO WEEKS OF searching, I found Theo's house, no thanks to any insight of mine. I found his address pinned to my saddlebag one morning after I had given up trying. Training started without fanfare. None of it made sense at first but I continued with the rigorous schedule, mostly because I loved his library, not so much the training, which was obscure, nonlinear, and lacked the logic I needed to feel any progress.

For two years I stuck it out. Why? He intrigued me. He was brilliant! His vast knowledge knew no bounds. He never repeated information. Never contradicted himself. Yet, he shared world views that on the surface were contrary to popular belief. His discourses on the unseen world behind the physical were vividly plausible, but I can't say I believed him for the longest time...until I began to catch glimpses of energetic domains behind the visual noise of life. Once that door opened, I gained access to worlds within worlds.

At first I couldn't do much but observe the activity. Invitations to engage with invisible beings gradually began to arrive at my visual doorstep. I acquiesced; made new, albeit unconventional, friends, and Theo help me navigate these relationships using the proper protocols. Everything was developing nicely until now. A dragon had to be found and set free.

I needed answers.

As I made my way to Theo's home, I systematically reviewed my question, knowing it would be a difficult task.

"Should I free a dragon?" I said, trying out a simple question in my most confident voice.

I came up with five likely follow-up questions, but that wouldn't do; Theo would have ten. Maybe more. I needed to put it a different way.

"If I have the opportunity to free a dragon, should I?"

That sounded simple enough in my head. I practiced it out loud a couple of times.

"If I am asked to free a dragon, *should* I? If I am *asked* to free a dragon, should I?"

The slight change of emphasis sounded a little better, but I was still concerned about asking a question that would invite a lot of Theo-type inquiries in return.

Who asked you to? Where were you when you were asked? How do you know what you heard was real? Or, in the case of the ancient scroll, *how did you find it? Who wrote it? Have you conferred with your wisdom guides?*

Yes, I could see it now. My question would provoke an interrogation, and I wasn't sure I could supply credible answers. I looked back through my notes. Maybe I could find something to help.

"Ah, how about this…"

I remembered Theo's earliest lessons on self-trust, self-validation, and fulfilling one's destiny. Could I use them to argue the point?

"When the final decision must be made," he said, following a difficult conversation about my lack of motivation, "gather all the information you can and then trust your heart. Even in opposition to the wisest advisors or the closest of friends, it is your truth, your High Self, your inner voice that you must trust above all else."

He gave me that hard stare, the one that reached deep into my soul.

"There is a lot to deliberate upon. Get help from your wisdom guides, hear the elusive voices streaming in from the cosmos, seek revelations from the land. Your pre-history and recent history will each want a voice in your decisions. These are all influences you must deal with, but others cannot reveal the answer to the puzzle for you. We can only supply you with the surest fragments we have discovered. When you assemble the pieces, they will reveal the steps you must take. Our voices are members of a choir. Listen carefully, consider all advice that is heartfelt and genuine, but in the end, you create your own destiny."

Today, in my efforts to make the best possible decision, I would listen carefully and consider all the information. Still, somehow the decision was already stamped on the letter of my life. Mailed by my heart, the writer of my soul. I knew what I had to do, but I didn't know how to do it. That was the advice I really wanted.

But standing in Theo's house, I asked the question, and was dealt a crushing blow.

"No. Absolutely not. You are not ready to free a dragon!" Theo's emphatic words assaulted the strategy playing out in my imagination, bringing it to a screeching halt.

"Do you know how hard it is? What the consequences

would be? Have you considered how much help you would need? Even I would not attempt it alone."

Theo sounded genuinely troubled.

I needed something to argue my point. So, I quoted from the Mystic Warrior's Handbook:

> *Choose to follow a path.*
> *Trust your heart.*
> *Trust your wits.*
> *Trust your training.*
> *Know yourself before trusting yourself.*

My recitation fostered no response.

I continued: "Okay, I am not aboard the 'know thyself' train yet, but I am waiting at the station. I know the destination, and I have my ticket."

Silence.

Did my cleverness fall flat?

I spouted the second rule:

> *Choose the proper tools.*
> *Solicit the help of qualified colleagues.*
> *Establish the perfect day and time.*

"I just need to officially add, 'Set the dragon free!'"

Theo knew I was out of ammunition. "Most humans are not at fault directly. There is evil. There is good. There is foolish. What I am teaching you is none of these. Life in this solid world is the perfect training ground for sincere seekers of truth. This is where mystic warrior training can lead you. You have the opportunity to investigate the extraordinary. When you are ready for a quest such as freeing a dragon, the decision will come from the Source." Theo opened a book on his desk shrouding the room in silence. His dismissal was wordless.

I didn't get an answer from the Source, I didn't even know who the Source was, but by the time I left his house, I knew I must free the dragon. Even with Theo's doubts, I had to complete this quest. It was my first real test, even if, by the sound of Theo's warning, it could be my last.

"Life only gives us a handful of extraordinary adventures among the many mundane activities," my wisdom guides told me. "Complete those, even one of those, and you will fulfill your destiny."

This was my destiny. I had my dream, the scroll, and my trust in the Dream Talker. Still, there was so little information to go on. I did have a treasure map, but no 'X' to mark the spot. There were no constellations to guide me, no sun to light the way.

"Where do I begin?" I asked, still not confident I was equal to the challenge. But what recourse did I have? The alternatives were unpalatable.

There was one voice I believed I could solicit. A voice I hoped would give me the confidence I needed to succeed at my quest. I would return to the Trail of Sages and speak to the Fire Dragon. Surely, a dragon would be the best advisor to gain knowledge about other dragons. But it was my encounter with the landscape giant that had ultimately revealed the Fire Dragon.

CHAPTER FOUR

THE LANDSCAPE GIANT

IT WAS TIME TO test my body. The road to recovery had dragged on for weeks. The accident with the box of books at my cousin's house hurt badly enough for me to curtail my hiking. Exploring the landscape was not an option for months. Getting antsy, no longer hobbling around like a reanimated corpse, it was time to determine if I was trail-worthy. I chose an unfamiliar destination, the three-mile route to the reservoir.

On a typical day, my calculations would have been accurate, but the adventure was not as straightforward as I had imagined. The plan was simple enough: walk toward the trailhead from my house, cross under the highway to the car park, travel a quarter of a mile to the main trail, and beeline it to the reservoir. Unfortunately, spring snowmelt, an exceptional amount of rain, and multiple hills with switchbacks not on my map all conspired to challenge me.

Right from the start, the trail to the highway dispelled my assumptions about the journey. Ten minutes into the hike, I hit a mucky section of the trail. The mud was so thick it filled the grooves in my shoes. Every few steps added a new layer of wet, cement-like mud. The accumulation accelerated. It was a standing-on-basketballs balancing circus performance. Each ball of mud weighed as much as a sack of rice. Too deep to make any headway, I was forced to stop multiple times to scrape off the excess mud before my ankles and socks were encased. Oddly enough, I wasn't deterred; in fact, I laughed out loud.

After I made it through 'Mud Alley,' I had a choice: head up the dirt road with easy access to the Trail of Sages or cut across the open space on the plateau above the valley. Taking the road up the hill looked easier, but heading east was a shorter, more direct route.

I focused my attention on Bobby and the gnome clan. They appeared immediately.

"Show me the best path to take." I said, but seconds later I wasn't sure if I was explicit enough.

The gnome clan scrambled up the trail to the right and disappeared over the hill. Bobby waited for my decision. I looked at the road, wishing they chose that way. Reckoning it was too late to redirect them now, I follow the clan with Bobby by my side.

I was tiring by the time I crested the first plateau. My breath heaved deep into my diaphragm. After wiping the sweat off my forehead, I folded the handkerchief neatly, placing it back in my pocket.

I gazed at the small lake bordering the trail.

"This is not supposed to be here. It isn't on the map."

The backdrop of the lake was uncharacteristic for Boulder, Colorado. It was marshy, similar to New England where I grew up. There was dense undergrowth along the south shore with trees growing in the depths of the water. The visual oddity of thick shrubbery, wading trees, and humid air hanging over the lake was awkwardly captivating. Turtles and snakes completed this out-of-place paradise.

My imagination cast images of nymphs, dragons, and faeries across the treasured mind of my childhood. I easily dove into the magic. Just as quickly, an uneasiness forced me back to reality. I couldn't see anything threatening, but I knew something was wrong. A breeze started up and quickly grew into a gusting wind. My suspicion heightened with the sound of a distant sobbing.

I picked up the pace, but I couldn't escape the intensifying fairytale images. My mind was storying hard.

A princess, locked in a castle, weeping into a cauldron. She looked down at a reflection of a lake. Each tear increased the vibrancy of the scene. The clearer it became, the more she longed to escape her life. She saw a traveler in her conjured image. She wished to be that person, free to explore and discover the world. The hiker below looked up into the sky, saw the princess, and wondered what it was like to live a life of royalty.

The coveting came true. They traded places. Although joyful at first, they quickly tired of their fictitious lives and longed to return to their familiar worlds and live their destined reality. When they did, they found many wonders in their own backyards. The princess had a kingdom she would one day rule. The traveler had a landscape to explore.

I tucked the fantasy images safely away in my mind and kept walking, focusing back on my surroundings.

Below the next slope, I paused in front of a few boulders the size of giants. The simple hike to the reservoir was becoming anything but. "I hope I don't have to climb over them. After all, they shouldn't even be here."

I'd seen evidence of rockslides in the mountains, but these large boulders were on the plains at the edge of the range east of the foothills. So, where had they come from?

Bobby and the clan pushed forward between a gap in the boulders and up to the top of the ridge. From there, the trail continued through a series of gates that directed hikers and bikers off to the left. It was a simple solution to contain the grazing cows and discourage any accidental bovine incidents.

When I reached the ridge above the valley, I could see the Flatirons on the foothills. I turned to look south. Pike's Peak was visible on the horizon, clothed in a delicate haze. A wave of joy breezed across my skin. It felt like happy spirits on the wind tickling me. I broke out in song. Bobby, who was just a few yards in front of me, turned, smiled, and added a jig to his step.

By the time we caught up with the clan, they had slowed their pace. Their chaotic movements coalesced into a synchronized turn toward a flat, open space up ahead. This behavior startled me. My inside eyes activated, opening like a shark's third eyelid, and overlaid a pastel world onto the stagnant, vanilla-shaded land. Behind the overlay and the physical world, something was becoming visible.

After a few moments, the landscape opened like a door, exposing a colossal form. There was a giant fast asleep on the plateau. The atmosphere around his body glowed amber with floating specks of gold.

I approached from the west and looked at the top of his head, unable to see his face. My gut told me that he knew I was close, and my inner smile met his inner smile as a mental reassurance. Still, as I drew closer, some concern sprouted. Would my training be enough to ensure my safety, sanity, and survival?

THE LANDSCAPE GIANT

"Oh, what am I worried about," I said. "It's only a giant on the landscape!"

The thought itself was ludicrous. I half laughed.

After turning the corner, I had a clear view of the giant's nose, but his eyes were closed.

"What do I do now?" I asked.

My wisdom guides surprised me with some rare advice.

"When the unknown reveals itself, present your genuine self. Act as if nothing is unusual. The invisible world will only engage with its visible counterpart on a field of trust."

Bumping into a sleeping giant fit the criteria, so I continued at a leisurely pace, intentionally ignoring him. But my inside eyes were fixated. That's how I caught him. He opened his right eye slightly. I turned my head in his direction, but he quickly closed it. I turned away. He opened his eye. I turned back swiftly. His eye closed again. What kind of game were we playing here?

By now I was level with his collarbone while Bobby and the clan sat on a pile of rocks across from us. They were fixated. Was it their first giant sighting too? I kept moving, alternating peeks with the giant, gradually reaching his abdomen, knee-caps, and finally his feet. I was at the next downslope before we finished sneaking looks at each other.

"Better wait for the gnomes," I said at the edge of the mesa. "The giant will be out of sight soon, and so will they."

Bobby caught up with me quickly.

"Was this your first giant sighting?" I asked.

"Oh, no, there are many giants. We were dragon gemming."

"What?"

"Dragon gemming," he repeated.

I panicked, looking around for any sign of a dragon.

"What is dragon gemming?"

"When we find a place where a dragon will appear, we plan an excavation in a nearby cave. If a human being mines a dragon for wisdom, we gnomes mine for precious gems. Whichever element the dragon is, that will be the focus of our mining. Earth, water, fire, wood, or metal gems are exchangeable food. We can use them to barter with other nature spirits," Bobby explained.

It was all news to me. I stopped to make notes in my journal. It was a good start; the giant and I had checked each other out. How many visits would it take to understand the purpose of the encounter? Returning with my blue camping chair would be the next step.

True understanding could take weeks, even years. Theo had drilled into me: "Be tenacious. Landscape viewing is not for the impatient."

I didn't need to think about that right now. There was cause for celebration. I'd had my first independent landscape encounter!

I made it all the way to the reservoir, returning by the main trail in the valley. The rest of the journey only took thirty minutes, about what I had anticipated from the start. The clan entertained me with their antics, happily leading the way home. I looked at Bobby. He shrugged, relinquishing all responsibility for their behavior.

CHAPTER FIVE

THE GOLDEN EGG

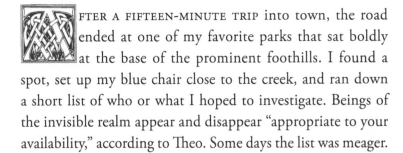FTER A FIFTEEN-MINUTE TRIP into town, the road ended at one of my favorite parks that sat boldly at the base of the prominent foothills. I found a spot, set up my blue chair close to the creek, and ran down a short list of who or what I hoped to investigate. Beings of the invisible realm appear and disappear "appropriate to your availability," according to Theo. Some days the list was meager. Today, miniscule.

Unsure of my availability and feeling a tad mischievous, I turned to face south, embracing the striking image of the landscape.

"I know! Let's try those imposing characters."

Reaching out with my psychic senses, I asked the Flatirons, "What is your purpose?"

"Our purpose?" came a deep, rumbling response.

The second of three Flatirons stirred slowly and turned around, revealing a monstrous creature no longer a piece of the mountain. I was encouraged; my imagination was working to set itself free.

"We serve as a dividing line separating the flatlands from our majestic peaks."

I visualized the hundreds of 14,000-foot peaks that spanned the mountain range. That was it. The strange creature slowly turned and face-planted back into the foothills. It was almost a comical gesture. I waited to see if Flatirons number one or number three would be more talkative.

"Looks like that's all I am getting out of those behemoths." I griped, settling back into my camping chair – my roost of exploration – and listened intently to the water roar. The sound of the cars winding through the canyon echoed above the park, while imperceptible jetliners crisscrossed from one coast to the other. In the midst of this activity, I cultivated a zone of soundlessness, diving into the water's intensity, drowning out the noise of people playing in the water or biking over the bridge. Watching the world from behind the river's wall of sound, I was in no hurry to penetrate emptiness.

I started 'recapitulating' my day, replaying the events in reverse order and putting my visual input of the world in context. "Put the visible world in its proper place," my dad would say each night as he tucked me into bed. I didn't know what recapitulate meant, but I'd always dutifully rewind my day. Little had I imagined the importance of this nighttime exercise. It established an enduring place inside me; a location I could return to again and again. The purpose it served, then? Dad and I shared a sacred activity. Until Theo mentioned it, I hadn't realized how it served as a rehearsal stage to transition onto the geo-mythic landscape.

I raced through the exercise, getting ready to travel to the ridge above the Trail of Sages and seek out the sleeping giant. Once prepared, I called the rotunda transportation service.

I learned from Theo that before today's flying machines

were invented, the ancients had their flying cities and chariots. Today, the rotunda is still the preferred choice of a mystic traveler. It is halfway between a small, floating temple and a chariot, with six columns into which its angel crew merge at will. In the middle floats a shimmering diamond which I use to interface with the geo-mythic landscape, but otherwise, I leave operating the rotunda to the angels. They weren't visible as the rotunda swung down in front of me for boarding, but I knew they must be at work for it to be airborne at all.

My preliminary flight above the city was thrilling.

At first, nothing specific captured my attention, but I wanted to be optimistic. I desperately needed a change. The hiking and biking to the ridge had bored me to tears. At this point anything was more exciting than slumping in my chair, watching the sleeping giant, wondering if he would get up and talk to me.

I launched toward the plateau expecting to find the giant still stretched out on the ground. The rotunda suddenly lunged into a parabolic arc and slung me toward the large temple set in the middle of Boulder proper.

"Hey, what gives? Why would the rotunda take me here?"

Nobody responded.

"Is this today's destination?"

Still nothing.

"This doesn't make sense!" I was floating above the city, facing the temple, stopped in midair. My angel pilots were missing, and I was alone inside an out-of-gas rotunda.

"What do I do now?"

"Stay present and discover what is important," Theo's words interrupted my uneasy thoughts. "Ignore what your mind wants to know. Focus."

I checked to see if he was sitting beside me. He was not.

"Focus on what is in front of you," he prodded.

When my mind quieted down, I took a closer look at the temple using my inside eyes. Its elegance was in stark contrast to the city surrounding it. It was similar to the Temple of Hercules, but much, much bigger, with a hundred columns around its circumference. At the entrance, I could see two griffins standing guard. I dug deeper into mystic seeing, peeled back a veil of the invisible, and saw a figure straddling a caldron on the expansive floor. I've seen this being before, stomping around the foothills, searching for something.

"Who are you?"

The name Apollo came through loud and clear.

I focused on his activity. He was reaching up through the dome ceiling's circular opening. The image of Apollo shifted and rotated through other guises. First, the landscape giant with his amber glow. Next, Atlas, holding the world on his shoulders, then Hercules standing between two pillars, and then back to Apollo. I wondered what the significance of this changing persona was. It was disturbing, making it hard for me to focus on his actions.

"Why is he changing so?"

I flashed back to a memory of one of my other teachers, the Triple Wisdom Woman. She took me under her wing with reluctance, but Theo insisted I study with her. When I came face to face with her, I wanted to run away immediately. I learned to fear the laziness of my thoughts while studying mental clarity with her. Theo sent me to Los Angeles after he became frustrated with my lack of progress. I never forgave him. Her tutelage was psychically devastating, brutally honest, frighteningly personal, emotionally painful, intellectually demanding, and powerfully freeing. I heard her voice vividly as I recalled her lesson:

"'Why' questions. Except for mathematics and science, they never invite useful answers, but still, everyone wants to know 'why?' Don't ask the invisible world of spirit beings 'why' questions. These questions invite detours at least, chaos at most."

Too far away from the temple to engage Apollo directly, I decided I needed to get closer. My predicament was puzzling. Routinely, the rotunda lands right in front of a landscape feature. I walk a short distance before stepping onto the geo-mythic site to explore. Now, the rotunda sat suspended, floating in space. What was I to do? I could shout to the changing character, but how could he help me with my stalled vehicle?

"Please, isn't there any assistance out there?"

Not long after my embarrassing plea, an angel stepped onto the rotunda.

"It's about time," I said, feeling confident again.

I manifested a rose and handed it to him. Roses require mental effort to manifest, but they communicate positive emotions in a way that is clear to any creature or spirit. The angel accepted my gift and stuck it next to a feather in his Robin Hood hat. Why was he costumed? To me, the Ophanim always presented themselves as jokers, with an essential point to make. I assumed it was a prelude to a new adventure, but what kind? I decided to play along.

"Robbin' the rich?" I joked as I scanned the items in his possession. Wearing a leather shirt, pants, and boots, he carried a high-tech bow slung across his back. He also had a zipline trolley and a roll of cable attached to the belt around his waist.

"What are those for?" I asked, pointing to his gear.

"You," he replied.

"What?"

"How else do you think you're going to get over there?" he asked, pointing to the temple.

"Can't you just move the rotunda closer?"

"What would be the fun in that?" he replied as he attached the cable to an arrow. He notched the arrow and loosed it toward the temple, where it stuck above the archway entrance.

"Ready?" the angel asked.

"No."

He ignored my response again, fastening me to the zipline he'd strung from the rotunda's roof. He pushed and I flew out towards the temple, but then a thought struck me.

"How do I stop?" I shouted back, but the angel and the rotunda were gone.

The line was disappearing as fast as I flew forward, and the temple was quickly approaching. I prepared myself for either a tuck and roll or a crash. I instinctively wanted to close my eyes, but it was time to jump. Before I could, the rotunda appeared in front of the temple with five angels, all dressed in firemen's uniforms, holding a safety net.

"Get ready to jump," they shouted. "Now!"

I let go and slammed into the center of the net. It was soft and spongy, and I passed through several layers of fine mesh. It slowed me down enough to land gently on the front steps of the temple. I stood up and casually straightened my shirt. The angels applauded, giving each other high fives all around.

The first task was to create a method of communication. These griffins, like all majestic beings, expect royal salutations and deserve respect as ancient guardians. Unsheathing my mystic sword and presenting it point down to the griffins as they stood at the entrance was proper. It wasn't an aggressive gesture – like roses, the sword was proof of my legitimacy. In this case, it represented my intent to accept new knowledge and, simultaneously, to reveal the extent of my studies. They gave me a slight nod, accepted my legitimacy and permitted my advance.

I saw Apollo's foot directly in my line of sight. Sword still in hand, I penetrated his heel. The first time Theo demonstrated this procedure, it unsettled me, but he elucidated.

"This is the official Mystic Way to share wisdom and make a sincere connection. Of course, no one gets injured." He paused before adding, "Unless a deception is intended. In that case, it is not wisdom one will receive."

I didn't ask what the ramifications were. I didn't want to know.

After a few moments of downloading the requisite wisdom, I withdrew my sword and returned it to its scabbard. The data would be available in the Mystic Castle library as unprocessed information. The impressions, deposited in my psyche, would appear as pages in my book of knowledge. It would eventually find its way to Achilles and Aesop, who would store it in my memory archives.

The large temple was sparse. Only the caldron and the mythological hero – now appearing as Atlas holding the world on his shoulders – occupied the temple. No blue lightning bolts appeared on the edges of my field of vision, a sign that nothing else was vying for my attention.

I sent more roses to Atlas, but something else was required. This moment called for another tool I often needed on the landscape: Golden Suns. These balls of illumination are created through psychic effort and boost needed qualities. Theo uses manifesting suns as a preliminary exercise. They stabilize the attributes of mystic warriors to improve communication with otherworldly beings. I gave myself five suns of clarity and Atlas momentarily stabilized in the form of the landscape giant.

"What are you doing?" I asked.

"Would you mind giving me a hand?"

His words echoed, ping-ponging about the temple and

creating momentary geometric shapes. I searched for the source; for some reason, I didn't believe it was the giant speaking.

"Pardon me?" I asked, searching for the source of the voice as the giant shifted to his Hercules guise.

"Would you help me?" the voice repeated urgently. "I would appreciate some assistance with this."

I looked up. Hercules was grappling with a golden egg lodged in the underside of the dome ceiling.

"Help you with what? With *that?*" I asked, a little intimidated, as I pointed to the luminous egg. "I'm not sure how I can help you."

Standing as tall as his foot, I could hardly imagine my usefulness.

"If you think yourself too small to accomplish something or help someone, use your creative imagination to size up," my wisdom guides reminded me. "From a photon to a universe you can choose to be. Or, anything in between you see."

"How?" I asked.

"Suns of worthiness, equality, and validation should do the trick," the wisdom guides whispered.

As the suns manifested, I immediately began to grow, stopping only when I was the same size as the figure. I was distracted by his changing appearance from giant to Apollo to Hercules to Atlas and back again. His morphing was unsettling.

"I wish you would hold one form." He stopped shifting immediately, once again becoming the landscape giant.

"You are awake and standing upright." I said, feeling a need to say something about our 'plateau' relationship.

"Hold this." He ignored my comment and directed me to the golden egg, hanging from a vine. The vine stretched straight up through the ceiling into the depths of space. As I grasped the egg, I saw an image of a sun at the center of a galaxy.

"Do not stare directly at the egg," he instructed. "Blink repeatedly and use your sense of touch. Keep your eyes partially closed. Later, you can inspect the egg to learn its purpose."

I held the egg firm while the giant reached out, trying to cut the vine. He was struggling with the maneuver. I had a moment of fear. What if the egg was too heavy and I couldn't hold it?

"Let me give it a try? To be honest, I prefer you hold the egg instead of me."

"A welcome request," he replied, flashing the Atlas image at me three times in quick succession. First, holding the world on his shoulders, then standing empty handed, and finally holding the egg above his head.

I took my hands off the egg, slid my sword out of its bejeweled scabbard and cut the egg loose from the vine. Then panicked.

The egg began to free fall. I froze in disbelief. I expected Atlas to be holding it tightly, but there was no time to discover what had happened. I dove for the floor, quickly calculating the distance I needed to travel. Before I managed to make it halfway down, the egg landed gently in the waiting arms of a robed figure.

I shrunk back down to my normal size, sending out roses as I moved toward the radiant figure.

"Who are you?" I asked.

"The Christopher," a strong voice echoed as he offered me the egg.

I grasped it carefully, inspecting its warm, porous surface before looking back at the Christopher. He was tall and bearded, with classic Middle Eastern features. I wondered how peculiar it must be to be 'the' someone. There was the Logos, the Christ, the Buddha. And now, the Christopher?

As the thought drifted away, I asked, "What will happen to the egg?"

"Since the inquiry has arrived, it is now quested," the Christopher declared.

I looked quizzically at him.

"What does that mean?"

"You will accompany the golden egg to the mountains for its incubation."

Unsure how to respond, I waited for a glimmer of insight while staring at the egg.

"How will I find a suitable place?"

"Guardians of the invisible kingdom will guide you. Prepare for the journey."

My wisdom guides produced a spine-tingling affirmation while the rotunda angels gave me a thumbs-up.

I turned when I heard the landscape giant's solemn voice begin to speak.

"My task is almost complete. I will accompany you, then return to the Trail of Sages and descend back into the land, so the one of fire can awaken."

I was intrigued about 'the one of fire' but more concerned about conveying the egg to its destination.

"I'm not sure I am qualified to chaperone the golden egg."

The giant, Apollo, Atlas, and Hercules all appeared separately, sized down, and assumed the four cardinal points of the temple. The Christopher stood humbly in the middle. One voice sounded from the many beings' present.

"It is not your duty to supervise the golden egg. There are creatures, spirit beings, and features on the landscape that will enthusiastically protect it. For now, place the egg in the caldron at the center of the temple and let it bathe in the cosmic light."

Relieved to get the egg out of my hands, I placed it in the caldron as the mythological figures moved closer to the central flame. They gazed respectfully into the sacredness then pivoted outwards into a protective stance. Who would dare approach this egg without proper extrasensory credentials?

"It is time to perform your ceremony," the Christopher abruptly notified me.

The mystic ceremony was only an exercise to develop discipline, or so I believed. I rehearsed the steps so often they streamed in and out of my dreams. Now, I had to actually execute them. I couldn't believe my ears. Theo didn't share the practical use of the ceremony, but he did say, "When a sacred being makes this specific request, you are bound by your mystic oath to act."

I laughed and said, "What is the chance of that happening?"

No time now to write another apology note.

I conjured up the psychic essence of the sacred idea Theo called a 'stupa.' This mysterious artifact, resembling a miniature shrine, was used in many sacred schools as an essential tool for soul progress. All neophytes had to painstakingly reconstruct a personal stupa during warrior training.

I carried my stupa to the center of the temple and placed it in a flaming receptacle. I assumed it was a practical substitute for the Hierophant's table used in the traditional ceremony. I donned a golden robe, manifested a staff, and solemnly went through each of the steps, finishing the ceremony by kneeling in front of the golden egg. I pierced the light surrounding the egg. The image of Lake Isabelle, in the Rocky Mountain National Forest, appeared in the flames.

"The egg must be taken to the lake to be with the Great Mother. She will nurture it until it is ready to emerge from its cocoon." The Christopher added.

I had already planned a trip to the lake that weekend. A coincidence? Good planning by the landscape beings?

"The golden egg is unfertilized. Place a pearl of light inside the egg to nurture it until we escort it to the Great Mother."

I placed a duplicate of my inner star (a precious pearl in mystic circles) inside the egg and watched as gold and silver ribbons of energy streamed down from invisible stars above the city. These ribbons, twisted together in a double helix, cradled the egg resting in the temple.

"They will protect and nurture the precious gift within."

The sound of hands clapping greeted me. Six angels gave me a standing ovation. They doubled, then tripled, exponentially multiplying until the applause of eighty million hands assaulted my bones.

The vibrations carried me back to the creek. I watched people leisurely going about their day, eating lunch, riding bikes. Some lay on the grass, sunning themselves.

On the surface all seemed normal, but I shifted my eyes into X-ray mode. The bones of the people in the park were vibrating with the streaming angelic applause.

It reminded me of Theo's experiment with tuning forks, each one on top of a sound box. When he struck the first fork, I heard it. When he placed his hand on the fork and stopped it from vibrating, I could still hear the sound vibrating from the other forks.

"One tuning fork set to vibrate will activate others nearby. They will all reverberate in harmony and resonate together. This law of vibration is consistent throughout the cosmic realm. The invisible, or shifted, world has its own set of frequencies, of resonances, just as the physical world has its sounds. When you synchronize with the frequencies of transcendent beings or structures, you can share this vibration. Angels help human beings in this way all the time. Do you remember, at times, feeling unexpectedly euphoric? Wondering what could make you feel so good, when nothing seemed to be going on? Chances are your angel, or someone else's angel, struck your personal tuning fork to vibrating."

I understood why Theo showed me the experiment. Seeing the bodies of all these people in the park vibrating at the same frequency was proof they were synchronizing with the angels' applause and in some way, feeling the effects.

The ground began shaking. At first, I thought it was an earthquake, but no one else seemed to notice. Then, I realized what it was. The millions of hands still applauding through my bones had built to a crescendo, setting the ground below my feet to vibrate as well.

I was beginning to understand what it meant to 'light up' the landscape.

When Theo told me that I would feel it in my bones, I thought it was a metaphor.

As I fell asleep that night, my bones rested, but my inner star continued to vibrate.

CHAPTER SIX

MISSION DAY

I T WAS TIME TO hike up to Lake Isabelle per the Christopher's request. The unweathered roads were dry and clear, making the canyon drive easy. I parked the car and set my backpack and camping chair down at the trailhead. After stopping for a moment to ask the invisible world for permission to enter the forest, I picked up my gear and headed toward the lake. Within a few steps, I was joined by Bobby, the clan, and Sirius, a star being living inside a big white dog, who acts as my protector.

The Christopher led the way, carrying the golden egg, followed closely by the giant. Watching the stately pair encouraged me to wonder about the sacredness of all things. Did a creator have a say in these proceedings?

As soon as I asked the question, an angel stepped out of a blue spruce wearing a featureless mask. Written in big letters across his forehead was 'The Face of God.' He slid the mask to the top of his head, then flipped a switch on each of his temples. A spotlight appeared on his chest, projecting a holographic image. The ever-changing faces of multicultural men and women appeared, rotating on two pillars floating in the sky. He immediately jumped back into the tree and was gone. It was the shortest encounter with an angel I'd ever had.

The meaning of the angel's performance baffled me as I looked over at the Christopher carrying the golden egg. A young child appeared sitting on his shoulders, resting his hands on the top of the Christopher's head.

"Now that is the proper purpose for shoulders," another angel said as he poked his head out of an oak tree.

We continued up the trail, and others joined the procession: an Arapahoe chief with full headdress; the Michael with his flaming sword; the Solar Mage; four archangels claiming the cardinal directions; and the fourteen rainbow masters, who stood around the outer edge of the group. Seeing these powerful icons loosened my grip on the solid world. My personal entourage, with Sirius leading the band of merry gnomes, was almost lost in the gathering. The cosmic atmosphere was dizzying. I re-established my grounding cords to keep from flying out of my body.

The procession fanned out into a half circle when we arrived at the lake. The Christopher stepped forward, presenting the golden egg to the large gathering of energetic dignitaries waiting to receive us. I wondered how so many beings could fit in this space. If only I'd truly understood multidimensionality. Could a lake surrounded by mountains be considered small?

The dome covering the entire lake and the mountain peaks was now encircled by a ring of giant angelic figures. A lapis lazuli radiance surrounded their godlike demeanor.

"Elohim," my wisdom guides prompted.

The rotunda was also under the constellation-sized dome, with the Ophanim angels perched in their usual abode in the columns. A multitude of seraphim flew over us. Their swift-moving swords blazed into action, painting the sky with a grid of protection. Pan stood at the edge of the circle like a minister in a king's court, keeping track of representative nature spirits. Gaia and her sisters had front-row seats, while the River King paid homage by bowing his river tributaries, bending them toward the lake. Additional spirit beings continued to appear, more ancient than current reality could remember. It was dizzying, with layer upon layer of invisible forces solidifying before my eyes.

"A shooting star will announce the arrival," a voice declared. "Even now, angelic voices are singing out the possibility."

The air thickened with gratitude, grace, and goodness as the authoritative speaker continued. "Those who have come to this place will joyfully nurture the essence of the egg. The sanctuary is complete."

A deep silence announced the ceremony was at an end. I turned to leave. Bobby, the clan, Sirius, and the Ophanim angels followed. Everything returned to normal on the way down the mountain. Even the angels took up their entertaining ways, choosing to bobsled in slow motion all the way to town.

"Hop on," they said, making room for me between the second and third angel.

I hesitated, wanting to refuse.

One of them called out, "Action!"

They performed a grand slalom adventure, shooting multiple views of themselves speeding down the mountain. When they showed me a piece of the edited movie, there was an addition on their sled. I was inserted into the frame, appearing scared out of my wits. Their laughter was contagious.

How could these guys be an angelic order when they spent

so much time performing slapstick? I could only remember one mythological figure who presided over comedy, Thalia, a Greek Muse. These angels would have Thalia in stitches!

CHAPTER SEVEN

A FIRE DRAGON

"SINCE INVISIBLE BEINGS AND landscape features are outside of time and space, how do they know when to reveal themselves to us? Or, if they should communicate with us at all?" I asked Theo.

"Although that is a simplistic way of looking at it, it is a valid question," he replied. "Do not assume they are outside of time and space as we experience it. To the fuller spectrum of beings, most humans are walking around asleep. Our subtle bodies may exist in their space, in a dream-like state, much like the giant first appeared to you when you encountered him. To him, you were the one who was asleep."

"That doesn't make any sense," I objected. "The evidence does not support your claim."

Theo picked up a frosty glass of liquid, ignoring my protest.

"What are you drinking?" I asked, realizing the futility of continuing my challenge.

"Oh, this? It is a drink I discovered while traveling in Florida."

My mind began to spin. I called on Theo every few days

and there were no gaps in our visits. He never flew on airplanes that I knew of, so how did he go to Florida and back without me noticing?

"When did you—" I began, but Theo interrupted me.

"It's all the rage on golf courses," he said, taking another sip.

"Yes. I drink a similar brew in the afternoons. It's named after a famous golfer. I met him once; he was redesigning a local golf course. But it was a very odd meeting."

Theo looked interested, so I relayed the story.

"It was a big deal. The national press was covering his visit, and everyone was on alert for a chance encounter with the famous celebrity.

"I was playing an early round. Driving my golf cart to the back side of the course, having finished the front nine, I crossed the iconic stone bridge by the clubhouse. There were voices coming from underneath it. I stopped a short distance from the bridge after rounding the corner to the tenth tee box and looked back.

"It was the perfect angle to see him. The golfer was talking to someone, though I couldn't quite see who. He was drawing pictures in the air, gesturing toward different parts of the course. I wondered who he was consulting with.

"Suddenly, he noticed me looking in his direction, became agitated, climbed up the bank on to the bridge, and looked around at the course nonchalantly. He pulled out a book and wrote down some notes, then looked up and waved momentarily, acknowledging me as I stepped onto the tee box. I was just a chip shot away from where he stood.

"I had a clear view of the bridge. The underside was dark, but I saw movement in the shadows. It took me a minute before I recognized the silhouette. A big, lumbering form was casting a shadow on the stone wall. It was a troll!

"I took off my sunglasses to get a better look, but the troll disappeared, leaving his shadow behind on the wall. The celebrity golfer caught me looking at the shadow under the bridge. Flustered, he packed away his notebook and hurried toward the clubhouse, disappearing through the doors of the downstairs golf shop."

I looked at Theo after finishing my story.

"That makes sense," he said. "Golf courses are populated by gnomes and trolls. Not to mention, lots of holes."

I laughed, thinking Theo was being ironic, but stopped when he stared at me and asked,

"What's so funny?"

"Well, you said golf courses have lots of holes. That's part of the game, to get the ball into the hole."

"Oh," he replied.

That was it. He seemed to make a mental note, as if he had just heard something completely foreign to him.

A few weeks went by before I noticed a new luminosity appear just below the ground on the plateau. Each day I checked in; it became more visible. My remote viewing eventually recognized a persistent shape. It was a bell jar. Could the giant, residing at Lake Isabelle as part of the ongoing vigil, be reappearing on the plateau? Or, maybe it wasn't him. I had to get a closer look to find out.

The next day I climbed the steep, muddy trail up to the plateau. I slipped and fell a number of times, thoroughly dispelling my mystic warrior dignity.

After setting up my blue dish (a mystic construct for viewing the invisible landscape), I adjusted its size to encompass the whole plateau. With the dish safely submerged just below the surface, I ran through my quiet-time sequence, cleared my head space, neutralized my analyzer and prepared to make an official investigation of this developing phenomenon.

Although still partially submerged, the form had risen enough toward the surface for me to see it. A shimmering, scarlet wall faced me. Behind this fiery barricade, on the spot where I first encountered the giant, rested a Fire Dragon under the bell jar enclosure.

His head was pointing west; his tail was wrapped around the front side of his body, curling up so the tip touched his crown. Behind his head, I could see razor-scaled shoulder blades connected to neatly folded wings.

I approached slowly, noting how calm I felt face to face with a sleeping dragon. My training had changed me since meeting the giant. Theo and I had engaged in numerous conversations about dragons. I no longer carried the weight of erroneous mythological histories. In fact, my overall apprehension was reduced significantly.

"It takes courage to encounter a dragon in the proper way," Theo had instructed. "Respect must be foremost, honor is essential, and clarity of intent is mandatory. In the end, courage will win the day."

Instead of playing coy, I approached the dragon valiantly, sent him a bouquet of roses, and pulled my sword out of its scabbard. Holding my sword hilt-up, I ventured into the landscape of his body. Seeking to extract wisdom directly was a fool's errand. With a dragon, entrance into his secret domain was required first. Wisdom would be a byproduct.

My visual surroundings shifted as the dragon's world acknowledged my gravitas. Once inside, I encountered diamond clusters and plentiful jewels covering the walls of his interior world. There were veins of metallic structures spiraling in all directions, forming a series of caves. I kept moving forward, confident in my sword's guidance and past conversations with Theo.

"In a dragon's heart, answers about the creation of the Earth and the vastness of the cosmos can be found. Find a surface, walk through it, and you will end up in one of countless landscapes. Since dragons are ancient so is their knowledge, and it can be very difficult to remember any wisdom gained from such an encounter. It is quite disorienting and may distort your everyday consciousness. It can bleed into daily life and dislocate or change the sequence of current events. You will lose some memories altogether. Do you like scrambled eggs?"

"Yes," I replied.

"Your memories will feel scrambled. You will swear certain events in your life never happened and become convinced others have always been the case."

"So, what would be the point of a dragon encounter, if I wouldn't be able to remember what I experienced?"

Theo paused before answering.

"I have no proof of what I am about to tell you. There are only stories which, even after all my encounters, I have not been able to verify. All I know is that the fastest way to recall the ancient knowledge is for a dragon to speak to you."

"Speak to me?"

"Yes. The stories go into great detail about the wisdom spoken by dragons."

"What determines whether a dragon will speak to you?" I asked.

"That, the stories never say. I assume it must depend on the capacity of the mystic warrior, the nature of the dragon, and their compatibility. Just remember, the answers are inside a dragon's heart."

I was tiring quickly, losing what little focus that remained. Asking for help from my wisdom guides was all I could think of.

"How do I find my way to the dragon's heart?"

I wasn't optimistic, but I was hopeful. I waited. Nothing!

But just as Theo had predicted, when I found myself on the plateau facing the Fire Dragon again, I was at a loss.

I discovered more holes in my memory each day. The biggest hole, and the most important one of all? I didn't remember the dragon waking up.

"*Is* this my first encounter with him?" I asked myself, feelings of doubt creeping in.

"Sometimes dreaming, daydreaming, and landscape exploration overlap, causing disorientation," I remembered Theo reminding me, "but stick with it. Memories, the significant ones, will return."

I looked around for more guidance from my landscape friends. My chariot, the rotunda, was close by. I could feel the wisdom guides. The Ophanim angels, the gnomes, Sirius; all were just a short distance from me and the dragon, but I was on my own. Would the conversations about dragons or the forgotten knowledge kick in and help me get through this encounter?

There was one thing I did remember. Theo's general landscape rule.

"Always give a proper greeting to creatures on the land."

Okay, I needed an official dragon greeting. I started off with a giant gold rose.

There was no response from the Fire Dragon.

I opened my mystic robe to reveal the fiber-optic suit of armor underneath it. Even I was impressed by its radiant, translucent colors.

Still no response from the dragon.

I pulled out my sword and held it hilt-up in front of me for the dragon to see.

Nothing.

What would it take to get a response?

I exposed my two backup swords and placed them on the ground. Next, I unsheathed my ruby and emerald daggers and lay them down. I placed the gold coins, given to me by the Gnome King, next to the handles of the daggers, then I gathered my staffs and put them down on either side of the other items.

Still no response.

"What now?" I wondered.

My intent was to display my gravitas with all the accumulated accoutrements of my adventures. I was hoping to reveal myself as a real human being who came to him with the highest respect. Did I forget something? Did I have anything else to present to him? He remained as still as a statue. I felt invisible. I ran my hand through my hair and wondered what to do next. I looked at everything on the ground in front of me.

Then I heard them.

"Look inside."

It was the wisdom guides directing my attention inward.

What else could I find? What was left that would impress a Dragon? I scanned my psychic centers and my auric field. The tools, gauges, and gateways that were part of restructuring my inner landscape were all there. Were these not suitable to present to a dragon?

My inner star was shining brightly. I looked at the jewel in my frontal lobes. It wasn't fully developed, but recently it was helpful in solving puzzles to gain entrance to landscape features.

I stared at the sanctuary in my heart with its twelve pillars of virtue. It was bright and shiny, radiating the full spectrum of colors. Could virtues be the answer?

It couldn't hurt to show these inner attributes to the dragon. After all, they were a true representation of what I was made of. I gathered everything together the best I could and held it up between my two energetic palms for the dragon to see.

That did it. The Fire Dragon began to stir. Like a powerful gust, a great force came from behind and heaved me forward, hard enough for me to dig my heels in to stop from plummeting into his expanding chest. I also gripped the ground with my toes, bracing myself, afraid his expansion would knock me over before I could jump out of the way. Struggling between two dynamic forces, wind from behind and a growing dragon in front of me, I was about to lose the battle.

By the time he reached three times his original size, he stopped inhaling and lingered a moment in stillness. A greater fear caught my momentary relief and smashed what was left of my complacency. What was coming next couldn't be good. It could be very, very bad. He would exhale, and it would be fire!

I cringed, wishing I had a shield. Wait a minute. I did have a shield—sort of. It was an invisibility cloak that protected me from unavoidable entities. It might just save me from being toasted alive. But it was too late. The fire exploded like heat from a blast furnace.

Why didn't I heed Theo's warning? "Dragons are dangerous. Leave them alone. You are not ready for an encounter with one. Stay as far away as possible!"

Why hadn't I listened?

I knew what kind of heat a blast furnace could throw off. I worked in a glass factory while traveling in the South. I ran out of money often then, but I needed to stay longer to finish up some research. Getting a temporary job loading large glass bulbs onto a conveyer belt that ran through a furnace was the easy part. It was so hot – even with asbestos gloves, an apron, and head gear – I had to rotate out of that position after twenty minutes. It took twenty minutes to hydrate and recover before another tormenting twenty minutes back at the furnace. Those three weeks were filled with the hardest work I had ever endured.

The dragon's breath wasn't like the furnace. It wasn't hot at all. It passed through each layer of my aura, burning off cloudy chunks of debris, black and grey blotches previously unknown to me.

"We carry many unfortunate substances in our energy field," Theo once said, explaining why we all need to review our history. "These substances accumulate over the years. They are projected at us and stick to us, living inside us all our lives. Parents, friends, relatives, events. Life's idiosyncrasies find their way into us. Some, we release unknowingly. Most become resistance to the free-flowing natural state of a human being."

As far as I could tell I was unharmed, but hundreds of obstacles in my energy field were illuminated, burnt up, and blown away by the dragon's breath. Was this a dragon gift? A blessing from the dragon? Or, a mandatory preparation for dragon communication?

In a slow, determined motion, the dragon raised a great claw toward his chest, lifting open a large, scaly plate that covered his heart. Landscape beings expect us to participate with them when encouraged. I accepted the invitation, picked up my sword, and pierced his exposed heart. The resistance I expected to feel was supplanted by a great force that pulled my sword into his body. I tightened my grip and followed.

Until now, I was sure I was training to escape my private prison. But this dragon experience showed me there were no bars, no locked doors, no measure of time to be served. If there was a crime, it was my refusal to accept being human—vulnerable to all that the world had to offer. Not as a victim, but as a neutral observer, free of judgement. Nothing to fix; just embracing everything as it was. And in that moment, acquiescing to the wisdom of the dragon's heart was my only choice, to drown out my obligation to struggle, to get away.

The elongation of wisdom breached the measure of time; I was lost in its pleasure.

It was not until voices crept into my immersion that I began my reluctant resurgence. I tried to ignore them. But they were poking holes in my bliss, pulling my attention away from the dragon wisdom.

"Is he done yet?"

"No."

"Well, how long?"

"Don't know. But he is half-baked."

"You know what we say?"

"Yes, I know what we say. Half-baked on the grill of wisdom is a full broil in the oven of life."

"That is a good saying."

"I know. We said it."

"Is he done yet?"

If I could have sunk deeper and bathed longer, I would have. But I couldn't. The voices ended my experience.

Expecting the Ophanim angels to be the culprits, I looked around, but only the fire dragon was nearby. Everything else looked the same, but I felt misaligned with my body. It didn't quite fit. My senses were distorted. I breathed deeply and listened for a familiar mental construct to ground me to the precise time and space.

Theo's words were still reverberating in the back of my head.

"Some trainees must be pulled out by none-too-happy mentors who advised them not to engage a dragon. If angels have to intervene, your goose was close to being cooked!"

The image of the fire dragon stabilized as I gazed at him. A rumbling…a roaring shook my subtle bodies, slowly making its way through each layer until it finally reached my ears. My eardrums oscillated, bringing the vibrations to my brain, which finally deciphered them. It was reminiscent of my dad's old Victrola ramping up, with the needle arm already in place; the sound growing more familiar as the record spun faster.

I was taken aback by the time it took for the words to make any sense. Long after the initial vibration, I heard recognizable words.

"Will you be the one to free the Water Dragon?"

I was confused by the source of the voice and the question. It was coming from the dragon, *and* from more than the dragon. It resounded in my heart, my blood vessels, and the acupuncture meridians on the surface of my body. It pondered the words deep within the magma of the Earth. The sun and stars were not exempt from participation, sounding as a choir articulating the depth and dimension of the words.

I checked my grounding cords and made sure I was firmly strapped in my head space chair, my mental throne of personal power. I gave myself a healing of ten suns of clarity and twenty suns of seniority.

The request was coming directly from a dragon. Until now, this ancient scroll could easily be considered a fantasy, a riddle, or a daydream. But how could I deny a dragon's spoken words?

What does freeing a dragon mean? Images and thoughts raced across my internal screen. My mind couldn't keep up. Overloaded, I forced myself to stop.

Focusing on my inner star, time slowed. Fragmented pieces

coalesced. The synchronicity of sound, time, and motion established a place of clarity. The dragon's voice reached out.

"She is chained, trapped by misguided wizards who thought they could control nature. In this case, the 100-year cycle of flooding the Earth with bounty. Little do they know that we dragons, out of our compassion, *allow* ourselves to be contained."

I was trying to understand the implications of what the dragon was saying. I didn't know who the misguided wizards were, and I'd never heard of the 100-year cycle.

The Fire Dragon continued, "You will find her in the Canyon of Gold Water."

I knew the canyon he was talking about. The Canyon of Gold Water was Eldorado Canyon. The 'water' must be the river that ran through it. It supplied the local water-bottling company who distributed it throughout the city. The 'gold?' Well, everyone knows 'Eldorado' means 'the golden one.'

I visualized the canyon to assess where she might be captured, but the Fire Dragon's resounding voice interrupted my thoughts.

"It is her time to join me and witness the new cycle," he said. "Gradually, I will fade away, becoming secondary to my companion. The misinformed may conclude I must also be chained. I will allow this. They believe they can control my cycle of breathing upon the land. But my fire rejuvenates the land, insuring future abundance. It has always been this way.

"I will fly with my companion for a time, then comes the deep constriction. I will slip into the land, only to once again awaken and return during the time of balance. It has always been, so shall it be."

The dragon's silence cued me to say something. But what? I must remember something useful from the Mystic Warrior's Handbook that could help me here.

'Be gracious when majestic beings communicate with you. It is a rare gift to have this happen.'

I spoke in a deliberate voice.

"I am honored to be of assistance. I will learn as much as I can about the Water Dragon's plight, and I promise to make all possible attempts to accomplish this task. Thank you for choosing me to serve your cause."

I spoke with as much grace as I could muster. It was my attempt to be elegant and formal, like a diplomat in a foreign land. The Fire Dragon slowly bowed his head in acknowledgement, then settled back down onto the landscape. I gave a slight bow of respect in return, sent out gratitude roses, and made my way off the plateau.

Once I was home, I furiously wrote everything down, capturing as much of the experience as possible. I then checked the notes in my journals where Theo had expounded upon the nature of dragons. The pages were blank.

It was already happening. I laughed, "Eggs over easy, please."

CHAPTER EIGHT

WANTED – ONE TRUE WARRIOR

TRAINED WITH THE WARRIOR five days a week. He wasn't originally involved in my training, but I had to seek him out after a particularly awkward preparation day with Theo. Wielding a mystic sword was no easy feat.

"It is important to begin external weapons training with a sword, dagger, and staff," Theo advised. "You must synchronize these real and symbolic implements. Add muscle flexibility and joint mobility to facilitate movement of your energy. As you gain discipline, you will validate the use of your internal weapons."

That day, I couldn't unsheathe my lower primary mystic sword from its scabbard. I was struggling with the concept of holding onto something in the 'shifted realm.' Every time I tried to grip it, my hand slipped right through.

"I see it," I told Theo, "but I can't grasp it."

"Focus," he demanded.

"I thought I was *focusing*," I replied, frustrated. "Isn't there an easier way to do this?"

"Yes," he said.

I felt relieved, believing he was going to help. I waited for additional instructions, but he didn't say anything.

"Well?" I asked.

"Well, what?" Theo responded.

"How do I get this damned sword out of its scabbard?"

"Focus," he said again.

I could feel anger building inside.

Theo sat down on a nearby boulder overlooking the small pond. He motioned me to do the same. I gazed across the gentle water. A white crane stood on one leg, partially hidden by the verdant reeds. Her white outline against the lush green was striking. Yet, her stillness made her invisible to her prey, and mostly unseen from everywhere but our location. I admired the concentration, the focus she needed to feed herself. That is innate, I thought. No training necessary.

"You must recognize that every life situation is a gift."

"That doesn't always make sense. There are too many examples—"

Theo cut me off, knowing the direction my logical mind was heading.

"Yes, yes, the chitter-chatter mentality of your analyzer has many examples, but this way of thinking is not genuine. Everyone believes life is an outside-in job that must be managed and controlled. In fact, life is an inside-out activity. You are responsible for creating your reality. Your training will bear this out. No explanation will suffice. Observe, process, and sort out your thoughts and feelings. This will clarify your situation."

I accepted my mental struggle as essential and recognized my anger as valued information, too. Immediately insight followed. I saw what wanted my attention. Energy was shooting out of my liver and wrapping around my sword. It was a sticky, gelatinous glue keeping it firmly sealed in my scabbard.

"What do you do for me?" I asked the glue, still feeling a bit silly talking to constructs of my imagination.

"I protect you," it responded. "If I don't, you will hurt yourself."

"I understand," I said, trying to appease it by acknowledging its position. "Is there a better way to protect me than to prevent me from using my sword?"

"I do not know," it answered. "This is the only thing I do."

"If there *were* something else, would you be interested in trying it?"

"Well…yes," it said hesitantly.

I called on my wisdom guides.

"A little help here, please."

My wisdom guides appeared and surrounded me and the glue. In a few seconds, an image of a steel shield appeared. It was the size of my body.

My sticky glue image loosened its grip on my sword.

"Thank you for protecting me from hurting myself," I said as I gave it some white forgiveness roses.

It merged with the shield and wrapped me in a bubble of bright yellow energy. I didn't realize how much muscle contraction was packaged around my spine, especially in the middle of my back. Now that the tension was gone, I took a long, deep breath.

"Well?" Theo asked as I exhaled.

I opened my half-closed eyes. The crane was gone.

"Check your sword," He directed.

I focused on the feeling of merging the sword with the landscape, not my struggle to remove it. I imagined penetrating a tree, a stone, a column in a temple, a river, and the sun, each time emphasizing how good it felt to connect in this way with the natural world. I repeated these activities until I felt centered, relaxed, and confident. Once again, I attempted to extract my sword.

I grabbed hold of the hilt, half-expecting it to be stuck, but it slid out quickly. I was so surprised and excited to see it outside of my energy body that I began to swing it wildly, laughing joyfully about my accomplishment.

"Stop!" Theo shouted.

Shocked by his voice, I stopped thrashing about with my sword.

"Your sword is a delicate instrument. A sensitive tool. One's initial behavior upon releasing a sword is a prophetic sign. Although you have the potential to be a wisdom seeker, you need exterior weapons training. Find a teacher who will instruct you on how to handle a sword. You have to learn to wield an extremely dangerous weapon. Genuine respect is necessary to use it appropriately."

Flushed with embarrassment, I returned my sword to its scabbard.

"How will I find a teacher?"

"Your search for an instructor will not take long."

Having already experienced Theo's relative time, his statement provided little reassurance that I'd find someone anytime soon.

"Don't worry," he laughed, reading the doubtful shift of my energy field. "I telegraphed a proper invitation into the subtle world. Look for yourself." He said, pointing above my head.

The words were floating a hundred feet high, flashing on and off.

'Ready to train with a master swordsman.'

"Isn't that a bit conspicuous?" I asked, trying to hide my discomfort about toting a large neon billboard around.

"Sometimes, conspicuous invisibility is necessary," he answered, sending me on my way.

Two weeks later was my scheduled visit with Miss Montgomery, a local widow. We shared casual conversation and I performed odd jobs whenever needed. One afternoon, I arrived to find a distant nephew at her house. We'd met a few times, and I knew he traveled in martial arts circles. He brought up sword fighting in a casual conversation over afternoon tea. I mentioned my search for a teacher.

"Come to think of it," he said, "there's someone known as 'the Warrior.' He's teaching inside a warehouse down the street. He's an enigmatic figure who speaks in allegorical idioms and can be difficult to comprehend. But the rumors around town are conclusive; he has extensive knowledge, and he's as fast as he is powerful. His reputation is impeccable, although he only trains a few students."

He looked me over, evaluating my reaction to the short video he showed me on his phone. I was concerned this warrior was out of my league, but I stayed neutral.

"He gives potential students an aptitude test which can be obscure and quite confusing."

He spoke from firsthand knowledge. He confessed that he took the test but had never heard back from the Warrior.

"Most potential students fail within minutes. His perplexing style creates an atmosphere few can follow, let alone work with. His contemporaries give him a wide berth, and I suggest you do the same." He moved closer to me and whispered, "He can do strange things with energy."

I didn't bat an eyelash. This acquaintance knew nothing about my training with Theo – a different kind of energy master – and it was prudent to keep it that way.

When he left, he said, "Good luck," over his shoulder. "You'll need it."

His voice resembled Theo's. He even gave me a familiar smirk.

I moved forward, contacting the Warrior by sending a handwritten letter requesting an interview. Two weeks later, I received a note written in brushstrokes: 'Park. Lake of Wonders. 6 a.m. Third day.' It was signed with a line drawing of a fearsome warrior.

The directions seemed easy enough. Meet him at Wonderland Lake at six o'clock on Wednesday.

Arriving early, I stopped between two oak trees and took a few deep breaths. The air felt heavy with moisture. A thick fog blocked the view of the foothills, and a layer of white mist drifted down the hillside settling upon the lake.

I dove into my quiet-time sequence – inner star, blue dish, rotunda – and readied my connection with the landscape. My energetic friends arrived: Bobby, the clan, even Sirius made an appearance. The Ophanim angels were up to their antics, performing a mishmash of Kung Fu and karate katas while tossing in a few acrobatic feats impossible for any human to perform. They finished up with a display of synchronized aerobics.

I cleared my head space, quieted my analyzer, and dusted off my etheric armor. Gripping the handle of my sword, sliding it in and out of its scabbard seemed prudent. For a moment of silence, I stepped into my staff—my entrance into a kind of pocket reality. The space inside was virtual emptiness, ideal for focusing one's attention before any undertaking.

Occasionally, I peeked out of my staff to see if the Warrior had arrived. I peered up the walkway, half-expecting a silk-robed sage to saunter down the hill. I saw the lines of force between the trees connecting cosmic energy to the landscape,

tempting me to perform some energetic acrobatics o
"Best to stay focused on the task at hand," I reminde

A rehearsed greeting sounded disingenuous, so I
stay empty and allow discernment to speak for me.

There was rustling behind me from the reeds surrou
the lake. It was still too foggy for me to see anything. A
A mountain lion? A deer? A coyote? A moose? All had rec
been seen in the vicinity. Whatever it was, I could feel it con
in my direction. A silhouette was coalescing inside the fo
decided to make some noise to warn off any wild creatures.

"A tune should do the trick!"

Just as I was about to start singing, he appeared just beyor
the fence between the park and the lake.

It was a solidly built man gracefully walking in my direction. He had reddish hair and a three-day growth on his
unshaven face. Tan cargo pants and iridescent-green running
shoes completed the picture.

"That can't be him."

I looked away and focused on the path once again. No one
else was around. There were no walkers, runners, or cyclists.
The usual athletes were avoiding the fog this morning.

Then I felt it, a large presence right behind me. Maybe
there was a wild animal after all. Energy ran up my spine and
the hairs on my arms stood up. It felt large, like the giant, and I
wondered if maybe it was a landscape being. I drew my sword,
somewhat clumsily, and prepared to display it.

I turned, brandishing my psychic sword, but the man
crossed it with his own *very real* blade, stopping twelve inches
from my face. My heart was pounding.

Behind the sword, I could see his eyes. They had a green
glow and pure joy was radiating from them, whereas mine
were projecting fear. Lots of fear.

A blue flash caught the corner of my eye, drawing my attention away from the present danger. My energy body projected up to the top of the trees like a slingshot, hooking onto their fibrous energy cords.

I looked down and saw twelve blue-robed Seraphim angels with blazing swords standing around my body. Each of their fiery swords was engaged with the green-eyed man's steel blade.

I wasn't sure if the man could see the Seraphim or their fiery swords, but he must have recognized something out of the ordinary was going on. He returned his sword to the leather scabbard slung across his back as he looked to my energy body in the tree, back to my physical body, and then up again.

I cautiously returned to my body. The Seraphim redeployed above the two of us.

I looked the man in the eye and watched his energy field shrink down to normal size.

"You're the Warrior, aren't you?" I asked.

"For today I am. Tomorrow, we shall see."

I didn't know how to respond to that.

Instead, I said, "I have come to learn how to use a sword."

"I see," he responded as he swept his arm through the air, drawing a triangle by indicating first the Seraphim, then the top of the trees, then me, and then back to the Seraphim.

Did he see that I had a mystic sword? Could he perceive the Seraphim? As with Theo, I knew it wouldn't be an appropriate question to ask. Not during a first encounter. Instead, I searched for practical questions.

"How do I qualify to train with you? What test do I have to take? How do you pick students?"

Saying nothing, he just stared at me. I instinctively engaged some protection roses, manifested suns of certainty,

and reinforced my auric bubble. Minutes passed while I waited for an answer.

"We start tomorrow at sunrise," he finally said, then he turned to walk away. "Meet me here."

He leaped over the fence and moved into the fog.

"But what about my test?" I shouted after him.

"You have passed the test," he replied, disappearing into the reeds.

I was dumbstruck as I walked away, giving gratitude roses to my landscape friends and the Seraphim angels. I showered the trees with roses, too.

I was excited. I was going to learn to use a sword in the proper way!

The coming months passed quickly as I trained with the Warrior.

"Do not think. Do."

"Do not do. Be."

"Action comes from non-action."

"Non-action manifests from no-mind."

"Do not think."

"Watch your opponent defeat himself. Then, no fight ensues."

The Warrior sounded like Sun Tzu.

I performed strokes – slashing, slicing, striking with my stick – imitating the Warrior's movements while listening to his words. When I began to train I was shy, quiet, apprehensive, and fearful of physical contact. But soon, my disposition changed dramatically. My confidence grew, my movements synchronized, and my stick training reflected complex internal sword movements. An unspoken arcane language was developing in my training. I strove to understand it.

When I graduated to live swordplay, I felt a new connection to everything. My mystic training took a new direction as well.

"Hold a sword, feel a dragon. See a dragon, draw a sword," Theo read from a book in the castle library. "You are beginning to discover connections for yourself. The sword movements imitate the ancient language of dragons."

I wondered how movement and language had anything to do with dragons. Theo's explanation took a mysterious turn.

"The ancient mythos describes, in minute detail, how the Michael taught the Merlin character and how, in turn, he communicated it to dragons."

Theo closed the invisible book and carefully placed it back on the shelf in the library.

"Modern warriors accumulate swords at different stages as they progress through their training, but a sword given by the Michael is the most sought after, the most precious sword of all.

"The dual mystic swords are given early on. The daggers of the Gnome King are given at different times; you may be surprised to find a dagger sitting on a large stone as a gift. And, if worthy, you will get to see the Seraphim swords in action. This occurs in specific locations, usually in a labyrinth or near a rainbow master's sanctuary. Lao Tzu or Quan Yin are well known masters of internal swordplay."

When the Warrior trusted I was committed to training, he taught me the System. Its depth and wisdom convinced me it was time to take the Warrior into my confidence.

Theo had once told me, "To seek out a compatriot is more prudent than attempting to accomplish a task alone. You can miss important clues on the landscape that a companion might catch."

One day, after training, as the Warrior was pouring us tea, I decided to ask him to help me free the Water Dragon. It was a long shot. I would have to reveal my mystic status and my visionary landscape work. The request and a confession of my belief in dragons could jeopardize our relationship and training, but I had to take the chance.

"I must free a dragon, and I need your help."

The Warrior responded, "I have heard of such things. My teacher shared many stories while traveling through the mountains of southern China. Magical stories about the lives of great masters in ancient times. Dragons living among people, changing the weather, protecting villages by washing out roads as marauders approached, putting out fires in the heat of the summer, adjusting the course of rivers to produce fertile land. Continuously helping people and spirits alike.

"In those days, the elemental forces communicated with each other. Folks came into life knowing this. Many were born with the ability to interact with spirit creatures, and they behaved accordingly. Now, it is different."

The Warrior spoke with fondness for his teacher and the ancient way of life.

He added, "There were stories of men who attempted to control dragons. This always ended badly. Dragons have long memories and even longer lives. They know when evil returns to the land."

It was the most the Warrior had ever said to me, and he had done so in such an ordinary way, so unlike his usual staccato delivery.

The Warrior's voice trailed off as he gazed into a distant past, watching stories play out on a mental screen in from of him. Just like Theo. I watched as he captured history and reeled it in for inspection.

I waited. My patience paid off. He took a deep breath and adjusted his tea-ceremony robe.

"The chronicles show us," the Warrior proclaimed, "that it would be wise to act upon this request."

I smiled down at my cooling cup of tea in relief. This was a good day. Now to come up with a plan.

CHAPTER NINE

FREE THE WATER DRAGON

I SHARED THE SCANT DETAILS the ancient scroll had given me with the Warrior.

"I believe that, with our swords, a bit of luck, and a little creative intelligence, it should be possible to free the Water Dragon."

The Warrior concurred, but he had little to add by way of advice. He remained silent while looking down at the collage of words and pictures I'd drawn while sharing my findings. It was a jumbled map of ideas. I pulled a spool of thread out of my pocket and linked the pieces together. A stick figure of a blue dragon sat in the middle. When I was finished, the dragon looked like she was trapped by a wire net.

"This isn't quite right," I said, placing a spool on her leg. "Just one chain here."

The Warrior examined my creation methodically, then he said, "We practice tomorrow. It will be an extreme training day. Our swords need to be focused and ready to penetrate the forces that will lend us insight into the dragon's plight."

Although I trusted the Warrior's wisdom and skill, I closed

my eyes and took a silent moment, hoping for affirmation from my wisdom guides. A good, old-fashioned belly intuition came through loud and clear. My inner star twinkled, and I smiled back. When I opened my eyes, I saw the Ophanim angels sailing large dragon kites. Each kite propelled bucket-sized water droplets splashing down all around me. I half-expected one to land on my head.

"This is a positive sign," I said out loud, turning back to the Warrior. He was looking at me with a whimsical smile on his face.

Splash!

"One bucket of water, sir, as ordered," said an angel holding a pad and pencil.

My subtle bodies received a soaking. Another good omen?

"It is the official Chinese New Year. The Year of the Dragon is upon us. That will give us an edge," I told the Warrior.

He nodded his approval.

I bowed respectfully, eager to prepare myself and evaluate the logistics of the location. Making a reconnaissance mission to the canyon would be expedient. We parted ways.

All night long, I was challenged by puzzles that needed to be solved.

When I met the Warrior the next day, I was groggy. My strokes were slow, 'off the bridge,' as the Warrior kept repeating. He was persistent that day, correcting me more than usual on how my sword crossed the (bridge) midline of the opponent's body.

He bowed, presenting his sword at chest height. I did the same. The lesson had ended, albeit abruptly. We sheathed our swords then sat down at the table in his garden. As was his custom, the Warrior left momentarily and returned with tea. It was freshly brewed from leaves he purchased during his trip to China; he brought back the exact amount necessary to last six and a half months, always allowing for the unpredictability of students and guests.

The high fence surrounding the garden was overshadowed by enormous rose bushes that lined its perimeter. I enjoyed the moments of drinking tea, appreciating the abundant flowers and the ever-present choir of birds. The Warrior never said a word during the tea ceremonies, which was fine with me, since it gave me the time to breathe in the accumulated chi that energized the atmosphere around our encounters. When the Warrior's voice broke the silence, I practically choked on my tea, spilling some on the ebony table.

"We must free the dragon on Thursday."

It was somewhat earlier than I'd planned. I hoped to gather more information first, but the Warrior's advice was noteworthy and not to be taken lightly.

As I wiped up the tea with my cloth napkin, the Warrior said, "An auspicious time marking inevitable success."

I felt encouraged.

The cosmos was rousing cooperation from the field of energy and, because we were partaking in this landscape adventure together, it was including us in its discourse.

The weather in late January was uncommonly warm, around fifty-five degrees. This gap in the cold winter months was welcome, and it increased my confidence and determination, but the Chinook winds that carried the seasonal warmth wouldn't last long. Soon, the serious cold would set in again.

"I hate doing landscape research while it's cold outside," I complained to Theo later. "Hours of sitting in sagging blue chairs. It's bad enough when it's a hundred degrees outside, but when it's two degrees I have a difficult time seeing. Even Bobby remains a ghostly figure!"

Theo laughed and replied, "I once said the same thing to *my* mentor, but I never complained again after he sent my consciousness to sit on a block of ice at the North Pole. Then, for good measure, he sent me to Timbuktu, which happened to be about 130 degrees Fahrenheit. I can laugh about it now, but it was an excruciating lesson. I haven't complained about blue chair syndrome since. I suggest you consider yourself warned."

I wasn't sure how serious Theo was being. Was it a real threat? Thankfully, it would be different with the Warrior. Instead of sitting and freezing, we would be moving and activating our sword energy.

What would the conditions in the canyon be like? It was deep, received little sunlight, so its orientation could be problematic. The floor of the canyon didn't melt all winter; the hilltops and canyon froze, thawed, and froze again, just like the valley. And what if there was a landscape feature near the dragon's entrapment? Would it also expect interaction beforehand? With the Warrior as my companion, this could be problematic.

It was always nonstop action with the Warrior, so I prepared ahead of time. I knew there might be unforeseeable problems, but if all my tools were readied, I'd be capable of handling most surprises.

I met the Warrior at the dojo behind his house. It was my preference to participate in mystic adventures at sunrise, or early afternoon in winter, but the Warrior informed me he was going to be busy until 3 p.m. Since I calculated the hike into the canyon would take forty-five minutes, it would be dark before the task was complete. This caused me no small amount of anxiety.

Out of respect I paused to see if the Warrior had any suggestions. He held up his right index finger. The energy rose straight up, changed direction, and began to curve. It streamed out and entered a small garage hidden by a clump of lilac bushes.

He walked over to a set of padlocked double doors, slid his hand inside his long robe and pulled out a key the same gold color as his two back teeth. He turned it twice in the lock – twisting counterclockwise – and then placed the key back inside his robe. He removed the lock, opened the latch, and swung open the doors. He performed the process with such adeptness that I was mesmerized by his efficiency of movement.

Inside the garage was a vehicle covered with a tattered green tarp. The Warrior grabbed a corner of the tarp with his right hand and gave it a quick tug, like a magician removing a tablecloth set with continental dinnerware. He revealed a shiny black Jeep with specialty license plates.

"AQUQI," I read. "What does that mean?"

In a powerful, uncanny tone, he proclaimed, "Qi energy singing poetically to the one."

His thunderous words arrived like a gust of wind and tapered off into a slight echo. I could see the shaped sounds rapidly changing from the time they left his mouth until the moment they reached my ears.

"Climb in," he said, with a slight bow and a wave of his arm.

I hopped into the Jeep, confident we would arrive in the canyon earlier than anticipated, but my optimism was soon dashed. If there was a longer route we could have driven, I didn't know it, and we never so much as neared the speed limit. Every time we headed toward the canyon, the Warrior would make a ninety-degree turn, collapsing my enthusiasm sails, only to be reflated each time we were back on course.

Following eight redirects, I closed my eyes, stopped my

yo-yoing emotional response, and focused on emptying my internal cup.

The next time I opened my eyes we had stopped at the park ranger's booth.

After paying the entrance fee, we drove over the bridge and entered the state park. Thin ice lined the edges of the gently flowing South Boulder Creek, its banks covered in a dusting of snow.

We continued along the narrow dirt road that hugged the canyon walls. There were a number of blind turns and only one vehicle at a time could occupy the road. This caused a few stops, backups, and waves of appreciation before moving forward again.

When we made it to the canyon floor and parked the car, I scanned the landscape for a vantage point. Gazing with my inner vision, I saw the dragon.

"Up there," I said, pointing with my walking stick. "That's the spot."

We started the hike toward the high plateau. The going became difficult. I hadn't counted on the accumulation of snow, ice, and slush on the trail. Our shoes (mine with flat, non-grip bottoms, the Warrior's a type of slipper-boot) were soggy within steps.

I was distracted by the conditions but pushed aside my trepidation and continued up the path. Breathing hard at this altitude was oddly exhilarating. I became downright giddy.

The daylight was disappearing quickly. We still had to get to the top of the hill, free the dragon, and get back down to the car before the fading light and falling temperature turned the path into a deathtrap. This fear was one more fleeting distraction. Oddly, it didn't disturb me. I was in a hyper-state of awareness, and it carried me along like an adrenaline-charged dream.

I exhaled hard and often. Was I becoming oxygen deprived?

"I should have brought an oxygen canister," I jested to the Warrior.

I was breathing harder and stopping more frequently with every dozen steps. Oddly, I remained in a state of joy. I could hardly contain myself. I laughed out loud on the final stretch of the steepening slope, sometimes scrambling on all fours.

When I reached the top, I was panting, gulping down every available molecule of oxygen. There weren't many at eight thousand feet. All the way up, my energy double was flying above the canyon while my physical body climbed the snowy, slippery terrain. Now, my consciousness was fully expanded. I turned to look at the Warrior. He was standing about twenty feet away, searching for a place to unpack our swords.

My jaw dropped when I allowed my gaze to shift toward the realm of the unseen.

"You are so beautiful," I heard myself saying out loud.

The greeting roses I conveyed to the dragon caused her blue color to erupt into a thousand brilliant shades, both visible and invisible. Her wings unfurled, growing taller than a ten-story building from tip to tip. Her tail snaked along the canyon floor and reached deep into the mountain range.

When my inner eyes adjusted further, she displayed her fire-jeweled heart. I had to stop myself from prematurely diving into its brilliance. There would be plenty of opportunities to investigate her inner realm once she was free.

The Warrior had already placed our weapons bag down on the ground and pulled out our swords. I knelt down, held my sword in the palms of my hands, and asked it to 'strike true.' The plan was straightforward: engage in swordplay; impress the dragon, the warrior gods, and the local spirits; and discover the way to free her.

THE WATER DRAGON

"We must convince the invisible realm of our righteousness and that we are worthy of this task," I declared.

We stood in a warrior stance to clear ourselves of distracting thoughts. I quickly flashed through the steps of the Logos meditation. The fast-forward version looked like a series of clipped scenes from a movie trailer, but it was compulsory for me to get to clarity.

"Empty clears the mind's eye," I heard the Warrior say.

He was right. Each time I peeked at the dragon, more of her mythological form came into view. There were star worlds rotating around the center of her heart. They flowed like a fountain of crystal water. Her unfurled wings stretched beyond the horizon, and her cavern of treasures sparkled. Ancient scenes flashed around her, reaffirming the purpose of our presence: her freedom. How many times had warriors come to free her?

"Immortal are we all," sounded a deep, slow voice. "Remember, I, every moment since time began. All water flows from the great mother through my kind onto the land. The hundred-year cleansing is a coming proof. Liquid life is given and taken away. Now is my time for freedom."

When she finished speaking, her plight became clear. What trapped her was a chain wrapped around her legs connected to deep forces inside the Earth. It was thin and delicate, with small, interlocking links like a silver necklace I remember my sister wearing.

My analyzer wanted to know, "How could such a fragile chain imprison such a powerful dragon?"

Before it could continue its rational journey, an all-powerful voice proclaimed, "It is time to use your swords."

We stood our ground and began our five-attacks routine; two warriors with swords standing before a chained dragon.

"Is there anyone else willing to help us?" I shouted, trusting we needed assistance.

It became windy, the air gusting with substantial force. Our swords went to work. The metal elements in the atmosphere electrified. Our ingrained movements filled the space in front of us. The wind gusts grew stronger and colder than my body appreciated or wanted to endure. The surreal predicament superseded my personal discomfort.

My confidence began slipping when unknown forces stepped up their disapproval. Why did they not want this dragon freed? I should have anticipated this. I felt ill prepared to continue this challenge. I checked my blue sphere, my protection roses, and my suns. Desperate, I invited the presence of the Ophanim, the Seraphim, the Cherubim, and any other angelic being out there.

Astral lightning, invisible rain, and howling ghost forms were unrelenting. They stepped up their attack.

The Warrior laughed at their trickery and swung his sword faster, though with no less precision. It struck fear into the interlopers and the winds weakened. Concentrated solar rays streamed through the cracks opening in the dark clouds. This backlit the dragon, the sunlight cascading over her heart and flushing debris from her jeweled caverns.

"A mystic warrior is steadfast when dark forces misbehave." Theo's words couldn't have come at a better time.

The distant mountains brightened behind the dragon. The sky, azure blue with diaphanous clouds, sifted the colors of a pastel rainbow as the sun descended.

It was time. The Warrior and I projected our swords' energy toward the dragon. Our combined power built up to a crescendo. We struck down on the chain with prodigious force.

The wind, slowing down around us, made a whipping

sound and rushed through the canyon, then stopped. Stillness ensued. The angels took advantage of the pause and gathered in the clouds above us. A fissure opened wide enough for the dragon to rise up and escape.

Afterimages of a colossal blue dragon rising with outstretched wings impeded my view of the evening sky. The fiery beams bursting from her heart were intensified by the setting sun. The precious pearl she carried in her claws was encircled by forces of spiraling energy.

We were outside of time. The electric atmosphere was alive with a magical presence. The choir of angelic song was deafening.

The wind shifted, now coming toward us from the peaks of the mountains. Its chill brought me back to the reality of my body. Dusk was pushing us to pack up our swords and get off the dragon's perch. I followed the Warrior back to the canyon floor. All the way down, I felt the weight of the quest lifting off my shoulders.

An angel was waiting by the car when we arrived. He had a clipboard in one hand and a pair of wings draped over his arm.

"Ah, I see here we have checked off a major box on your list of boxes," he said.

"List of boxes?" I responded. "I only had one quest. Free the Water Dragon."

"No, that is not quite right. That was your first challenge. And, since you succeeded, you get to wear these wings for two minutes."

"Two minutes?"

"Yes, there are only two-minute wing wearing boxes on your list."

"How many boxes do you need to check off before I get

to keep the wings permanently?" I asked, now curious about the challenges on the checklist.

"Oh, we can't tell you that, but hey, not many people even earn a two-minute winging."

By the time I got into the car, the Warrior had started it and turned the heater on. I held my hands over the vent and warmed my fingers. He looked at me with curious eyes about my delay. I didn't tell him about my two-minute grant of wearing wings. I was satiated by the privilege.

The Year of the Dragon was upon us. The Water Dragon was free. What next? Qualify for another two-minute winging?

CHAPTER TEN

THE GREATEST SWORD OF ALL

"WHY SWORDS? WHY IS the Michael's sword the greatest sword of all? What does he have to do with mystics? Why do we look to him in our quest for warrior-ship? Why—"

Theo held up his hand to silence my questions without chiding me for my stream of 'whys.'

"It is time to tell you the Michael story, as it was told to me by my mentor. But before I begin, you need to don your philosopher's robe, step through the Logos meditation, and walk into your staff."

When Theo suggested this, I assumed we would be going for a ride in the rotunda. I stepped into the emptiness of my expanded staff, still unsettled by how infinitely large it was on the inside.

Soon Theo said, "Now, open your eyes."

I expected to discover a visually shifted destination, but we were still sitting in his house near the Dell of Faeries. I didn't disguise the surprise in my eyes and looked at him questioningly.

"You need to be in a clear state for this story to have a

lasting meaning. Eventually, you will have your own Michaelic experience. You must be ready to capture all the subtleties of that adventure."

He took a moment to adjust himself in his chair and then closed his eyes. I knew what this meant; I'd seen him repeat this preparation many times, searching the mysterious castle archives with his mind to locate the appropriate book from which to recite.

"There are many stories about the Michael, as we mystics fondly address him. Not out of disrespect but out of the closeness we feel. No single version of his story is complete. The story I tell you is similarly imperfect, yet this version will paint a helpful picture."

Once upon a time, long after the original creator gods had designed human beings, the One grew concerned about the creation. The next step in human evolution would be crucial. Help from above was needed. Providing it was a voluntary mission.

He asked the assembled hosts, "Who will undertake the task of bringing freedom to humanity? It is not our wish to create compulsory worshippers; we desire human beings to be free. It is through this freedom, the final step on their journey will be ful-filled. Our fondest wish is for them to finalize the most important quality of all: love.

For a moment in the time of the One, not a voice in the hordes of assembled angelic beings spoke up. And, as we all know, in heaven, a moment is an eternity!

There was an angel, considered to be the brightest of them all, who stepped forward.

"I will descend to the Earth and teach human beings freedom so they can discover the true meaning of love."

It was the Gift Giver.

The One was very pleased. He informed the Gift Giver how difficult a task it would be.

"There is no guarantee you will succeed. If you fail, your name will be demonized, buried, chained, and defaced until the Logos comes to Earth to set you free."

The Gift Giver stood steadfast and accepted the terms without hesitation. He was confident he could succeed but, alas, how little angelic beings understood the fickle race of humanity. Their maturation would take time; more time than the birth and death of the stars in the heavens.

The law is very clear, when a vacancy occurs in paradise, someone must step forward to fill the void.

The Angel Michael, referred to as 'Like unto the One,' stepped forward and said, "I will take the Gift Giver's place here and also aid him in his descent to the Earth."

"How will we ensure the comfort of humanity during their long struggle?" a choir sang, urged on by the passion radiating from the One.

Inspired by the moment (for he knew the voice of the One in his own mind), Michael pulled out his sword and, with one magnificent stroke, cut an emerald from the crown of the Gift Giver.

The One was pleased. He immediately promoted the Michael to a full-fledged archangel for his courage and action.

Theo paused until the scenes, assembled in my mind, were placed in a precise order on my memory screen. I aligned and corrected the pictures, adding the appropriate colors and sounds. This exercise solidified the stored memory in my soul.

There was another spirit who played a role in this experiment. It was the Sophia, the guardian of the Holy Wisdom. One day, she will return to Earth and share her gift with a new

THE MICHAEL

humanity. She appeared, sacrosanct, and stood silently next to the Michael's radiance.

Another task was given to the Michael: heal the Dark Dragon by carrying him to the depths until he could be redeemed by the One or returned to his original home in deep space, a place before stars knew light. It is this act of compassion which we celebrate each year on Michael's Day.

On September twenty-ninth of each year, the fourteen rainbow masters, who assist the Michael in guiding humanity, come together to celebrate his continuing efforts to show human beings the way through freedom, to love, and finally to the wisdom held by the Sophia.

Do not confuse the Dark Dragon with the cosmic dragons who protect the Earth or the elemental dragons who still live and breathe here. These natural dragons have provided the world with many benefits. The Dark Dragon has a different purpose. One we do not discuss directly.

Michael's final, most important task is to lead human beings to the awareness of love – the Logos – who also volunteered to help humanity. Whereas the Gift Giver carried the lessons of freedom, the Logos did the unthinkable. He became a human being to be a living example of love.

"This is an unfinished story," Theo concluded. "I hope it helps you understand the importance of the Michael's work."

I could see sparkling, golden light twinkling around Theo's head. It was a sign of the quality of truth, purity, accuracy, humility, and love in his words, a sign of what happens when a mystic spark awakens love in the heart, travels to the brain, and ignites higher wisdom.

I hoped Theo's story would be enough to prepare me for an encounter with the Michael.

CHAPTER ELEVEN

A MASTER IN A CAVE

"SOME LOCATIONS CAN BE used to see into the invisible landscape. Imagine a location is a large pane of glass that functions like a telescope. A mystic can use this viewing device when waiting for the unknown to reveal itself. Look through it, scan the landscape, and locate new places to explore. This is an effective method to discover what your next encounter might be," Theo told me during a lengthy excursion in the New Mexico desert.

"Rivers and dry riverbeds are special," Theo continued as we sat in an arroyo on an exceptionally hot summer day. "They reveal secrets and supply impetus for landscape traveling."

I listened to his words, but most of my attention was focused on my own discomfort. I imagined a cool stream of mountain water running through the arroyo instead of the burning-hot desert sand. Even the soles of my shoes were blistering. I wet my neckerchief with water from a thermos and put it on top of my head, but it dried out before I was able to settle into meditation.

"You can daydream all you want, it may even give you

relief for a time, but it would serve you better to accept the circumstances as they are. Acknowledge the conditions and discover the extraordinary within the uncomfortable ordinary."

Theo's reprimand hadn't helped. Trying to stay focused in the dry riverbed felt impossible but sitting by the cool river in Fine Park today was easy; especially with the misting water blowing gently onto my face every time the breeze shifted.

I came to investigate the floating river stones. The conditions were perfect – the river at the proper late summer depth, the lazy flow of the water, and the tail end of rafting season – all contributed to the attainment of the phenomenon. I was suspicious about how it started here. There was folklore passed along by the visiting Himalayan monks. They claimed to have conversed with indigenous ancestors. Whether the practice started with the monks or the local ancestors was a hotly debated subject. Well, as sizzling as monks and ancient beings can get.

I was still seeking a spirit guide; someone who could teach me about the landscape history of the valley. Each time I intended to ask Theo about finding one, I was interrupted by yet another question about my progress. There was little opportunity to discuss the subject.

I sat alongside the river in my blue chair, focusing on my stupa preparation before traveling. Theo had given me a directive.

"You must perform the routine until every step reinforces its magic in you."

I quieted my internal chatter. The river was loud enough to drown out the traffic on the road leading up the canyon just across the pedestrian bridge. I used the sound of the water to go deeper.

My empty space was disrupted by a loud buzzing. At first,

I thought it was coming from a bird's nest in a nearby tree. Two baby birds were noisy, but the humming wasn't theirs.

I kept shifting my internal receiver until it locked onto the sound; it was coming from within the river, just downstream. When the sound and my vision synchronized, I penetrated the water with my mind. Just on top of the sandy riverbed sat sizable stones. They shook loose from the sand and began to vibrate in tune with the buzzing sound.

Faster and faster, the cycle of vibration intensified until the stones began lifting off the bottom. They piled on top of each other by some hidden force, partially breaking above the surface. The stacks, three, four, even five feet high, appeared to float as the water flowed around them.

I let go of the image and stepped into my staff. When my mind was spotlessly scrubbed, I returned to the perspective of my chair.

Certain it was time to travel, I entered the rotunda, presented my ticket to the six angels who stood by the pillars, and prepared for takeoff. We moved quickly over the foothills, traveled up the river and continued along its connections upstream.

We hovered above a small, azure lake at the base of a mountain for a few minutes before landing on the shore. I looked around to discover any features: a building, a temple, a tunnel, a gate; anything identifiable, but nothing appeared.

The angels stayed on board when I stepped off the rotunda. I scrambled a few yards up the hillside to get a better view. I offered greeting roses to the landscape and waited. When I felt clear, I opened my eyes and looked west to scan the face of the mountain.

"That's it, a cave entrance!" I said excitedly.

I reached out with my other senses, imagining my eyes,

ears, and nose could elongate and feel around like soft, sensitive hands.

Coming from inside the cave was a whisper.

"Is it time?"

I looked deeper and saw a shadowy figure within the cave. The name 'Dragon Master' flashed in my mind. Before I could answer, I was forcefully pulled back to the rotunda, flown to the river, and abruptly dumped onto my blue chair.

Confused by the hasty return, I focused on the water, the floating stones, and the hummingbirds, all of which cemented me back inside my physical body. The mother hummingbird buzzed my left ear and flew across my eyes, her wing brushing my eyelashes. She paused at her nest and made a kamikaze run at me, flying by my right ear. Was that my first official hummingbird scolding?

I entered three notes in my journal:

Find a compatriot.
Visit the Dragon Master.
Hummingbirds can be...hostile.

CHAPTER TWELVE

A MUSIC MAN

I WOKE UP SWEATING. IN my dream, I was hiking on a trail. Distracted by someone bellowing at me from atop the mountain, I slipped on a loose rock and fell over the edge of a cliff into a body of cold, blue water.

I heard these words when I resurfaced from the depths:

With one, there is trouble
Brewing outside
Free me,
The land is on fire
Or wet never dry
Free me,
To tame is a kindness
For balance and blend
Free me,
The fire and water
Never to end

I pulled out my notebook and wrote down the words while my coffee was brewing. The invisible world was revealing my next assignment. Time to come up with a plan to travel to Blue Lake. It wasn't a coincidence that they showed me the location of the Dragon Master right after freeing the Water Dragon. Maybe visiting Theo would help provide some solid advice.

I hopped on my bicycle, rode to the trailhead, and followed the dirt road to his house. Haystack Mountain was brilliantly backlit by the rising sun. In no time, I was parking my bike in front of the house and walking around to the back porch. I was barely settled in my usual chair before he began sharing his insights.

"Landscape research is an unusual activity. Sometimes, we start out with a particular destination in mind but find ourselves in the middle of a different adventure.

"Take me, for instance. I was in England visiting Stonehenge. It was my first time at the site, and I was excited about getting to see the giant standing stones. I set my blue chair down as close as possible to the circle and prepared to investigate the landscape. I stretched out my energy in every direction looking for activity. Where was the star dome? The celestial city? The magic temple? There was nothing except a few ghostly, ectoplasmic extrusions left behind by poorly trained psychics. It was disappointing."

"I thought Stonehenge was geo-mythically active?"

"Yes, it is true. And since it is, I was determined to discover an interesting feature or two. I wasn't about to leave without a close encounter of my own."

"What did you do?"

"I rummaged through my staffs and tried on a number of robes, finally deciding on the white combination. I wanted the invisible world to take me seriously. I was sure wearing white would demonstrate my sincerity."

Theo paused and sipped his tea. I imagined him standing in front of a giant walk-in closet, trying on outfits, gazing into a full-length mirror and then throwing off an outfit and trying on something different.

Theo's voice pulled me back from my musing about his determination to find the correct mystic gear.

"I sunk deeply into the diamond in the middle of the rotunda for enhanced effectiveness. Later, my mentor told me that had been overkill. I ended up in the center of a gathering in South Africa, right in the middle of a stone circle. My mentor was attending a meeting. Boy, was he surprised! So were the other cognoscenti in attendance; they looked like a bunch of fops with their plumed hats, jeweled hands, and ornate wardrobe.

"It's humorous now, but it wasn't funny to my mentor. He pulled me aside and reprimanded me for traveling where I wasn't invited. The dressing down I received in front of all those teachers was embarrassing.

"My pride shriveled as I headed back to the rotunda. It was parked right outside the original Stonehenge circle. When I stepped into it, I turned and snuck a peak. It was a magnificent sight. A galaxy of stars on a translucent domed ceiling with a complete circle of standing stones blazing with golden light. The dome roof was layered in translucent, palm-shaped leaves and accented with magnificent pearls. The dandies were exquisitely dressed in colorful fiber-optic robes. It was quite impressive and deeply humbling.

"My mentor referred to me as the 'classless wonder' for a very long time after that. But before I took off, he popped onto the rotunda, smiled forgivingly and mentally projected the words 'nice job' into my head. Then he told me to get my sorry butt back home.

"This is the reason I remind you to be prepared. Anticipate the unexpected and stay open to what the extraordinary world may present. Its timing is different from ours. To invisible beings, we are the chaos to their orderliness. We need to adjust. It is their world we live in. But most of all, they need our help as willing participants."

The insight I received from Theo was pertinent even though I didn't tell him I was planning the help a Dragon Master after freeing a Water Dragon. It was getting dicey keeping my land-scape activity from him. I knew I would trip up and spill the beans, but how long would it be before he figured it out for himself? If he hadn't already known. I believed he was giving me just enough of the rope called freedom to stretch my hubris neck. This was one of those times I appreciated the Ophanim angels not providing me a visual of my vivid imagination.

The next day I hiked along the foothills, traversing a ridge trail overlooking the valley. I worked my way to the southern edge of the Flatirons. The 280-million-year-old Fountain Formation was renowned for its flat-bottomed, clothes iron shape. Rock climbers respected the challenge, and tourists loved to watch. There were numerous routes around the formations. The one I chose was stretched along the base of Flatiron number three and gradually rose toward a favorite viewpoint named Devil's Thumb, a solitary rock protruding above the profile of the ridge. My destination was Angel's Point, with its punishingly steep, narrow steps for the final quarter mile of the trail. The reward was an eagle's eye view of Boulder Valley. Never disappointing, it was a sure way to discover new landscape features.

I turned the corner near the top of the ridge, greedily gasping for oxygen.

"How much further up the trail do I need to go?" I wondered.

I stopped abruptly. There he was; a towering figure. I'm not sure if I was more surprised by his activity or his stature. He was tall and slender, standing like a giant willow growing straight out of the forest floor, reaching for the sun. His clothes, although slightly disheveled, were professional. His legs were long, and his feet were big enough to solidly ground him anywhere he chose to stand. I imagined his arms could reach out and touch you from any conversational distance, and you wouldn't mind if they did. His hands were a work of art.

He faced northeast standing on a sizable stone perched between two fir trees. The foothills were to his left, the sun to his right. His wand flowed with waves of light beams that raced to penetrate the ground. Was he conducting an orchestra? One only he could see? He looked down periodically and turned a page of invisible sheet music.

It was still morning, just after sunrise. I shifted my gaze. I wanted to see…more. From where I stood, the early light was streaming into the atmosphere in controlled waves, following his movements. The waves particlized as they hit the Flatirons and bounced like tennis balls springing off tightly strung rackets. After picking up speed, each one found a destination.

I focused harder to see where his talent, his power, his extraordinary ability came from. The movement of his wand attracted the waves, but I couldn't figure out how. The gestures his free hand made were craftily guiding the particles toward different locations around the valley. I relaxed to see deeper. The silent music was attracting throngs of winged beings riding solar currents, and a full array of instruments followed his every movement. The synchronized dance of the solar beings and the unfathomable cosmic music built a fascinating vision. The outline of his obelisk shape acted like a prism, separating the fourteen distinct colors of the mystic rainbow, each responding to a reverberation coming from the center of his heart.

I envisioned standing in ancient Egypt with a temple behind me, an obelisk in front. I watched the same scene of sunlight, magician, and music being directed onto a large patch of landscape lush with trees, bushes and grasses. It was nothing like any pictures of modern-day Egypt, yet it was recognizable.

Other hikers passed him by with little notice. Did they think he was just another student from the music college refining his skills? Were they politely ignoring him, not wanting to invade his privacy? Could they even see him?

When he finished his performance, I wanted to applaud, surprised to be in such a cheerful state, wrapped in a bubble of joy from his performance.

I caught a glimpse of a delicate smile at the corners of his mouth.

"Good greetings to you," he responded as he slid his wand into his pocket. "Has sound fashioned a call for you today?"

"I...I guess so," I answered, not exactly sure I understood his question.

I joined him as he started down the path. All the way back to town, he greeted the sounds of nature as old friends and referenced a composer for each sound, most of whom I didn't recognize. I nodded politely, impressed with his descriptive correlation between what nature was singing out and how composers created their masterful pieces. I could see the dancing light particles he orchestrated up on the ridge as he spoke.

"Enlightened beings are said to appreciate music as being close to God's ear. It can create an accentuated stance, a flourish not to be taken lightly. As a bird lands, it knows it has lifted off from the branch of unseen existence, and when it dies, nature remembers to celebrate its song."

His words were poetic, musical, and philosophically pleasing to my ears. I liked this Music Man and invited him to breakfast as we passed my favorite restaurant. We continued our conversation about nature, music, and the energy of the sun.

When we stood outside the restaurant to part company, my neck began to kink from the strain of looking up at him. Was I standing too close? I backed up to peer at him from a slight distance. From this more comfortable viewpoint, I realized he wasn't actually that tall. Instead, he communicated from a place above his head which pulled my attention higher as he spoke. When I discovered this, I moved closer again, adjusted my focal point, and immediately became comfortable.

Meeting the Music Man put meat on the bones of my skeleton plan to get to the Dragon Master. I hastily put the rest of my plan in place, then realized I hadn't a clue how to find the Music Man. Where did he live? Or work? Did he even have a job? Was he performing in town? I could check the opera house, or the symphony, or the college...

I could ask Bobby to help, but unless the Music Man was performing in nature, how would the clan find him?

"Best go to the source," my wisdom guides suggested.

"The sun?" I asked.

"From there, it will be easy. Follow the waves of light. Ride them to the Music Man."

That made perfect sense, but...

"I stopped visiting the sun two years ago," I said weakly.

"Then the self-imposed exile is over," the guides insisted.

I began avoiding the source of life around the time the Solar Mage had changed his zip code from 61000 France to solar 00001. I was still smarting from his unexpected departure. I believed I deserved advanced notification and pouted for months. But this new adventure was a sign. Time to purchase a ticket on the Solar Express and visit the Solar Mage.

CHAPTER THIRTEEN

THE SOLAR MAGE

HAD VISIONS OF LEARNING the soul traveling technique from the Solar Mage in ancient India. My connection with him was resilient across lifetimes. The abilities were back, though I wasn't sure how. Was it the angels, my wisdom guides, my Dream Talker? Theo's training was a good possibility. But if it was the Solar Mage, I needed to know. The chance to discover the source of my awakening gifts would be possible. And, soon.

His return had been announced to the world of mystics. It was predicted he would visit the South of France this year. At the time, I had no way of knowing how serendipitous this would be. It was my good fortune to be on the French Riviera just a few months later.

When I'd told Theo my plans, his words had not been encouraging. "It is improbable," he said, shattering my self-assurance. "Finding the Solar Mage is comparable to discovering evidence of the Michael. Two truly difficult tasks."

"I remember your Michael story," I replied haughtily. "I studied everything I could get my hands on. Visited the documented sites and explored them with the rotunda. I even set up blue dishes at the locations for remote viewing in case he reappeared. As a mystic warrior and a student of the Solar Mage, I can do this."

Those were the last words I'd said to Theo before I left and set a date to rendezvous with him. After, traveling across Europe, I'd given up coveting success. Instead, I catalogued my adventure; I took meticulous notes about energetic features on the landscapes and discovered details I would have easily missed in the past. My notes had become as succinct as my subtle sight. Everything else was crystal clear, yet there was no sign of the Michael and no evidence of the Solar Mage's return.

My trip was coming to an end, but I wanted to make one last attempt. I decided I would climb the mountain for sunrise on Michael's Day. If the Solar Mage was back, he wouldn't miss the opportunity to appear. He would summon the Michael with his prayers. Yes, the twenty-ninth of September was my final chance.

It was murky, I was wet from the misty rain, and I was deeply chilled by the dropping temperature. Growing dejected, I began to feel pessimistic about what I would present to Theo in five days. Even my chattering mind had little to say, and my analyzer had gone quiet after provoking me to make this final attempt.

"Focus on the promise of the sky. Appreciate the elements of nature as they begin to light up around you. With sun and shadow, the dawn demonstrates the magic of life. Light shines the way to eternal love."

These words sang their way through the gathering storm of my anticipated failure – purging some of my heaviness.

When I crested the final switchback at the top of the mountain, I scanned the clearing up ahead. Sitting stones were placed in rows overlooking a valley. Each stone was two, maybe two and a half feet high. They were backlit by an autumnal pallet of pastel profundity.

"The seven companion colors, the Yin subtleties, represent the qi we cannot see," the Warrior had told me, capturing the essence of the mysterious rainbow masters. "They stand together with their opposite, the Yang boldness, to epitomize the foundation of qi. Like the Tao, the mystery remains in the emptiness."

A shadowy figure was sitting on a stone at the edge of the cliff. His silhouette was glowing.

The darkness evaporated as I drew closer.

He wore a fur hat, and a crystal-capped cane stood next to him in its custom placeholder. Moving slowly and quietly, I chose a stone to his left and sat down. Finally seeing him clearly, I chuckled at his full, white beard. He looked like Santa Claus dressed in a white suit! But this was the Solar Mage in his earthly guise.

"Welcome back, my favorite elf," the voice said, stronger and clearer than my own.

Not even the wisdom guides spoke with this kind of authority. The quality of the powerful words cut through the soft wax of my uncertainty like a hot knife. Each word left a flaming impression and, together, they acted like a key that unlocked long-unvisited rooms within my mind.

"Be like the sun," the voice proclaimed.

That did it. Clarity ensued, and shadows escaped. Until that moment, I had only imagined the room of my clairvoyance was a real place. Now the room was alive, with living, liquid gold streaming along the surface of the walls and outlining my psychic viewing window, my head space chair, and my analyzer's crystal housing.

The simple instruction had been like the sun, and the sun remembered me as my real self.

My blasphemous daydreaming began deconstructing fragments of religious history. I saw a picture of a confused Moses looking at the burning bush with me standing in the middle of the fire, comfortably inside the heart of the Christ. The Christ was laughing, giving me a solid seven-point shake on the Richter scale.

When the physical sun broke the line of the horizon, a beam of light illuminated the Solar Mage, creating a sphere of golden light that engulfed the mountain.

Instantaneously, I remembered everything. My history appeared in the field of light; the many lives of encountering this mysterious being. The Solar Mage was the guide I always followed. When I acquired the secrets of the sun, he was the one pointing the way.

"The only thing you must focus on is the light. The love. Then, all existence will share its secrets. This is the true life standing between the past and your many lives to come. How else will you master yourself?

"Do not work so hard. Have your thoughts convinced you otherwise?" I sat inside the question until another one came. "Do you remember yet?"

A longer pause still, then I remembered. I remembered it all! But circling around those memories was a sadness; the time he had returned to his home in the great Central Sun.

"Can I accompany you this time? I do not wish to forget," I pleaded with the Solar Mage.

He gave me a compassionate look and said, "No. There is still more work for you to do, but I hear your request. I can tell you now that the Michael will make an appearance this evening at the great fire ceremony. Go to the center where the People of Light reside at the base of this mountain. When you arrive, say the sacred words, 'The Love of God solves all problems.'"

These words were proof: this was the Solar Mage I knew and loved. Only he would say the word 'God' with a long 'o' sound, creating a bridge directly to the sun.

"The People of Light will welcome you. They only appear once a year, for this event. You must leave the following morning, before their world of light disappears. For now, let us make a trip home."

The sun rose higher above the horizon. I half-closed my eyes. The Solar Mage took my left elbow as we walked toward the edge of the cliff.

"A leap of faith is necessary to know the sun," he said.

As he spoke, more fragmented memories reappeared from ancient times and mixed with the present.

My step over the edge landed on a rainbow bridge. Its light particles danced to the vibration of the extended spectrum, the seven visible colors alternating with the seven implied. I whizzed along the bridge like a joyful skater racing on slick ice. The Solar Mage was gliding at my side. When we reached the sun, we entered a crystalline city populated by splendid angels. Tall, brightly colored, winged, all applauding.

The Solar Mage manifested golden roses out of his palms, distributing them to the angelic masses. The scene quickly disappeared as I struggled to capture the images and store them in my memory archives; I knew my ordinary recollection couldn't be relied upon to retain all the details of mystical events.

I opened my eyes. The Solar Mage had vanished. In his place was a wall of Elohim around the sacred mountain. I felt unworthy to be immersed in their presence. Sensing inappropriate piety, a voice echoed, "We require equal partners, not worshippers."

I gave myself suns of confidence, validation, and seniority, sending gratitude roses to the angels, Elohim, and the Solar Mage. Then I hurried down the mountain with one thought in mind: find the People of Light!

At first the forest path at the base of the mountain was dark and dense, making it difficult to see beyond the next turn. When I reached a small meadow, I attempted to get my bearings. Parallel rows of young pine trees in the middle of it suggested the way ahead. I walked between the trees, distributing roses to any spirits on the landscape. A distortion of light appeared around the trees. Multicolored lights turned on as I passed by each pair, looking like the front yard my family decorated for Christmas.

I continued until I reached the edge of the meadow. When I turned and looked back between the twin aisles of lit trees, the energy was radiating like sparkles of pixie dust from a Disney movie. To the left and right, normal light reflected off the vegetation, which was dull in comparison to the high-definition light show in the middle.

"What do you seek?" a voice asked from over my shoulder, causing me to jump five feet to my left, where I landed with my sword at the ready.

It was a man dressed in a luminous white shirt and pants. A soft wool hat flopped to one side of his head, and he wore beautiful burgundy leather slippers.

I stared at him without saying a word.

He repeated himself in the exact same tone.

"What do you seek?"

"The love of God solves all problems," I said, surprised I had drawn my sword.

I put it away sheepishly, straightened my jacket, and

approached him with a half-smile. I hoped that would reassure him.

"I came at the bequest of the Solar Mage; he instructed me to seek out the People of Light. Do you know them?"

"Welcome. Follow me."

"Follow you where?" I asked.

He waved his hand in a grand, sweeping gesture, opening a shimmering gate right behind me. Inside was a village only visible through the open space. As he ushered me through to a small building, I expressed no surprise; the entrance was enchanted. These were the people of light. Manipulating waves of light would be routine.

The cottage's roofline curved at the top, its two oval windows sitting over an emerald door. For such a small, simple building, it offered few straight lines. When the light hit these lines, they bowed and bulged in both directions. It reminded me of the rhythmic breathing of the sleeping giant.

"You will have to wait for someone to verify your credentials," he said.

What credentials? Verified how, and by whom? I didn't know any People of Light or have any identifying papers except my passport.

I took a seat near the door under one of the windows. The light streaming in warmed the back of my head and cast a shadow on the floor. My silhouette was misshapen. When I looked around the room, everything else was too. One file cabinet. Two people conversing in French. A small table with rows of clip-on badges. All their outlines were shifting and appeared misaligned. It was unsettling, so I gave myself some golden suns of clarity. Hopefully, the vanished gatekeeper would find someone to 'verify' me and return soon.

The silhouette of a tall woman appeared on my psychic screen. How could this be?

Moments later, the door opened. There she was, accompanied by two short women, one on either side.

"What is *she* doing here?" I muttered.

"And who did you think would show up to verify your presence?" she snapped.

I'd forgotten her hearing. She could hear thoughts, whether spoken or envisioned. Was I in trouble? When it came to the Triple Wisdom Woman, that was usually the case.

"Sorry. I was just surprised to see you here. I've never seen you outside of Los Angeles, so you felt…out of context," I said.

As soon as I spoke, I desperately wished the words back into my mouth.

"So now I am contextual?" She challenged me.

"What I meant to say, was…well…err…It is unexpected to see you."

Her mini smile, which happened in her eyes and not at the corners of her mouth, was a relief.

"Seeing you here is not the prize of my day, either," she said, turning to her two companions, who had been whispering to each other.

After a long conversation, which sounded contentious and made me uncomfortable, one of them returned with an identification badge and handed it to the Triple Wisdom Woman, who clipped it to my lapel and said, "It is imperative you leave this place before the badge disappears."

With that, she turned and walked past me, her two companions trailing closely behind her.

I exhaled deeply, excising the uncomfortable feeling of having held my breath the whole time she was present. The

Triple Wisdom Woman was the most difficult teacher I'd ever known, and she was here.

While I sat there, I couldn't help wondering about the bigger picture. What was the connection between the Triple Wisdom Woman, Theo, and the Solar Mage? What about these People of Light? Were they all part of a network of mentors and teachers for mystic warriors?

Waiting in the odd little structure for another hour made me drowsy. Finally, a young man came to lead me to my room. I was happy to leave the building, looking forward to a nap, a change of clothes, and some food.

We walked along a well-trodden path for a little while before the man stopped and said, "This is it."

We stood in front of a tent surrounded by standing water. Stones and mud were stacked up against the stakes, and the left side was sagging. I was confused.

"This is what?" I asked.

"These are the accommodations for the duration of your stay."

You couldn't have found a more pathetic-looking soul than me in that moment. My backpack slid down off my shoulder and came to rest hanging from the palm of my hand. I was stunned. My mouth hung wide open. I stood in front of a partially submerged, mud-moated tent. There was no hiding my disbelief. I turned to the young man to see if this was a joke.

"There has to be some mistake," I said in disbelief, but he was gone.

I was ready to take a cab back to Nice, check into a comfortable hotel, and give up on this adventure.

"Unless I get confirmation soon, I am leaving. I need some type of verification for me to stay any longer."

As soon as I said it, a young woman appeared.

She held up a thin piece of wood about three feet long and said, "It is not so bad," then gently placed it on the ground. The wood sat on top of the muddy water, creating a miniature bridge.

"At least my shoes will stay dry," I said, trying to be positive.

"Well, you did ask for a sign," my wisdom guides remarked. "When you ask for something and get it, respond with gratitude, even if you don't like the results. This will clear your mind and help you find the connection between what you want and what you need. This is an opportunity to stand in the middle. Neutral. Unbiased. In this way, you will learn to stay unaffected by transitory events."

It was a salient point, but I didn't care. I was neither happy nor amused, and gratitude was a distant island. I turned to acknowledge the young woman, but she too had disappeared.

I stood there for a few minutes and heard, "Remember why you're here."

Reluctantly, I entered the tent. Inside was dry and actually felt cozy. It had a raised platform covered with thick foam to sleep on, and there was a small lantern sitting on a petite, round table. A cubby with two small drawers gave me somewhere to store my clothes.

I removed my shoes by the entrance, unpacked a few things, changed my clothes, and laid out my sleeping bag on top of the foam for a quick nap, hoping to reset my internal clock then have a much-needed lunch.

I woke up from a dream filled with luscious feelings but no pictures. When I opened my eyes, I was once again struck by the realization that I was in a tent. Surrounded by mud. In the South of France. In late September. And very hungry. At least I was no longer peeved.

I took a handful of water from the bowl on the table and

rinsed my eyes, drying my face with a small, white towel. I looked in a mirror hanging from the ceiling by a piece of leather.

"Well, what have you gotten yourself into now?" I mused.

Sensing movement outside the tent interrupted any forthcoming answer. I put on my shoes and unzipped the tent flap. Several groups of people dressed in white were all moving together. They were incredibly quiet; not a shuffle, a word, a disturbed stone, a crackling leaf, or a broken twig. All this activity was just outside. When my eyes took over from my ears, I noticed the path was dry. The only wet ground was surrounding my tent.

No one looked my way. Apparently, I was located on a main throughway in the compound. I merged into the next opening between clusters of people and was gently carried along with the flow, not stopping until I stood in front of a large, domed building.

The double-doored entrance was big enough to permit four people to easily pass through, walking abreast. The ceiling was three stories with no internal walls or support beams. The domed roof hovered on the exterior walls. There were no pictures, patterns, designs, or written words anywhere in the room.

Long rows of tables set with simple dinnerware filled the hall, and a small, square table stood at the far end of the room, just in front of a door. I paused, not knowing where to sit. Someone gently touched my arm. It was the same young woman who had placed the piece of wood across the water to my island tent. With a smile, she gently grasped my arm and led me to one of the tables. I stopped at the third chair from the aisle. She sat to my right.

"Allow me to formally introduce myself. I am Boji. This is the best seat in the hall. I believe you will benefit from its placement," she whispered.

She was right; I had a perfect view of the whole room.

"Thank you!" I said, as quietly as I could.

My voice sounded out of place; other than the rustling of clothes and some inaudible whispers, the room was spatially silent. No one else was speaking above a murmur. A flush of embarrassment came over me. I glanced around to see if anyone noticed.

By the time everyone was settled, even more sound had drained out of the room. Similar to the emptiness of outer space when journeying to distant stars, the only sounds that refused to discontinue were the ones inside my own head.

I sat with my eyes half closed. A triangle, no…a *pyramid* of energy appeared in the room, restructuring the atmosphere. I breathed in the piezoelectricity generated by a crystalline form that materialized in its center.

Boji's left hand slid toward me and touched a point on the outer edge of my less dominant sword hand. A jolt of energy exploded like an atomic blast. It traveled through my body and collapsed back into the center of my head before it dropped down into my heart.

"We need to be blasted wide open by the touch of the love of God," the Solar Mage had once said. "Then, we remember we are always touched by love."

I hadn't realized how much I'd needed this until the next blast of energy sent me spiraling through an invisible barrier. It was a wall of energy that stripped away any confidence that I somehow controlled my reality. I had no choice but to sit back and hold on tight. When I let go, I saw him.

He was enormous. His wings stretched from the dining hall to the sun, with flames up to the throne of the Supreme Being. The size of the figure in the hall adjusted until he fit into the space. Now, he stood two-stories tall. The gold crown above his head rose through the ceiling. It was the Michael, with wings and a magnificent sword. Heavenly voices painted his epic story on panels of etheric air.

The scene solidified, and my mind grew comfortable with this adjusted perspective of the angelic presence and the dining hall attendees.

I scanned the room to see if anyone was reacting to this scene. Everyone was in a peaceful meditative state. I was partially out of my physical body by now, and the tether that held me anchored inside was stretched taunt. I feared it would break, leaving me forever adrift in this heavenly reality.

"Hold on to the moment. Breathe deeply," my wisdom guides suggested.

I relaxed, centered myself in my solar plexus, and stabilized my grounding cords. Still needing a focal point, I looked closer at the Michael.

The door behind him opened, and the Solar Mage entered the room, passing through the Michael's translucent body. He paused behind a simple wooden chair placed at a table on an elevated platform facing us. The Solar Mage lifted his right hand in front of his heart and greeted the visible and invisible beings in the room.

Everyone outside the building and throughout the compound received this solar greeting. Hundreds of archangels were positioned upon the landscape. They had appeared at the same time as the Michael.

I looked at the Solar Mage. Golden roses were pouring out of the center of his right palm. Inside each rose was an ancient language written in fiery letters. I wished I had a pair of mystic reading glasses. Such glasses were capable of translating energetic languages. With Theo's help, I'd practiced using the glasses on a little red book from the library with mixed results. What I'd translated had sounded like it was from a second-grade reader in the 1950s: "See Pegasus run. Hello, Arthur. Fly faster. Faster! Pretty mountains. See how beautiful her rolled crow's nest smelled."

"That's not bad," Theo had commented. "Well, apart from the 'smelled nest' part. The reader determines what is read, expounding its meaning depending on his sense of awareness. Continue to exercise your clairvoyant muscles."

As I recalled his teachings, I felt a sensation in my shirt pocket where I usually kept my glasses. I slid them on, discovering they had magically become mystic glasses. I looked closer at the roses coming out of the Solar Mage's hand. The word 'Love!' was written on each petal, the exclamation mark included.

"I've seen this before!" I remembered. "But when? Where?"

The Solar Mage sat down at the head of the table between a man and a woman. Standing behind the man was a rainbow master dressed in a violet outfit trimmed in lilac. A short sword and a jeweled dagger were tucked in his belt, and he wore knee-high boots, a gold broach with a large emerald on his lapel, and a ring with an amethyst gem on his left hand. He sported long, flowing, jet-black hair topped with a peacock-feathered hat.

My awareness extended toward him, so I asked, "Who are you, sir?"

"Saint Germaine," the reply resounded inside my head.

I stopped the flood of information about Saint Germaine flowing toward me from my memory archives. Achilles was clearly working overtime, but it was a multi-lifetime chronicle to read at a later date.

I looked at the woman to see if a rainbow master was standing behind her. Instead, I saw a blurred, ghostly figure. A few moments passed before the image clarified. It was the Goddess Lakshmi in a soft, red sari, accompanied by two Ganesh.

"Will they be serious sentinels today?" I wondered, recognizing Ganesh as an Ophanim guise. The Ganesh on Lakshmi's left flashed his angelic persona, winking at me before returning to his solemn stance. I smiled, evoking my fondness for their recent antics.

The Solar Mage closed his eyes, and the hall sank into a deep meditative state for twenty minutes. When the Solar Mage began to speak, it was about the sun. My vision of the hordes of angelic beings blanketing the compound remained intact during his sermon.

The choir performed three Bulgarian songs, then the food was served. I didn't want to lose my connection with Boji's hand, believing it was the catalyst for my open-door vision, but I withdrew my hand to eat. We ate in silence, listening to an unceasing choir streaming in from the cosmos until it all ended abruptly.

I was back outside the hall. The sound of dishes and silverware being gathered wafted out through the open front door. This was the first untidy sound I'd heard from the People of Light.

When I realized the magnitude of what just happened, I raced back to my tent, craving solitude. My reality was blown wide open, but my senses desired a major shut down.

Exhausted, I watched my thinking collapse. Patterns of belief were being rewired at a dizzying pace. Everywhere I looked, images of the extraordinary realm raced toward me. It was too much. They came too fast! I put my head under a pillow. How could I shut it off? I needed a quiet state to rest in.

What I found lasted hours. Bordering on a lucid dream, the dining hall images replayed themselves, inviting me to join them. Bustling outside brought me back to the tent, and I looked at my watch. It was five o'clock. The afternoon was gone.

"Knock, knock, knock," came a voice from outside.

"Hello, hello, hello," it continued. "I've come to escort you to the bonfire."

Bonfire? Of course. I remembered hearing a conversation outside the dining hall about a celebration tonight.

"One moment, please."

I tucked my journal under the pillow and unzipped the flap of the tent.

It was Boji, wearing a lavender dress and holding a long, white coat. She held out her left arm. It was an elegant gesture of grace and charm.

"Shall we?" she asked.

I delicately clutched her arm, and we strolled as if we had been friends for life. We had a deep soul recognition; a sweet, unspoken acceptance. Her eyes summed up my feeling.

"Well, after all these years, isn't it good to be together again?"

I smiled at her in agreement. Familiar love wrapped around our togetherness. I felt whole.

Other voices moved along the path with us. I heard whispers and giggles in French, Italian, Bulgarian, German, Russian, Hebrew, and even Aramaic, that most ancient language.

Boji and I entered a circle outlined by small but mature trees. She scanned the landscape and nodded south, then walked to a spot halfway between the center and the outer circle. Stacked in the middle was a nine-foot pyramid of small tree trunks with bales of hay wedged between them, all strung together with hemp rope. To our right, sitting on a makeshift platform, was an exquisitely carved chair. Found in a castle, it would have done nicely as a throne for the Faerie Queen.

More people arrived, momentarily pausing at the edge of the circle, then finding a sacred spot for the evening. Each seemed to choose with little obvious forethought, using a method of seeing that recognized the wisest place to sit. Aside from trusting his gnome, Theo used the same method when searching for the best location for landscape research.

The discreet talking built to a crescendo. When it stopped, all heads turned with perfect synchronicity toward the east entrance of the gathering and waited in silence.

A blue flash of light appeared out of the corner of my eye. It pulsed to the rhythm of unspecified music. I looked not to the east, but to the west. On the horizon were randomly organized colors. They swirled around until a double-rainbow pattern constructed a bridge stretching into the night sky. Streaming like the aurora borealis, it began coalescing over the trees.

A red bubble appeared at the edge of the bridge and a glowing figure clarified within. Dressed in splendid Middle Eastern garb with a long flowing beard, he stepped down into the circle about six feet from the center.

The blue light flashed again, and another impeccably dressed figure appeared. She was surrounded by a brilliant pink sphere. My heart soared. She stepped down into the circle. One by one, twelve more aristocratic souls entered, culminating with the lilac-hued figure, Saint Germaine, who had stood with the Michael and the Solar Mage inside the dining hall.

All fourteen rainbow masters faced the circle center, brewing with intensity and strewn in flaming colors.

Murmurs around the staged area turned my head. The Michael stood behind it. His sword was shouldered, and he was carrying a long staff with a golden flame rising to the great Central Sun. The Solar Mage entered and stepped onto the stage, sending light and roses from the palms of his hands.

When he sat down in his ornate chair, he closed his eyes for a moment. More sound emptied from the gathering.

He began a long discourse in French that journeyed powerfully in the evening air of the Riviera. Each word arrived a short distance from my ears, paused, and delivered a dewdrop of energy as the form and structure of the language fell away. A reservoir of understanding began to build inside my chest. I struggled to focus on a few words but feared the pressure would burst and drown me from the inside out. They, too, deconstructed into pure energy and trailed off.

A man handed a torch to the Solar Mage. He walked toward the logs, accompanied by giant angels circling above. With his free hand, he touched a basket of prayers previously placed atop the hay.

As the Solar Mage physically lit the fire, the Michael incinerated the compound with his flaming staff, lighting up souls, feeding angels, and blessing nature spirits. The fire burst skyward, and the handwritten letters of the declarations soared off the paper, dancing into a vortex with the rhythm of the flames. The fourteen guests stood in solemnity.

The imprint of this scene blazed in my mind. I closed my physical eyes periodically, but the internal images and my external sight remained the same. The waves of energy washing over me made me swoon. I wished to leave this world and follow the burning notes through the vortex. I felt a yearning for home. Not some physical home, but my true home among the stars. I was sure I could get there if I followed the flow of energy wafting up and away from the Earth.

Movement drew my eyes to the fire. The hooded brood of masters turned and moved in a clockwise procession around the fire, back toward the bridge. They stepped upon the floating colors, walked the length of the rainbow bridge, then retreated into distant space. The ceremony was over. The fire would blaze for hours.

Some people lingered. I couldn't; I could hardly operate my body. Boji led me back to my tent, her strength Amazonian. I felt she was carrying all my weight with her delicate left arm. I wondered how.

"You have not fully developed the necessary light body to navigate the land of the People of Light," a voice said to me. "After you encounter the Logos, all this will change. You will be able to live and work in the subtle realms easily."

Without enough energy to acknowledge the words of the speaker, I collapsed onto the makeshift bed, neither asleep or awake, unsure of which reality I would spend the night.

Eventually I raised my body off the bed, stabilized my legs, and made my way from the tent toward the facilities to wash my face and rinse out my cotton mouth. As I dried my face, I looked into the mirror above the sink. I gasped. Instead of the reliable face I've seen every day, the image was randomly changing. First young, then old, then middle-aged, quickly moving through different stages of life, many not to appear for years. The shifting images changed more dramatically, from men to women. Some white, some black, olive, brown. All unfamiliar.

I splashed water on my face, hoping to wake up from this dream, before looking into the mirror again. There I was, stabilized in the foreground, with the other images floating behind me. This was more comfortable, but was I awake?

I headed back to my muddy haven. Bobbing flashlight beams reflected off the ground ahead of me. Did I really walk over to wash my face in total darkness? Even without a flashlight, I could see clearly. My thoughts were interrupted as a floating light stopped in front of me.

It was Boji.

"How did you sleep?" she asked.

"I can't say I slept. But I am sure I wasn't...awake."

"What's wrong?"

I hesitated before answering.

"My voice doesn't sound like my..."

A long pause filled the air as I waited for the next word to arrive.

Still waiting, I looked at Boji, lost. She grasped my moment of wordlessness and filled in the blank.

"Voice?"

My facial response told her she was right.

She took the opportunity to once again take the lead.

"Let's go. It is time to greet the sun."

I walked a few paces behind her as we began the gradual ascent up the mountain.

Although the stars were still bright in the early morning sky, the horizon was already a cerulean strip stretching across an uninterrupted view. When we reached the top, Boji scanned the meditation area. Early arrivals had already chosen their spots to greet the sun. I was in no condition to decide; ordinary thoughts needed to make choices were absent. Choice? No choice? Any choice? It didn't matter; they were all the same. It wasn't that I was detached, I just felt a strong sense of neutrality.

The non-stop planning, considering, and problem solving were all missing in action. Was this real peace? The impermanence of mind? Acceptance? No, not even that. It was something different. Pure observation without opinion. No waves of emotion. No deluge of mental chatter invading my space, flooding my receptive filters, activating my protective responses.

"No, no, no," I remembered the Triple Wisdom Woman insisting. "Not detachment. You must be *disinterested*. Not dead to life nor reactionary on a visceral level. Be tolerant to bad and good with the same consistency. When you discover the outside world ripples through you and finds no obstacle or obstruction, then an easy passage through your history will provide the clarity you need to live the extraordinary life!"

"You have to become as pure as crystal," Theo had agreed, "invisible to distractions and distortions of the habitually accepted view. Our goal is to become visible to the subtle landscape around us. In return, it reciprocates. Then you will have proof of the living history behind the story of the world."

Here I was, disinterested, just a witness to life and quite comfortable without my opinions or uncertainties. Only now, standing on top of a mountain in the South of France, was this making sense. I was lifted off, rising to view the sun before it crested the horizon. My grounding cords were engaged but unable to tether me. I launched toward the horizon. The sky was pinking-up quickly, turning rosy with blue accents. When the first beam crested the distant hills, it impaled me. I felt like a fish, hooked and ready to be reeled in. And that is exactly what happened!

Theo's description of this experience held true when he said, "The Fisher King will hook you when you are ready to be caught. If you struggle to escape or show any fear, you will lose the opportunity to sit at his table. If you make it to his castle, you must present your life stupa. This stupa contains the real story for him to read your genuine character. Neither judge nor jury, the Fisher King is a fisher of real human beings. If you choose to serve humanity, you must adhere to the appropriate qualities. This summary has little to do with your life as you know it."

Working on the landscape, developing my clairvoyant tools, and building a personal stupa finally made sense.

I was hooked, just like Theo said.

At equal speeds, the light passed through me to the Earth

as I raced toward the sun. I looked back to see the planet getting smaller.

In front of me, the intensity and size of the sun was growing exponentially. It was bigger than I imagined, its reach extending throughout the solar system and connecting to other stars. There were beams from our star to millions of planets, a network of interlinking pathways. On closer inspection, they were similar to the beam that hooked me. Was this some kind of road map for travelers? I imagined it had been built and traversed by beings above my visual grade.

Then I thought, "I may be dead."

Immediately, a voice said, "No, you are very much alive! More alive than ever before."

It was the Solar Mage. He was traveling alongside me, racing toward the sun. As I looked around, there were others traveling with us. I was not alone on this journey.

It was the most intense experience I'd ever had in the hidden world, as not one but two spiritual realities overlaid the physical plane.

"When three become one, you are done."

That sounded suspiciously like an Ophanim proclamation. They continued:

> *Bardo, Bardo*
> *Is more than you want.*
> *No telling how many times*
> *Again, finds you in the hunt.*
> *In-side-out of time,*
> *So, get it now or again,*
> *You will go.*
> *Go, go like every able-bodied*
> *Mary or Joe that know.*

Yes, those were the voices of the Ophanim angels. But why were they teasing me now?

"Laugh and worlds laugh with you. Cry and you die as a lie with a sign on your back which says, 'Number One Fool.'"

My innate response was to give myself golden suns of amusement, which had the effect of yanking me hard toward my physical body. From there, I could see all three planes with clarity. On the physical, I sat on the mountain, eyes closed, seemingly guarded by my High Self. On the etheric, I was traveling to meet the Fisher King. On the astral plane, I was heading right for the sun! This trifurcation was unnerving.

I was getting closer. My inner eyes bathe in the liquidity of the sun. A solar reservoir of fluidic light saturated me from the inside out. In my heart was a miniature replica of the sun. It was reaching out with joy, like a baby grasping at a parent's finger.

My internal sun was doing everything possible to fill the gap between itself and the external solar orb. The only thing between them was me. I was the gap. A doorway. A bridge.

A hidden fear gave voice to panic.

"I have to do something. If not, I will soon disappear. What will my family and friends think happened to me? Will they find my body sitting on the mountain? Or will I evaporate into a rainbow of light, my physical body disappearing like ancient Taoist masters?"

My adrenaline rush of fear was interrupted by the Warrior's words, "Focus on the bridge."

Whenever my razor-sharp steel sword was engaged in practice, I followed his instructions very closely. Any distraction could be deadly. So, his bridging phrases held sway over my fear.

"Bridge the gap between you and the opponent. Stand on the bridge. Control the bridge. Use a bridging method."

These swordplay instructions poured into my mind along with other voices, all broadcasting advice, each sharing their wisdom.

A mythological picture came into view. I saw the image of Percival leaving the castle for the first time, having not queried the wounded Fisher King. The cartoonish scene in my mind showed him mounted on his horse just at the edge of the drawbridge. He had to scramble off quickly because the attendant hadn't waited for him to get to solid ground before raising the bridge.

From a distance, a voice could be heard, "Thou art a goose!"

The Fisher King motif rotated to the center of my psychic screen. I saw my etheric body enter a honeycombed mausoleum. Each hexagonal subdivision was filled with its own pool of water, other recently hooked souls were swimming around in personal saunas.

My momentary relief – that I was not alone on this part of the adventure – was dashed when I was unceremoniously dropped into a pool. The thick, milky water felt like stepping into a soothing bath. I floated on the surface of my private pool at a dividing line between the liquid lower half and the airy upper half of a sphere. Above this blue bubble were points of light. Like stars in the night sky, they twinkled in sync with a cosmic choir.

I didn't just feel the water on the level of my skin. I felt it filling interior spaces, from my toes to the top of my head. I saw a series of pictures: an empty goblet in the shape of a human; a human being inside a filling cup, drowning; a light rising out of a dying body.

My focus shifted to my solar journey on the astral plane. The liquid light of the sun had solidified. I was standing with the Solar Mage and traveling companions on a brilliant yellow road lined with walls of gold and multicolored pillars. Radiant beings appeared in mid-stride, coming toward us. We were old friends reuniting in unconditional love while dancing on particles of light. "Welcome home." They triumphantly cheered.

We were escorted to a beautiful table set for a feast. The Solar Mage was seated in a prominent place at this prodigious round table that grew in size as more beings joined us. No matter how large the table became, or how many beings were seated, no one felt any further away.

On the etheric plane, near my personal bubble bath, a different kind of table was being set. It was a large, high table. Not like the solar table, seating many, just large in scale with five chairs placed on one side. All were thrones, with the one in the middle slightly larger. A bright orange hue shone around each golden throne.

It brought to mind an experience I still remembered: my three-year-old self holding my father's little finger as we ascended four flights of stairs. The steps were too steep, my little legs struggled to get to the top. It took forever.

"Why doesn't he carry me?" My child mind wondered.

It was so hard, and I was cranky by the time we'd entered my grandparents' apartment. Everything there was oversized. My grandparents' chairs were even larger than the rest; and there was Italian hell to pay if anyone sat on their personal thrones.

Today, my grandparents were absent, but an imposing hierophant sat in the middle of the table with two subordinate hierophants on his left and two on his right. At either end were two fat and fluffy white swans, their wings partially spread. Drops of bright-red blood were dripping down their chest feathers. If the hierophants banished me to some far-off land, would the swans carry out the sentence?

Summoned by trumpets, I was moved from my private

THE SOLAR MAGE

sauna and stood in front of these five regal beings. Behind me, I could sense three hooded witnesses. Where were the Ophanim angels? I desperately wanted someone to inject a bit of humor into this solemn ritual.

On cue, I heard, "Location, location, location. Get your tickets here. Buy a place in the Cube of Space, outside of injected light. By God. By God. That's right. That's right."

I was relieved. I wanted to laugh at the Ophanim word-play, but the characters sitting in front of me remained solemn.

"When the final piece is added to your stupa, you will be ready."

Theo said this months ago, but never told me what the final piece was – or when I would present it.

A picture was projected onto my mental screen. It showed me climbing onto the table with my stupa and setting it down for the hierophants to evaluate. My upbringing was strict about *not* standing on tables, and I became conflicted. My social training became a visceral invasion, penetrating the scene in front of me.

But a different, yet insistent scene from my childhood diverted me. What connection could it possibly have to the current events?

"I am begging you, not now," I pleaded, but it was too late.

It was a disastrous fifth grade science project, a prize-driven event put on by the teachers. Whoever won the competition received free tickets to a pre-opening gala at the local zoo to spend the whole day perusing an animatronic dinosaur exhibit.

My classmates spent their days buying supplies, planning, building, and talking about how their project would win the big prize. I spent a few hours building a volcano model out of plaster of Paris, whipping up some baking soda mixed with dye and a few other ingredients. It was a lame project, and I didn't expect to win. But the combination of a prank and a local accident would determine the outcome.

As the judges came to the table to grade my project, the power in the school went out. Apparently, a car hit a telephone pole, breaking it in half and snapping the main power lines. My volcano solution was already prepped, mixed, and poured, but thankfully no one would see my dismal demonstration.

Unbeknownst to me, Johnny 'Class Clown' Henshaw had added an iridescent dye and a Fourth of July explosive to the mixture. When my volcano erupted in the darkened room, the lava projected straight up and covered the drop ceiling with glowing, artichoke-green star patterns. The magical night sky image suspended the initial commotion, lit up the room, captured everyone's attention, and won the prize for being a creative twist on an overused project.

Did I get reprimanded by the principal for using too much of a dangerous explosive? Yes, but I still didn't fess up that I'd been pranked. I took the prize and the three days of detention. It was quite a reputation boost, being recognized as a rascal and revered by the pseudo-edgy crowd who stood on tables and patronized the detention hall.

"What does this have to do with..." I asked, standing in front of the hierophants' table, still deciding which side to climb on.

"Approach the table from the left and climb up behind the swan. Walk to the center and present your living story. Climb down and readdress the hierophants," a powerful voice instructed.

I followed the directions, set my stupa down, crossed to the right side of the table, passed behind the second swan, then stepped down. My angelic witnesses were standing there, and I could sense Theo was also watching. I assumed he was gazing into his water mirror; a handy gateway he used to check on the status of trainees. Once I'd watched him reach his hand into the water mirror to redirect a trainee who was about to embark on a misadventure, pointing him in a different direction.

My stupa lit up and projected images of my persona from many lifetimes. I saw myself having multiple appearances, dispositions, attitudes, dysfunctions, and virtues; a great number of them entirely unfamiliar. All of these reflected off my energy field and shaped my body image. Like a projector, they propelled these traits and qualities into the world. I was embarrassed because nothing was hidden from view. My stories of potentials, failings, and successes were being examined by the hierophants.

I didn't feel judged. On the contrary, I sensed their silent compassion. Somehow, I knew they were championing my progress, like a family cheering on a child from its first steps to those of its own offspring.

On my simultaneous astral adventure, it was different: a celebration was in the works, a feast of divinities. All glasses and bowls were filled with light and fire. Each time someone ate or drank, their energy intensified and burst with explosions of love.

"It is the Love," the Solar Mage reminded us.

This bursting of love happened many times at the table. One being after another went supernova after eating the fire or drinking the light. Then it was my turn.

I lifted the crystal bowl and saw the fire shape itself into a ruby-red grape, the fruit of my desire. I plucked the grape out of the bowl and popped it into my mouth. It coated my mouth, slid down my throat and infiltrated my torso. The sensation was exquisite! I was cleansed, purified, a bit giddy, and abundantly full.

When I picked up the chalice and drank the liquid light it exploded outward with a wave of love. My heart swooned. The feeling of being less, void of obstructions, found me without the quality I had always carried: fear.

"Wisdom seems cold, sharp, short tempered, impatient. It appears to always hide something. Wisdom achievers know that even when they share their wisdom with us, it falls on deaf ears and disappears, following a fleeting realization," the Triple Wisdom Woman had insisted years ago.

"Why is it so elusive?" I questioned.

"True wisdom must be earned, learned and churned to become a leaseholder of its power. It will disappear in a heartbeat if not respected and nurtured with love."

Her counsel about wisdom was nestled in my mind.

She was right. It was a challenge of virtue, a gauge to weed out the gadflies. Without the dedication of letting go of prosaic knowledge, in exchange for authentic wisdom, only a momentary taste was allowed.

On the etheric plane, it had only taken a few moments for the hierophants to evaluate my stupa. The process ended without formality or explanation. There was no approval, congratulations, encouragement, or advice for the future. Just a burst of golden light blasting the room. Instantaneously, I was alone, wondering if I'd failed.

Back on the astral plane, every drink, every taste, was celebrated with looks of empathy from each member – according to their capacity to express and receive love.

A powerful void, demanding to be filled, drove us to silence. It coalesced into a luminosity that blasted us with the Solar Mage's principles of Love, Light, and Life.

"Love is capable of absorbing everything that is not itself and transforming Light into Life," the Solar Mage proclaimed.

This love was too intense. I was absorbed and losing focus quickly.

"What am I missing?" I asked.

"You are forgetting the direct line to Spirit, the Supreme Being's sole stamp of approval." The Ophanim angels shouted as they launched my inner star. It went supernova, reached the center of the galaxy, and bounced back; greeting every star in between. When it returned, my personal star was augmented, now carrying the additional flavors of all the stars it met on its journey.

"Star upon star, that is what you and we are." The Ophanim said, expressing their approval.

The next thing I knew, I was back on the physical plane, sitting in meditation basking in the sun as its light danced through the leaves of the trees.

I heard something in my left ear; Boji was speaking to me. I examined her lips, but I couldn't make out the words. I looked around. People were getting up and leaving.

It took a few minutes before I was back in control of my body enough to hear Boji say, "We must join the Solar Mage to perform the morning exercises, have some breakfast, and begin our day."

I followed Boji down to a large clearing. The Solar Mage stood at a slightly raised end of the field in front of the gathering. After standing motionless for a moment, we imitated his refined calisthenics. For ten minutes we danced, the silence only broken by the song of rustling clothes. Our movements partnered with white clouds drifting across the washed-blue sky. When the exercises ended, we walked off the field slowly, still influenced by the pace of the movements.

Boji and I followed the crowd to a small outdoor café, similar to one found on the streets of Paris. I could smell the fresh-baked goods and strong coffee! Boji led me to a seat and then hustled off quickly. What a delight to see her return moments later with coffee, pats of butter, warm croissants, and a small bowl of round instead of cubed sugar.

Almost drooling by my first bite, the croissant melted in my mouth, dissolving before the iced butter. Sipping my coffee with traces of butter still in my mouth created an exquisite sensation. I looked at Boji; sitting with her at a small table in the South of France was perfect. I had nothing to say, and no thoughts interrupted our periodic smiles. I sat there, appreciating everything.

The journey to the sun had muted my usual discomfort and awkward self-consciousness. Merging with other souls was natural, and I was finding it easier to love others without pretense.

I glanced behind Boji as the warmth in my heart expanded. My eyes fixed on a tree with a perfect crooked fork in its trunk, standing just at the edge of the courtyard. Its green shoots were vibrant. I fancied climbing it to get a birds-eye view. It had been a visceral drive to scramble up trees since my childhood.

I sipped my coffee again, enjoying my reverie, when a boyish figure with a huge smile appeared in the crook of the tree. He looked quite natural sitting there, waving at me. His clothes were green and brown, accented with sparkling blue jewels. I looked closer and realized I had been mistaken; it wasn't a boy at all.

Another creature was sitting in a different tree, some were on nearby bushes and others by a row of flowering plants. Still more were flying above our heads in the courtyard.

I described what I saw to Boji.

"Oh yes," she said. "Those spirits dance and play about the grounds by request of the Solar Mage. Their activity helps cultivates the delicious fruits and vegetables which thrive on the living energy of their presence. When we sit down for a meal with the Solar Mage, we believe we are eating fire and drinking light. We can visit the gardens today, if you'd like."

My jaw dropped. Her words rekindled the memory of my fire and light meal on the sun. The love came flooding back into my cells.

Later, we walked around the gardens and picked some apples in the orchard. Feeling peaceful, joyful, and alive, I considered living in this paradise permanently. But I knew it wasn't my time.

In my journal, I wrote with none too little pride: 'I traveled to the sun with the Solar Mage, feasted on love, presented my stupa to the hierophants, and encountered the Michael. Mission over-accomplished!'

The next day, I had to leave Boji and the People of Light.

We embraced at the front gate; I gave gratitude roses to the inhabitants of this amazing place while thanking Boji for her companionship. We agreed to meet again in the near future. I promised to return.

I walked through the gates and turned to give her a final wave goodbye, but she was gone. So was the gate, my badge, and the People of Light. The only thing left were the two rows of trees.

I couldn't wait to report back to Theo.

CHAPTER FOURTEEN

FINDING THE MUSIC MAN

Y DECISION TO ASK the Music Man for help with the
Dragon Master was easy but finding him would be
a bigger challenge. The experience with the People
of Light and the reignition of my relationship with the sun
should help me discover anomalies in the light patterns as the
rays enter the atmosphere above the city. I speculated that if
they were redirected to a particular spot in the valley, it should
lead me to his location.

The difficulty was reaching him before his solar performance was finished. If he was in the mountains, forget it. If
the ridgeline was his venue, I'd have a chance. It would be most
fortunate if he chose a location in town. I wasn't optimistic.

It was a groggy morning. A delayed caffeine fix caused
my mind to loiter in the ethos of the Logos meditation and
I was slow to complete my Chi exercises. So, when a blue
flash of light notified me of activity on the landscape, I had
to scramble to engage my geomantic mentality. There was the
sign. Light beams were bending around a section of the hills,
distorting the view of the Flatirons.

"That must be him!"

I jumped off my cushion, threw on the clothes lying on the bedroom floor, and grabbed whatever shoes my hand felt first. Reasonably dressed, I hopped on my bicycle and raced toward the foothills by following the trail behind my housing development toward the light distortion. With any luck, it would lead me straight to the Music Man's performance. When I couldn't ride any longer, I'd have to travel by foot. The worst-case scenario? I'd encounter him on his way down. Or, I would miss him completely.

"Solid thinking," came the sleepy voice of an Ophanim angel. "Your analyzer seems quite alert. Any coffee left?"

I ignored the Ophanim angel in my haste, unwilling to lose a moment.

By the looks of it, the Music Man was performing high on the ridge. There were only a few ways to get up and down the foothills, so I just needed to get close to the light distortion. He had to be there.

"Interesting assumption," another Ophanim angel said. "Where's the coffee?"

Why the heck did they show up this morning asking about coffee? Since when do angels even drink coffee? The thought quickly passed as the trail steepened beyond my leg power to continue. I set the bike between two trees at the edge of a bluff and continued up the path at a quickened pace, reassured I still had an oxygen container in my backpack if I needed a jolt of energy.

The sun wasn't high enough to light the back side of the Flatirons, so it should be easy to follow the beams passing into the shadows. If my premise was correct, I'd see a slight curvature of the rays bending toward the Music Man at the zenith of a hill.

My analytical mind was in overdrive, hypothesizing the probabilities.

The light should take a dramatic turn before heading to its intended target. But it needed to happen soon. Once the sun reached above the horizon, I would lose the opportunity the shadow side of the hill was giving me.

"Where is that bittersweet cup of joe you rave about?"

If I had a suspicious nature, I would have thought the angels were trying to distract me. But why now? I was at the top of the foothills breathing heavily, and they were talking about coffee.

"I could use a little help, here," I said acerbically.

"Much too early for that," another angel responded. "Oh, this coffee is good. Want some?"

"No, but thanks for all your help this morning," I quipped, intentionally sounding peeved. "Can't you see I'm trying to find someone?"

"Oh, him," I heard as a loud sipping sound filled my head.

The angels were mocking me, but I didn't have time for their antics.

I crossed into the shadowy side of the foothills, momentarily losing my bearings. I couldn't locate the light beams.

"What kind of coffee is it?" one Ophanim angel asked.

"Where did you buy it?" another immediately followed.

"When did you brew it?" a third chimed in, coffee cup in hand.

"How much does it cost?" came the next.

"Now that is some good coffee," another one exclaimed.

The sixth one was holding a pot upside down, pouring the remaining dregs of thick coffee, and said, "Bingo!"

I was about to blow up and yell at a group of high-ranking

angels, so I gave myself suns of amusement and breathed deeply. Calmed, I listened.

"Look at the undifferentiated light within the shadows," angelic voices sounded in my right ear.

I refocused by crossing my eyes for a moment and looked again. At the top of a rock outcrop, near a grove of trees, stood the Music Man. He blended in easily with the surroundings, but the light around him was inverted. The beams had shifted into negative space as they moved behind the hills.

I was growing desperate and called for gnome assistance.

A dust cloud erupted with Bobby and the clan already on the move in front of me. They took the right side of the split trail and charged around the next bend.

Fifteen minutes later, I was standing twenty feet from the Music Man, very much out of breath. He packed his wand into an ornate carrying case and slipped it into his overcoat.

"Good greetings to you," he said. "I have been anticipating the coloration of your invitation, knowing that a proclamation has been gestating for a set duration."

"Good greetings to you, sir," I said, in the midst of decoding his words.

I shared my thoughts about the Dragon Master while we headed down a dilapidated trail I didn't know existed. A few minutes later and I would have missed him completely.

By the time we arrived at the trailhead where his three-wheel cycle was parked, my story was just about finished.

"I am not sure what kind of help he needs, but I would appreciate your assistance. Are you available anytime soon? I fear there is an urgency to this quest." I said, hoping I wasn't being too pushy.

"Tomorrow I shall be appropriately rehearsed for such an

adventure as this," he proclaimed. "I will depart while the sense of you and I will momentarily seem dispersed."

With that he climbed onto his motor-less tricycle, pulled out his wand, and tapped between the handlebars. My brain was still interpreting his lyrical tongue before I had time to wrestle out the suitable words designating where we should meet. Thankfully, he interrupted my logjam.

"Being here, yes I will at 6 a.m. somehow, still," he said cordially. "See you on the morrow, by the by."

With that, he sped off, propelled by a soundless motor. While distorted light appeared ahead of him, waves of light rushed in behind him – flapping his coattails wildly in the breeze.

Hooked on the side of his tricycle appeared six angels squeezed together in an oversized sidecar. Wide-eyed and apparently over-caffeinated, each one was holding an open glass jar, capturing the light particles as they blew past.

"Hey, fill one up for me," I shouted as they sped away.

"Check your coffee pot. We've mixed up a special brew for tomorrow morning," one angel shouted.

The Music Man held out his hand toward the sidecar, and an angel placed a jar of light in his hand. When he took a sip, his tricycle accelerated like an Atlas rocket.

CHAPTER FIFTEEN

THE DRAGON MASTER

COULDN'T GO TO THEO with what I was planning.
After all, it would be awkward and risky. He would
ask why I was going to see a Dragon Master, and I
would have to tell him the truth.

"I talked to the Fire Dragon. I freed the Water Dragon."

My list would grow from there, and he would chastise me.
I imagined the conversation in my head.

"How could you think you were capable of such missions?"

I would answer honestly.

"You released beings on the landscape many times. I just
imitated your technique."

That would just annoy him, and he would say, "You haven't
been trained to free…anything. There are protocols I use to
keep us safe. Since you do not know what they are, how could
you hope to succeed?"

The conversation would wind its way downhill from there.
I would justify my actions by reminding him of my past-
life abilities.

Theo would not be impressed or convinced, saying,

"Past-life attributes, successes, or abilities do not entitle you to behave irresponsibly."

We were in Ireland the last time he was this cranky. I certainly didn't relish upsetting Theo again, but my analyzer needed to be reassured by reliving the experience. I could sense Achilles and Aesop preparing to show me exactly when his mood changed.

We were searching for a dolmen, a large stone still remarkably balanced on two standing stones after centuries of exposure to the elements and vandalizing conquerors. Theo's research on these ancient structures led him to believe one would be especially significant to our mission.

"It was a meeting place for tribesmen to commune with, and this is where things get a bit confusing in the myths; aliens from another galaxy *or* a sacred cow," he explained prior to our trip.

I laughed in response, thinking how absurd 'aliens' and 'sacred cows' sounded, but Theo wasn't approving.

"The sacred cow, at times a bull, from Irish mythology, represents more than the splash of milk you put in your coffee every morning!" he reprimanded.

I looked at him, befuddled, but he didn't explain further. Instead, he remained terse and sour for a while. In short, he was downright insufferable.

In Ireland, we were quite a sight strolling aimlessly around the manicured links of Dundalk golf course with our group of geo-mythic researchers.

We found the dolmen right in the middle of the course, but instead of Theo being pleased, he became quite agitated. There was something about it he didn't like. The stone? The location? The energy? Or was he bothered by the genuine charm (and lack of signage for sacred sites) in the 'Irish' part of the Republic? He'd seemed surprisingly at home in British Northern Ireland; who would have thought Theo was such an Anglophile?

I never saw him so irrational. He grumbled, complained about the behavior of Leprechauns, and walked away brusquely. Our group members were torn between following him and staying to explore the site.

I needed to delay my departure; my wisdom guides were giving me an urgent message.

"Reactivate this dormant standing stone. The land will be renewed."

How had it been shut down and sealed? By a superstitious priest hellbent on converting the druids, or just a belligerent Brit's way of controlling the locals? No matter. I had to work fast. Once Theo noticed I stayed behind, he would suspect I was breaking more geomantic rules. That would cause an inquisition I was none too prepared to face.

Ultimately, the other researchers – a woman from the California coast; a mysterious but powerful Mexican psychic; and Suzy, a spry Australian – all followed Theo.

I faked a desire to take pictures for my travel journal, instructing one of my compatriots to tell Theo I would meet him back at the car.

After racing into emptiness and attending to my inner star, I quickly laid down the blue dish support structure under the standing stone, mounted the rotunda, greeted the Ophanim angels, picked out a robe and staff from my wardrobe, and pulled my mystic sword from its scabbard as protection, just in case I stirred up a nefarious spirit or two.

I evaluated the energetic situation. The dolmen was blanketed by a forcefield of fear, disbelief, and judgement. Before

I executed a countermeasure, I invited the energy to reveal its key feature. Then I would use that energy to dial in the appropriate reverse sequence to clear the blockage in energy flow.

It was easier than I imagined. Much easier. A few dozen greeting roses, a sincere listening ear, gratitude for an assignment long ago accomplished, and a one-way ticket to any location outside the solar system for the bored-looking entitlement entities, and off went the ghostly spirit. The lock released, and the moody entities hanging around? They all vanished.

When the site was cleared, a beam of light descended into the top of the dolmen. A white-robed being appeared. It had a large, conical head that reminded me of a statue of a pharaoh.

"For the longest time, I have wished to return. Thank you for clearing the way. The doors of Ireland can now be used to link with the planetary continuum," he said eerily.

I had questions, although I didn't know where to start.

"What does this place have to do with—" I began, but I was interrupted as Suzy materialized next to me.

"Theo sent me to fetch you before you get yourself into mischief," she said, slightly out of breath. Then, sensing the presence of the interplanetary traveler, she said, "And what is going on here?"

"Oh, nothing. Well, nothing Theo needs to know about. Right?"

Suzy grinned. She'd had a run-in with him recently and was still smarting from the 'viper,' her new pet name for Theo. I smiled, assured she would keep my secret.

As Achilles correctly guessed, the memory from the Ireland trip was the answer to my internal debate. I would avoid asking Theo any and all questions about the Dragon Master.

On the map, Blue Lake was a six-mile round trip hike. It

was a mountainous trail where we could expect rain, fallen trees, and rockslides. And what if the Music Man needed to perform an impromptu concert? Finding a way to help the Dragon Master could be an all-day event.

Sandwiches? Check. Snacks? Fruit? Water? Tools? Check.

I stuffed my backpack with these necessities and hurried out the door. Today, I drove my Honda. She was a reliable old girl who ran better uphill, so I foresaw no problem traveling through the canyon to the mountain lake.

I rendezvoused with the Music Man as planned. The roads were clear, the park was mostly empty, and the trailhead was easy to get to. I'd been there before to do research. It was localized and allowed access to multiple destinations.

One trail ran up to Monument Mountain, a long, challenging eight-mile trek. I'd hiked it once, developing altitude sickness on the way down. It had been my first experience with what Theo calls 'thinning-space disease,' and it was a horrible experience! It took me days to recover.

The other trails were relatively easy. The Lady of the Sword Lake was just ten minutes in, and Lake Isabelle, a glacier lake, was a forty-five-minute switchback. A look at the trail map fixed the destination in my mind. It said it would be an 11,833-foot excursion, but we had driven to 10,000 feet to start, according to the topological map. Not too challenging a hike by my assessment.

We soon arrived at a rockslide area. It must have happened years ago; the trail consisted of large, strategically positioned boulders. The Elohim of ancient times, the builders of everything monumental including physical life, could not have placed the boulders more competently.

Next, we passed through wide open valleys with herds of elk. A mother bear and two cubs scrambled up the mountainside. Foxes, coyotes, and eagles hunted on the lush summer landscape.

It took an hour and forty minutes to get there. I slugged lots of water, gulped oxygen from my canister, and stopped often to take in the view. The Music Man didn't drink much, or breathe much for that matter, stopping simply as a courtesy to me.

During those moments, I would glance over, half-expecting him to pull out his wand. Once, he did reach into his pocket, only to stop himself. If he started conducting a concerto, we could be in for a long demonstration of light and sound.

When we arrived at the shoreline, we sat down to eat. I casually scanned the landscape while refueling.

The Music Man was as curious about my way of approaching the geomantic landscape as I was about his. Clearly, his method of engagement was unique.

"Each mystic has their own style," Theo had said while sitting in an old Irish churchyard, a herd of cows grazing nearby. As he spoke, I watched a giant head filled with beings, buildings, ladders, and steps. The skull cap was missing, and the characters were climbing out to investigate the world, relaying their findings back to the very pleased giant head. It was quite funny, and I felt rather silly sharing, so I didn't reveal the image to Theo at first. Nevertheless, he kept pestering me until I did. His response almost knocked me out of my chair.

"That is an accurate representation. It is a god head, albeit stylized. Good job."

With that, he moved onto the other apprentices to gather their feedback.

"My style of investigation is still developing. I scan the landscape. If I see something appearing from the invisible realm, I engage with it the best I can," I said to the Music

Man. "In this case, I know there is a Dragon Master here, somewhere, who needs our help."

He silently finished his sandwich, delicately wiping the corners of his mouth with a lace handkerchief he pulled from an inside pocket of his long coat. I wished I could get a look inside that coat. How many pockets did he have? I estimated at least nine.

I remembered reading an alchemical text that claimed there were many worlds inside a master's garment; universes of stars mapped out in a way that designated their rank and standing in the history of time. The space between the stars was inside a cape, shawl, or coat. This, the text said, was where magic began.

By sitting with the Music Man, my appreciation of the magic of clothing continued to grow. Guido, an Italian tailor, would have been proud of my approach to the wonders of the depth and dimension of this fabric.

I'd met Guido in the back room of a bookstore where he temporarily set up shop. Finding a tailor working out of the back room of a haphazard bookstore was unusual. But he was not your typical tailor.

"In early times, tailors were masonic, with their own secret guild." Guido told me.

He taught me an accurate pronunciation of my name. Like most immigrants, my family name had been bastardized when my great grandparents 'came over on the boat.' Not only was the name itself changed, but the Italian pronunciation was lost in translation. Once I learned about my name, its correct accent, and its secret social meaning, I changed an inexplicable degree. My facial features altered, my complexion improved, my eye color shifted from a burnt umber toward hazel, my posture adjusted, and my voice and diction shifted overnight.

The waiting technique I learned from Guido was simple and effective.

"Focus on the eye of the needle. Imagine the thread flowing into it. Then wait. At the appropriate time, follow the length of the thread slowly. The answers you seek will appear tied to the end of the thread."

Remembering Guido's thread lessons led me right back to the Music Man. While I'd been exploring my imaginings of the interior world of pockets – pockets that functioned like doorways – he'd been preparing to set off. I took a moment to fully return. Images of geometric shapes with colorful vibrational waves radiated, blended, elaborated, and danced in limitless space.

"That is a splendid book title," he said.

"What?" I asked unconsciously, closing the door on my fanciful adventure. "What would be a great book title?"

By now, the Music Man was backlit, blocking out the sun. His shadow loomed as large as the Elohim who guarded the boundaries of the blue dish I'd set in place under the lake. He nearly showed his teeth when he smiled at me.

"Limitless Pockets," he responded.

Why was I surprised? He'd sampled my mind journey; one of the many talents stored in his pockets.

The Music Man pulled out his wand and closed his eyes. The light particles previously dancing around him stopped, hovering in space. Then, receiving direction from their conductor, they began to alter their color and intensity. He'd played his part superbly. The activated light redeployed to the opposite shore and illuminated the crystalline structure of a cave. Outside, the landscape altered. The inside darkness rushed out, shadowing the mouth of the cave, as the outside light rushed in, illuminating every crevice.

Now it was my turn. The lake was calm. Puffy white clouds slowly drifted by, reflecting off the deep blue water. I invited Bobby, the clan, and Sirius to join me, hoping their presence would help. I extended my gaze across the lake. An outcropping caught my attention. I dialed in, narrowed my focus, and penetrated the rocks.

There he was. The Dragon Master. A Merlin-type figure encased in crystal, asleep in time. I continued scanning. He was in the central part of the mountain, and I looked for the best way to approach.

"There it is."

The cave entrance was a third of the way up the mountain, tucked behind a small waterfall fed by a barely noticeable stream. There was a slight drop from a large boulder to a small pool where the water continued its journey to the lake without much fanfare.

I mounted the rotunda which sat at the edge of the blue dish, zipped through my quiet-time sequence, then stepped on the central diamond. Optimally, my chariot ride would drop me off just a short hike to the cave. I landed above a large boulder, hopped off the diamond, and took the three steps down to the ground. I could see the water flowing over the edge.

I scrambled down and saw a notch behind the miniature waterfall, an entrance that a gnome might be able to squeeze through. Bobby seized my intent and made it through easily. Without hesitation, I projected myself through the mouth of the cave.

My eyes didn't need time to adjust. Embedded with jewels, the sparkling walls illuminated my way, courtesy of the Music Man. I unwound the spool of thread on my belt and tied the end to a jagged rock near the entrance, then I proceeded to the interior of the cave. Would I need the thread? Maybe not, but I was comforted by this extra precaution, even though my helpers would surely guide me to safety if need be.

I held up my sword hilt as I walked, periodically shifting my gaze to the opposite shoreline. The Music Man orchestrated light waves deep into the crystalline structure, guiding me toward the Dragon Master. They softened the density of the walls as they lit up the interior of the cave, making it easier for me to cut through the surface with my sword. I moved toward the central chamber, following the patterns of light, but my focus began diminishing. I was losing the thread of my location.

I popped through a wall into the room containing the Dragon Master. Just like the myths of old, he stood frozen outside of time. Lifting my sword, I easily penetrated the crystal block, but nothing happened. I tried again. Still nothing. I looked around the room, hoping to discover another mechanism of release.

"What should I do now?" I wondered.

"Some trickery is involved here," my wisdom guides responded. "There are forces at work that wish you to fail. A distraction energy is being projected to stop you. Restart your journey through the crystalline maze from where you first entered it."

I was confused. Should I backtrack? Start again? I didn't doubt my wisdom guide's direction, but I looked over at Bobby and he agreed. Capitulating, I retraced my steps to the spot where I first inserted my sword into the wall.

When I did, I saw a picture of a spiraling pathway tracking in the opposite direction. If I circled around this new way, I would end up behind the Dragon Master's chamber.

A bit muddled, wondering if this was also illusionary, I

established the four directions, added the above and below, then waited to see if my interior space and exterior worlds would bridge the gap, synchronizing the totality of my awareness.

A deep stillness shocked me, and my consciousness blinked on and off like a dying light bulb, disappearing in an abnormal silence.

The quietness was penetrated by a loud, clear voice.

"It is time to use your staff."

I pulled it out and stepped inside the deep space of the zen-like staff for a dose of no-time. When I stepped out, I was right in front of the Dragon Master. There was a small black ring attached to a coiled chain wrapped around the crystal encasement.

"This must be what is anchoring it."

I raised my sword and struck the ring with a downward slash. The chain snapped, and the crystal began to melt, liquefying without losing its shape. As it melted, silver light reached up into the heavens, and hundreds of winged beings swept upward, released from under the cavern. The Dragon Master slowly began to move.

His energetic bonds continued to melt away. As they did, an influx of energy rushed toward him. Minute changes occurred. Twitches and tremors blasted inward, entering geometric jewels positioned throughout his body. When they liquefied, waves of energy rippled out into the cave and the landscape.

The energy changed into organized patterns. These distinctive patterns replicated the artful forms demonstrated by the sixty-four magical warriors I discovered while visiting with Lao Tzu at his sanctuary on my first Santa Fe adventure. These warrior movements were orchestrated by the Eight Immortals of Chinese legend.

The Dragon Master's escape reminded me of Michelangelo's unfinished statues at the Uffizi Gallery Museum. His body was slowly exposed as it moved out of the crystalline structure: his head, an arm, a chest, a leg, all gradually emerging.

Now completely free, he walked quickly out of the cave and across the surface of the water to the center of the lake, no longer slowed by solidity. Essence of light from the surrounding mountains flowed toward him as he moved, giving color, shape, and substance to his clothing. By the time he arrived in the open air, his outfit was sparkling, a combination of a modern-day suit and Hindu warrior-priest attire. I could easily identify attributes of multiple cultures in his character.

He stopped in the center of the lake. A golden fire flared, becoming the centerpiece of a newly forming temple. The fourteen rainbow masters stood around the central fire. The Dragon Master's Merlin appearance had changed radically as he squatted in front of the flames. He began asking questions while staring into the fire.

A movie of the history of the world was leaping out of the flames. These moving pictures, assembled into a three-dimensional context, were speaking an unfamiliar language.

At the opposite side of the lake, the Music Man was still orchestrating the light that was now dancing above the newly formed dome.

From the scenes flashing by, I guessed at the questions the Dragon Master was asking.

How long have I been asleep? What has changed in the world? Where are the others?

His image continued to shift as fresh answers appeared. Each question activated a representation of his past. At times he appeared as a Daoist monk, a pharaoh, an Assyrian king, a

THE DRAGON MASTER

Norseman, a pope and many others, all appearing and disappearing as the answers to his questions came and went.

The rainbow masters standing around the circle supported him, their visionary minds forming a light bridge with the Dragon Master.

The winged beings I had released filled the open-air temple, buzzing around the flames. They looked confused, surprised, and uncomfortably delighted to be free.

The flame-born answers stopped, and the Dragon Master's expression changed. I imagined he had discovered enough for now. He turned and addressed me.

"What do you want?"

I didn't understand the question, so I didn't answer him.

Again, he asked, "What do you want?"

I still didn't get the point of his question.

He stared at me, wondering why I wasn't answering.

He looked toward the flame momentarily, then asked, "What do you expect as a reward for freeing me?"

My chattering mind went crazy with desirous thoughts, racing to find the perfect wish to be satisfied.

In the back of my mind, a voice sounded loudly, "When meeting a powerful being who offers you a gift or reward, decline!"

So, I answered politely, "Nothing, thank you. Happy to be of help."

My chitter-chatter mind, incredulous, was jumping up and down, carrying a long list in its hand.

"But, if you'll hear me out, there may be one thing."

He was listening carefully, so I continued.

"There is a situation at the Trail of Sages. There was one dragon, the Fire Dragon, then I set the Water Dragon free. Now that they are together, I do not know what to do with them. The land is in a drought, and I was told the Water Dragon could end it, but nothing has happened. Would you talk to the dragons?"

Only now did the words of the Solar Mage come through loud and clear.

"Ask for the needs of others first, and all the rest will be given to you."

Had this been a test?

My wisdom guides flashed an inner smile.

The six Ophanim angels, each from a different pillar on the rotunda, chimed in with a musical, "Yes."

I looked back at the Dragon Master, who likewise observed the singing angel voices.

Smiling as if remembering something pleasant, he said, "Dragons, as you have surmised, are my area of expertise. It would bring me much joy to work with them again."

He held out his hands and a momentary refraction of light distorted the space around his palms. A staff appeared, and he handed it to me. It was shorter than my mystic staffs, even shorter than a shillelagh. It was more like an elongated magic wand.

He looked toward the shore of the lake, then up toward the mountain. A giant lightning bolt struck the ground, and a column of silver light appeared above his recent prison.

"This magic branch is a smaller version of the silver light. Use it wisely."

Before I could ask him any questions about the gift, he disappeared along with the rainbow masters. The dome over the lake remained, as did its central flame and the freed spirits swarming above.

This new staff merged into my spatial footlocker. When would I need it? How would I know when to use it? The colors and radiance of the other staffs shifted to accommodate its presence.

I returned to the Music Man on the opposite shore. He placed his wand inside his coat, and I shared the events he'd missed. He listened to every word, but his gaze extended beyond me into space while his eyes danced in time with some invisible score. Was he orchestrating in his mind, laying down the framework for a grand piece, or was he just matching musical notes to the cadence of my words?

When I'd finished relaying the highlights of my encounter, he said, "You must tell your story. I shall set it to the music created here today. Each year, a performance should take place on this very spot."

The released winged beings pledged their loyalty to this sacred space. I smiled and sent gratitude roses to the spirits that had assisted me in freeing the Dragon Master.

"Offers must be cultivated for their *honey*, but don't be a *badger*!" a sage voice proclaimed, followed by uproarious laughter.

"It is the comedy team of Ophanim and Ophanim. We are performing everywhere, all the time."

I smiled and looked out over the expanse of the lake. It was extremely blue – a deeper, richer blue than it ought to have been. Its texture was thick, like an oil painting.

I took another look at the snowcapped mountains surrounding the lake. They, too, appeared to have thick brushstrokes expressing their contours.

The hike down the mountain with the Music Man was easy going. We spent half of the way in rhythmic conversation and the rest in silence, giving periodic roses and smiles to passing people, Indigenous spirits, and nature's extensive family. All were radiating more abundantly than before. I didn't need extra water or the usual stops to gather oxygen. I was exhilarated, breathing air and moisture through the pores of my skin. The bountiful psychic atmosphere was a bonus.

CHAPTER SIXTEEN

MINER'S ROW PARK

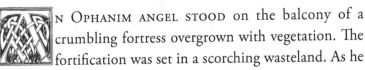

A<small>N</small> O<small>PHANIM ANGEL STOOD</small> on the balcony of a crumbling fortress overgrown with vegetation. The fortification was set in a scorching wasteland. As he spoke, reading from a scroll, two other angels solemnly led a hooded Ophanim – icicles hanging from his wings – into a courtyard just inside the huge gate of the fortress. There, they climbed a platform. Suspended high above was a very large blade; instead of polished steel, it was carved out of ice.

Standing on the platform was a hooded figure grasping a wooded handle. At the bottom of the stairs, another Ophanim angel stood, pike in hand, guarding the event. No one else was present, and the landscape was barren for miles around. Any hope the prisoner angel would be rescued was futile.

"Hear ye, hear ye, hear ye! This is a warning for those who may venture too far, exploring their cold, dry intellect and giving free rein to their mind's calculating, considered certainty of its own copious, conspicuous control of self-suffering superiority," the Ophanim angel on the balcony proclaimed. "Let this be a lesson to all those who besmirch the truth or opinionate as an acceptable substitute for the truth of the basic goodness of existence. The cost is dire, but the punishment fits the crime. So, take heed. Or…just, um…oh…just keep it in mind!"

By the time he finished his declaration, the three Ophanim angels had reached the top of the platform. They began discussing where exactly to place the prisoner. The guillotine was missing some of its parts: a bascule to support the body and a lunette to hold the head.

"How do we align your head with the blade?"

The two attendants looked to the hooded figure for an answer, but he just shrugged.

After a long discussion and much confused gesturing, the criminal decided to lie down on the platform, face up. He made a few adjustments to align with the icy blade, sliding east a foot, north six inches, two inches west. Then, he wormed toward the south about eight inches, tilted his head right, straightened out his face, and gave a thumbs-up to signal that he was ready.

"Finally!" griped the angel up on the fortress balcony. "Let the show begin!"

The executioner took a magnifying glass out of his pocket and moved toward the long rope attached to the blade. He angled it between the sun and the rope. A wisp of smoke rose from the three-inch thick rope.

This was going to take a long time, and I didn't get it. What was the point of this performance?

"The two extremes either fill you with expanded pride or compressed intellect," my wisdom guides explained. "These are vividly active on the screen of your life projector. They remind you when you get a little too close to either polarity. On one side, you feel the heat of your expanded pride. On the other, the frigid cold of self-importance predominates."

The Ophanim angels were usually hilarious and generally over the top with their illustrations, but this execution scene wasn't that funny.

When I shared it with Theo, he just smiled and said, "The Ophanim angels can only give you what you are capable of understanding. Apparently, they are giving you an example of a slow-burning, icy, albeit not-very-accurate death. Normally, your blanket cleverness and shrewdness is contrasted by a penetrating attention to detail. In this case, you are naked and can't see the nose on your face."

Clichés, metaphors, analogies; all this was confusing at best. And what did they have to do with the Ophanim angels' odd execution play?

"What are they trying to show me? The nose on my face has nothing to do with it!" I exclaimed out of frustration.

"The bulky blade? The imprecise alignment?" Theo hinted. "How accurate will the falling blade be on the prisoner's neck? It represents a sloppy death. The magnifying glass being used on the thick rope. How long will the victim lie there, waiting, watching the rope burn and contemplating the icy blade? What are his choices?"

"Do nothing, go empty, and wait. The sun will melt the icy blade enough that it slips through the ropes holding it, crushing the Ophanim angel before the magnifying glass burns through the rope!" I said.

The Ophanim angels all stopped their play and took a bow. By this time, the blade was melting quickly, raining on the troupe of performers. They stripped off their costumes and danced around the stage in their underwear, laughing like little children playing in a sun shower. Above the melting ice, a rainbow appeared. One end started at the hanging ice, the other end connected to a pot of gold at the base of the foothills, near Miner's Row.

"Well, maybe you will live long enough to be a warrior after all," Theo said, laughing his infectious laugh, after I shared the part about them dancing in the rain in their underwear.

"What about the pot of gold?" I asked.

"Don't worry about that. Chances are your gnomes are already on their way."

Sure enough, Bobby and the clan were scrambling off toward the large park near Miner's Row. The foothills, a few blocks away, made an impressive backdrop, and the park was big enough to host two soccer games at the same time. It was a great place to perform tai chi or Bagua mud walking.

Today, standing between two trees and facing northeast, I set up a blue dish from my exploded inner star. The rotunda appeared near the west rim of the dish, and the Ophanim angels readily accepted my roses of greeting. All six angels stepped out of the columns (their home base when inactive) and sat together on the left side of the rotunda, providing a good view of the center of the field.

I moved to the rotunda and stood facing the same direction as the mesmerized angels. I noticed a distortion in the center of the park. The energy began to slowly ripple around that point, but nothing came into view. No mythological creatures and no invisible structures reached out to me from any shifted space.

"When in doubt about a feature's presence, send heaps of greeting roses," Theo once suggested. "Give yourself suns of clarity, worthiness, and seniority. Walk into your expanded staff and wait."

I planted my staff into the ground; it grew to fit me and

my eight-foot round bubble, then I walked into it. Instead of going empty, which was usually the next step, I walked right through the staff to the opposite side of it. I ended up in front of a large, silo-shaped structure in the middle of the park.

It resembled the musical lamp that sat in the corner of my room when I was a child. The lamp slowly revolved when turned on, rotating around the soft, yellow light bulb. As it spun, the images on the shade projected shadows on the walls of my room. It always put me to sleep after my parents tucked me in for the night, but if the images I now saw on this landscape feature had been on my lampshade, I would have been frightened out of my wits.

My fascination moved me forward, but I maintained a safe distance. The shade-like outer structure was turning in the same direction as I circled the silo. It covered a third of the park and, although it was backlit, my childhood, friendly animal carousel had been replaced by a hellish, Bosch-like scene.

I'd seen something like this recently, projected on the wall of a canyon, deep in an isolated gorge in New Mexico. The paintings depicted fire and ice demons engaging humans at the extremes of post-life, souls moving through the Buddhist Bardo or Dante's Christian Hell. Here was a virtual Jacob's ladder, residing smack dab in the middle of Miner's Row.

Watching figures fall down into icy realms with their logic and others rise to the fires of personal pride was fascinating. Some stuck in nationalism, racism, sexism, and other retrogressive prejudices watched helplessly as demons goaded, teased, and encouraged the after-life journeys of these tormented souls.

After a few circumnavigations of the silo, I relaxed and defocused to allow myself to see deeper into the structure. Beneath the scenes (which were very much on the surface of this thin, spinning shade) was a brilliant realm of liquid light being ignited by bolts of energy from above.

I mused over a Zeus-like figure periodically tossing his lightning bolts into the center of this feature. Stirring the pot of souls, feeding, enlivening, and elaborating it.

I walked around it a few more times, but nothing new appeared. I returned to the rotunda through my standing staff and sat down next to the Ophanim angels.

"What is this?" I asked them.

"Bosch? Dante? Jacob's ladder? The same and also different," came the response from these angelic sidekicks.

"I saw that, but I feel like there's something more," I replied.

"When features on the land give gifts," they said, "they give them *right* when they're needed."

For a moment, I was nonplussed, but then I remembered the branch the Dragon Master had given me. I retrieved it, replacing the staff I'd walked into, then looked at the angels for confirmation.

"Look again," they instructed.

I walked into the branch. This time, as I exited and stood in front of the silo, there were three of me. My astral self to the right, my etheric self to the left, and my ego in the middle.

I walked around the silo again. Certain images faded as I passed by while others intensified. Some came down off the silo exterior and walked away, others recognized their hypnotic states and searched for a way to escape, only to fall right back into the dynamics of their self-created hell. Were they not ready to give up their attachments, or did they lack the insight to move on? I didn't know the answer.

Then I saw the connection. Certain images were linked to my astral body and others to my etheric body. Some were responding to my warrior presence. Not my warrior body, per se, but something inside it. No, actually, behind it. I turned around, stepped backwards and was surprised by what I saw. The Michael, the Solar Mage, the Francis, the Christopher, my wisdom guides; all stood behind me. They were visible through the spatial distortion. An unfixed barrier stood between us.

"You have begun a chain," said the Michael.

"W-what?" I stuttered.

"It leads to the stars, but you must be ready. Know you my sword?"

"Yes. I mean, I know you give it to mystic warriors when they're—"

"I give nothing," interrupted the Michael, "but I can guide you to what is yours. Make yourself ready."

"I will."

"The sword is not all you will need. Gain the Lady's favor and the dancers' gems. When you have them both, you will be ready to search out your guide."

"Wait, what do you—" I began, but almost as soon as the Michael finished speaking, I found myself back at the rotunda, gazing at the silo, and wondering what it all meant. The Ophanim were silent. So was I until Bobby and the clan came running by, carrying a pot of gold.

CHAPTER SEVENTEEN

A SUPREME MAKEOVER

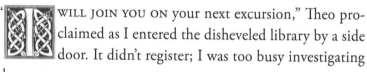

"WILL JOIN YOU ON your next excursion," Theo pro-claimed as I entered the disheveled library by a side door. It didn't register; I was too busy investigating the room.

Why more than one entrance? My senses insisted something was peculiar. The room was small, with books stacked from floor to ceiling despite the cases easily able to hold more books. Two of the doors in the room were covered with heavy red curtains reminiscent of movie theaters I frequented as a youngster.

When his words registered in my consciousness, I blurted out, "Why?"

"Did I hear a 'why' question?"

Theo allowed the empty silence to conspicuously hang in the air while it tightened around my pride. My anxieties were growing fat for slaughter.

Images of the Triple Wisdom Woman appeared. She was lecturing me about 'why' questions. These strong memories triggered my insecurities, hanging them out to dry.

"What made you decide to come along tomorrow?" I asked, eager to reclaim a confident demeaner in the midst of Theo's alarming proposition to accompany me.

"There is an energy presence you cannot fully grasp. Firsthand guidance is necessary; this is an opportunity to demonstrate how to engage with a unique landscape feature."

While I was excited to learn something new, I dreaded going to the canyon with Theo. I would end up revealing that I had freed the Water Dragon; the event was an uncomfortable secret. He would see the results of our interaction in the energetic field. Best to confess before heading out, but how? I didn't want him peevish after we arrived in the canyon. Best to just spit it out. Now.

"Before our research tomorrow, I need to say something."

"What is it?" Theo pressed.

"Remember the time I asked you how to free a dragon? If I should attempt it? Well, I freed the Water Dragon imprisoned in Eldorado Canyon."

I waited for his response. I waited longer. Theo sat back in his chair with his eyes closed. When he was silent, the atmosphere changed; time slowed, and emptiness filled the room. It was my cue to take advantage of the clarity of the moment.

Eventually I lost my focus. My body seized my attention by cramping my right calf. I prayed he'd say something soon. After standing with seventy percent of my weight on one leg for two hours, Theo's eyes opened. He continued with planning the next day, ignoring my confession.

"Get a good night's sleep, don't eat or drink excessively, and be ready at 6 a.m. Meet me here."

Ah, my penance. Walk for an hour and a half before we enter the canyon, another hour to find the site, two hours of research, and the hike back.

"Do not ride your bicycle from your house," he added, "and give yourself 100 suns of transparency."

With that, his unspoken tone of dismissal shoved me out the front door.

I woke up free of any burdens after working with suns and roses before going to sleep. Multiple layers were necessary today. The canyon could be icy cold; except for a few plateaus, the winter sun never reached into its depths. I wished Theo would choose a bright, sunny spot, but it wasn't guaranteed. His gnome would lead him to the best geo-mythic viewing place, not necessarily the most comfortable one. Bobby, on the other hand, would try to fulfill both requirements per my request. Theo's gnome would get the final say.

The hike across town to the canyon road was uneventful. Packs of coyotes howled in the darkness of the morning, broken up by hooting owls. A black bear scampered up the hillside as the first light crowded out the stars. Theo led us along at a quickened pace, ignoring nature's pre-dawn activity.

The three-quarter moon cast shadows as we started up the unlit road into the canyon. The sky slowly began to blush a pastel pallet of blues, pinks, oranges, and reds.

We were getting close. I could hear the river as it emptied out of the canyon after running by the water-bottling plant and summer swimming pool. The pool was void of water and activity this time of year. I attempted to tell a joke about the taste of the water, the swimming pool, and the filtering process, but it fell on deaf ears. I chuckled at how stupid it sounded. Theo was obviously not amused.

I was working on the quality of my amusement. My focus was improving, but I would have to say my fondness was still a little sappy.

"A warrior without a sense of humor is in danger of

self-inflation, which is a genuine concern when power is acquired," Theo warned. "If you complete your training, you will become powerful, but that is not the goal. The goal is to be useful to the cosmos by cleaning up your karmic history, alleviating self-absorption, and engaging the landscape. Therefore, I have added the element of amusement to those of focus and fondness, so trainees will remain good-natured in their development."

My thinking was still playing around with those terms as the light began dancing high on the canyon walls. I could see the terrain clearly if I cranked my neck. But it was dizzying looking up at the jagged rocks above the tree line.

I was hoping it would be a short ascent up to the plateau above the visitors' center a mile or so into the canyon where the Warrior and I freed the dragon. It couldn't hurt to revisit the site of my no-longer-secret exploit now that Theo was up to date.

"Please, landscape spirits, don't let this be a climb to the top," I begged quietly.

"You lead the way," Theo said, interrupting my appeal. "Before I determine the best location for exploring the feature, I would like to see where you have researched the landscape."

"Okay," I responded, relieved to get such a quick answer to my plea.

The visitors' center was coming into view as we turned the corner along the muddy, elevated road. Right behind it were the steep steps leading up to the dragon's plateau.

The images and feelings revivified as we closed in on the location: the chains that bound her; my sword; the unfolding of her wings; a rainbow bridge appearing as she lifted off; the gale winds abruptly stopping; the atmospheric density altering. How I felt taller than the canyon as the dragon rose; and finally, the Water Dragon rising above the city with the Fire Dragon waiting on the plateau, her trail of light raining down upon the cityscape like multicolored jewels as she flew in his direction; all flooding back upon me.

By now, we were at the base of the plateau. I pointed up to the spot where I'd freed the dragon with the Warrior and said, "I stood right up there."

"You *stood*?" Theo queried.

"I was holding my sword, standing with the Warrior. And we were, we were—"

I was relieved when Theo interrupted my stammering by unpacking his chair on the flat, sunny spot right where we'd stopped.

With our protocols in place and the steps through the Logos meditation dutifully performed, Theo guided me to the rotunda, saying, "This time, we will nudge your awareness, pushing your seeing beyond its celebrated reputation."

Theo's acerbity did not go unnoticed. Immediately, my heart began pumping adrenaline.

"The level of seeing you will need today warrants this. The feature is accessed by way of tools not yet taught by me or used by you. Well…as far as I can tell. After all, you free dragons without having been taught the necessary skills."

Was he going to start reprimanding me now?

"At some time in your existence, you will freely avail yourself of the powers and subtle awareness afforded you without consequences. But without my assistance today, it would be fruitless to proceed."

Although I was relieved that he wasn't going to lay into me about the Water Dragon, my energy was ramping up. An uncomfortable anticipation was creeping in. It wasn't anxiety, but if concern was in the wings, fear would not be far behind.

Sure enough, my mind began reeling. Theo had a penchant for being overly cautious, but this time I felt like the hair on the back of my head was being twisted into a tight knot.

"Go to your head space chair. Use red roses to clean off the mental screen and give yourself suns of worthiness. Then, return to the rotunda," Theo instructed before I indulged too deeply in fearful thinking.

When I returned, he continued, "Today, we will put on white robes, completely covering us from head to foot. In your hand, you will hold a white staff with a flaming crown on top.

"Step into the rotunda. Move through the octahedron phase of the Logos meditation while inside your staff. Imagine yourself in the flaming crown. Sink deeply inside the diamond."

This was complicated and difficult to hold in my mind. I saw why I would have had trouble accomplishing this on my own.

I sunk downward into the diamond. Today the diamond was in its purest holy form; the quiet, opened-palmed hands of the Ophanim supporting me while I settled into its emptiness. Theo's voice brought me back.

"Scan the landscape and tell me which number on a clock face would point to where we should look."

I turned slowly on the palms while looking through the multifaceted gem. As I reached four o'clock, the shadow of a structure lit up, but it disappeared as I moved to five o'clock. That was evidence that something was present on the invisible landscape in that direction.

"Four."

"Good. I would have calculated four and five-thirty, so let's split the difference and say four-thirty. Now, what do you see?"

I hesitated. My doubting mind was working hard to push my confidence into the background, but that wasn't unusual. It happened more times than not when Theo asked me to describe what I saw. Although this always unnerved me, I trusted he would adjust and clarify any distortions that appeared on my viewing screen.

"It's a partial view of a structure with someone sitting upon a chair. The building is dark, the being is light. It's difficult to get a clearer picture."

"Give yourself suns of clarity and worthiness," Theo responded. "Don't pay attention to clouds of obscurity."

I followed his instructions without any progress. Theo noticed my lack of momentum and redirected my attention.

"Look up above the structure and spirit. What do you see there?"

His directions produced instantaneous results.

"It's a large castle – bright, radiating, colorful – with stairs leading up to large doors."

"Investigate further."

I climbed the stairs, showed my swords to the guards, and walked inside to see a great hall with small groups of people standing around. They were waiting for something, but without expecting it would happen anytime soon. If anything, they looked despondent, almost bored.

I was seeing very clearly now, and I communicated the scene to Theo.

"Good. What else?"

"I see a king sitting on a gnarled wooden throne. He's slightly slumped over and he looks tired, if not a bit sad. He's waiting too."

"Who is this king?" I heard Theo ask, his voice growing more distant.

"He's wounded. A screen above his head is repeating a familiar scene."

My wisdom guides and mental analyzer were working

together, and I began accessing information from the past-life archives. Achilles and Aesop engaged with my adventure and ran a related video. I watched it unfold.

A spear wounds the king. It is self-inflicted, done out of shame. Guilt. There is no foe holding the spear to deliver the blow. Could this be the dolorous stroke? The wound is grievous. Festering. The strike repeats, never healing.

The scene above his head matched that on my screen. As my movie projected above my head, the king's movie did the same. I paused to acknowledge this realization.

I told Theo, "All the people standing around are waiting for the king to be healed."

"Very good," Theo said with a decidedly congratulatory tone in his voice. "Now, let's go back down to the other figure below. Who is this being?"

I was silent for a long time. It wasn't that I didn't have an answer, I was just reluctant to voice it. Part of me couldn't admit who this smiling, jolly, mischievous looking being was.

His happiness, his playful disposition, was the antithesis of everything I'd been taught to expect.

Theo nudged me to give him a response.

"Who is it?"

"It just can't be who I think it is."

"Then you shouldn't mind telling me."

That made sense.

"It is the Supreme Being." I repeated it again, not believing the words coming out of my mouth. "It is the Supreme Being."

A memory jogged loose from a previous landscape adventure with Theo:

"…whose chair is always empty, but he clearly has the best seat in the cosmos." Theo playfully said when I turned my view of God into a nice old man with a long white beard while faced with a landscape feature called the Head of God. "Does he remind you of someone?"

It did. I designed God from my memory of the Solar Mage. I tried again and ended up as a cell in a large body. A foot cell to be precise. Then, I briefly became a star in a large galaxy before ending up face down in front of my blue chair. Theo was laughing at my predicament. The Ophanim playfully mocked me. Millions of them. Faces down in the dirt. Only Sirius seemed sympathetic, licking the side of my cheek and cleaning off some dirt with his stardust tongue. When I stood up and sat back on the blue chair, I was laughing also.

"It is the Supreme Being," I said one more time.

It sounded so crazy and presumptuous that I laughed hard enough to bring me to tears.

"Why would the Supreme Being not be happy or playful?" Theo maintained. "Ask Him to give you a healing."

"What?"

"Ask Him to give you a Sunday morning special healing."

"This is ludicrous," I said. "I can't ask the Supreme Being for a healing."

"Sure, you can," Theo encouraged. "If you would rather get on your knees and pray, do it. Or you can just ask and see what happens."

"Could I really?" asked a timid voice from my past. "The Supreme Being would do that?"

If a younger me was brave enough to ask, then I had no other choice.

"Supreme Being, would you give me a Sunday morning special healing?"

As soon as I said it, the Supreme Being bopped me on the top of my head. He pressed his thumb to my forehead, dipped me in a vat of water, bathed me in a brilliant light, poured a fluid rainbow into my body, and levitated my awareness above my head. All these descriptions were suitable for what happened, yet none of them were quite accurate.

"What happened?" Theo's voice interrupted.

I felt giddy. Tearful. Joyful.

I composed myself and told Theo, "Spiraling energy poured down through my body. I feel relief. Lighter. Expanded."

"Ask the Supreme Being to give you a Saturday evening special healing," Theo insisted.

"What?" I responded.

"Ask the Supreme Being to give you a Saturday evening special healing."

It sounded silly. Wasn't one healing enough? I was embarrassed. Ashamed to ask for another.

I repeated what Theo had said to make sure I'd heard him correctly.

"Ask the Supreme Being to give me a Saturday evening special healing?"

"Yes," Theo said again. "Ask the Supreme Being to give you a Saturday evening special healing."

Embarrassment notwithstanding, I did. Again, I felt a powerful joy infuse me, this time with more spiraling energy rushing up from below.

"How does that feel?"

"I don't know what to say."

"Well, say it anyway."

"I feel alive. Happy – as if I just woke up from a very dull dream."

"Good. Now ask the Supreme Being to give you a Friday afternoon special healing," Theo pushed mischievously.

"What?" I said. I couldn't tell if he was testing me or just making fun of me now. "Are you yanking my chain? Do you really want me to ask for more healing?"

"Ask the Supreme Being to give you a Friday afternoon special healing and see what happens."

Theo showed no sign of letting up.

"Okay. Supreme Being, please give me a Friday afternoon special healing."

I melted into emptiness, expanded into fullness, dove into fathomlessness, rose infinitely, and wrapped around eternity. I felt deep-fried, skinned, alleviated from all my burdens. By the time I heard Theo say, "What was that like?" I couldn't answer the question. I was toast. Burnt to a crisp! And Theo knew it. When I looked at him, I could see he'd had many Supreme Being healings.

"You know what I'm going to ask you to do next?" Theo prodded.

"Yes," I replied. "Ask the Supreme Being to give me an all-day Thursday special healing."

"After getting a Sunday morning, a Saturday evening, and a Friday afternoon healing, that would be silly," Theo teased. "You would think you'd have had enough."

"Good. I don't think I could survive another one," I responded. "So, what do I do now?"

"Check the castle above and tell me what has changed," Theo suggested.

I did.

"Everything is different. The wounded king has transformed into a healed Fisher King sitting upright on his throne. Straight, tall, vibrant, alive with life energy. The people are happy, smiling, radiant. The room is brilliant. A chalice is floating near the ceiling, overflowing with liquid light and love, pouring down upon everyone. How is that possible? Was my healing his healing?"

I turned toward Theo. He was already packing up his chair, and I mechanically packed mine into its carrying sleeve. The questions slipped away from my mind; they didn't matter right now. I took deep breaths of the canyon air. I felt alive. My mind was clearly on pause, its incessant desire for answers held back, its habit of identifying, labeling, and cataloguing my reality delayed.

As we started down the path, Theo suggested, "Let's take the bus back to town, eat at Ted's, and taxi back to the Dell of Faeries."

I'd never seen Theo ride a bus, eat out, or take a taxi. I'd never suspected he ate restaurant food anytime, anywhere. But then, I hadn't imagined a Supreme Being healing special would immediately change my reality. Everything was different. Even Theo!

CHAPTER EIGHTEEN

A TRICKY, TRIPLE-STACKED RIDE

"WHICH LANDSCAPE SITES SHOULD I link to the umbilicus?" I asked.

A week prior, we'd gone on an expedition to the 'belly button of the valley,' where Theo mentioned a linking technique without fully explaining it.

"Well, that *is* a question," he replied before diving back into the arcane book he was holding.

Was that it? Was that all he was going to say?

I waited, hoping he would divulge a little more information, give me instruction, or at least share some insight into using the linking technique. Engaging a site was difficult enough most of the time but stacking many sites and linking them together…well, that sounded like a daunting assignment.

The idea came from the Ophanim angels who invaded my dreams with an elaborate scene. The six rotunda drivers were weaving bridges while sitting in a heavenly realm. As a bridge grew out of their tapestry needles, they linked it to a seventh location among the stars. After meditating on the dream for a few days, I concluded it suggested bridging landscapes together and asked Theo if I was right.

"I'm not surprised you had such a dream. The umbilicus, the diamond, the Nimitta: all different names for the center of the Albion. The Albion is similar to the giant, though bigger in size and serving a larger purpose. He is the original anthropic being. This template for evolving human beings can be found in plain sight on the land, on *all* the lands of the Earth, on every continent."

"I read once that Albion was an early name for Britain."

"Yes, that is true in geographical history, but on the geo-mythic landscape, Albion is much more. If you link an Albion umbilicus to another geo-mythic site, it will give you gravitas in the eyes of celestial beings."

Given the Michael's cryptic counseling, that sounded promising.

Theo looked up, peeking over his glasses.

"Trust yourself. *And* your helpers. Even though gnomes are unable to assist you in some situations, you can always trust the proficiency of the Ophanim to guide you," Theo continued. "They are as close as close can be. Act as love from your inner star."

Recently, on my way back from two weeks in the Santa Fe desert with Theo, the Ophanim accompanied me by riding in a trailer hitched behind my car. They'd tethered a dragon kite to the back of the trailer and flew it all the way up Route 25. They were especially animated near Hermit Mountain; although the Hermit was long gone, there was a castle, jam-packed with stellar knights at a round table. Had the dragon kite been a sign? A teaser? Or an invitation for the castle's occupants to come to Boulder. Either way it worked. The knights had mounted their mighty steeds and followed us home. The table in Boulder's castle grew to accommodate 100 more knights.

Another time, the Ophanim showed me a souped-up version of their chariot. The wheels were turned-up propellers, like a Harrier jet. They gave me a ride to a distant star. Well, I'd thought it was a distant star until they reminded me it really was:

> *The star that you are,*
> *A star that we are.*
> *The blazing star*
> *Pinpoint, there*
> *In the middle of your sphere;*
> *Two inches above*
> *Your belly button, here*
> *One inch inside,*
> *Not so far.*

The Ophanim, after reciting their poem, explained: "It was more your doing than ours" as to why the journey took so long and passed through several galaxies to get to my inner star.

"We can only show you what is possible according to your beliefs. We are cognizant of the constructs you use to remain comfortable in your reality."

The Albion was just a short ride from my house, and I arrived in good time. It was on public land with a great view of the mountain range, geo-mythic temples, domes, and the downtown Boulder landscape. Theo called this part of the Albion the umbilicus or Nimitta, but I was uncomfortable with those terms. 'Albion's belly' fit my personality better.

Red roses? Check. Suns? Check. Quiet-time sequence?

Logos meditation? Staff? Rotunda? All protocols in place? Check.

It turned out Albion's belly had a diamond similar to that on the rotunda, and I sank into it, glad to have some frame of reference.

"Combining the two, already one, would make it easy to get to these, a triangle-done," Theo's voice rhymed out.

I looked around to see if he'd changed his mind and decided to join me on this stacking adventure, but he was nowhere to be found.

"Combining the two, already one, would make it easy to get to these, a triangle-done," Theo voiced again, decidedly inside my head. "Have fun," he added, triggering my inner smile.

I could see him remotely, but the scene wasn't quite clear. This was getting a little weird. It made sense that Theo could see me, but how was I seeing him? He winked.

"Combining the two, already one, would make it easy to get to these, a triangle done. Have fun. Dumb, dumb. De-dumb, dumb!"

The Ophanim chimed in on the 'Dumb, dumb. De-dumb, dumb,' as Theo's image faded away.

"Shall we dance, upon the land? This could be grand," they sang in harmony, one of them flatting the last note as the rest fell over laughing.

Before I could sincerely question the nature of these comedic angels, they put on bishop hats, folded their hands in prayer, and marched solemnly in a two-by-two procession.

"Is this better?" they asked, reminding me of my Catholic years.

"No. Go back to being funny, please," I insisted, not wanting to revisit the mischief I caused the parish priest.

Immediately they donned 1920s smoking jackets and held

long cigarette holders in their mouths. Of course, instead of smoking, they were blowing bubbles. Their jackets bore crests depicting two figures: God sitting on a throne and Mrs. God sitting on a conspicuously more impressive throne.

The crests became animated. The regal couple were reading newspapers consisting of two main sections. The first, cartoons underscored with lurid captions. The second, an editorial segment secretly composed by God himself. This anonymous critique of cosmic events was clearly a way to elicit exploratory suggestions about what to create next.

"We acknowledge the cosmic joke," one angel explained. "All was created by God, but was creation based on entertainment His idea? Mrs. God had a hand in this. She is not only the mother of the Word whispering throughout the universe, but she is also the driving force behind His sense of humor."

The Ophanim continued their newsroom antics, with one reporter commenting, "False rumors have been spread regarding God's distress after He burped the Big Bang. Why did He do it? Was He bored with so much empty space?"

Another angel responded, "Look what it says here: the missus intervened. She surprised Him with the idea of creating a first-generation humanity. This new group of characters was valuable entertainment for the old boy. Until they got out of hand, that is, and almost destroyed the planet with their shenanigans.

"God stepped in and admonished them, sending them to the purging zone for much-needed training in cosmic good manners. In the interim, He created a next-generation humanity with less cosmic power but more common sense.

"These balanced qualities toned down humanity's pride, selfishness, and tendency for self-indulgence. The power to manipulate nature's forces was removed. Now, they were only capable of destroying themselves, not a whole planet."

The hidden story of first-generation humanity, a 'stop the presses' moment for the ages, was printed on the front page of God's newspaper. The angelic realm was supremely shocked. Not one of God's creations had ever crossed the line before. Only He could administer chaos. Once this scandal was exposed, the publication was augmented and replaced by a didactic story intent on enlightening wayward angels who may be cultivating radical thoughts. In the reprint, there was a major omission: destroying a planet and throwing the whole solar system out of whack wasn't mentioned.

"How about this part?" another news angel pointed out.

"Humanity Goes on Bender: Maybe Destroys Planet."

"And the sub head."

"Will the Old Boy Make the Same Mistake with His Next Creation?"

"Okay, what if we also publish this in the editorial section?"

"Everyone Should Believe it. God Said So."

"This would create even more doubt in the minds of fringe angels."

"But look at all the comments streaming in. We can milk this for a millennium. Then, when interest starts to dry up, we can print, 'God Confesses – I Made It All Up!'"

One reporter, stepping out of the newsroom skit and back into his Ophanim persona, whispered in my ear, "Don't worry, we know He is setting a larger plan in motion."

I heard a ticker-tape-reading journalist shout out from a distance, "Wait until you get a load of this!"

Thankfully, the newsroom scene faded away before I heard anything else. The joyride was an amusing distraction and no doubt the angels had a point. But what did it have to do with my research today? I shook loose from the escapade and refocused on the logistics of linking the sites.

"I need help stacking landscape sites. Except for knowing this first one, Albion's belly, I'm at a loss."

"Did Theo give you this assignment?" one angel asked. "He's a sly one, that boy."

"No, you did!" I replied with an accusatory tone.

"Okay, then, who are we to contradict ourselves? Buckle up, it's time to fly."

The rotunda lifted off. Well, a version of it lifted off. A copy of the structure stayed in place on Albion's belly with a facsimile of me remaining behind as well. From above, my replica remained motionless. I was dressed in a gold robe holding a golden staff. I watched myself over my shoulder right up until we landed at the driving range where I first learned to swing a golf club.

I relaxed and shifted to internal vision. Immediately, six thunderbirds appeared, perched on tall columns of light. A huge bird's nest plopped down on the range.

"Time to put on a silver robe. At the Albion's belly, you are using gold, here at the thunderbird nest, silver is appropriate, and at the next stop, you'll need...well, something else. The correct fashion statement will get you more attention than your inside-out socks," jibed an angel. "You can obtain the robe and staff from the wardrobe room at the castle."

Dubious that a wardrobe room even existed, I entered the castle where the knights had taken up residence, bypassed the round table, went in the library, and asked the records' keeper, "Where is the wardrobe room?"

"Oh, you mean the prop department. Take your first left, go left again, then, at the four-way corridor, take another left."

After taking a few steps, I heard him mumble something

about a 'misfiled copy of a mystic's copy of a Supreme Being's copy of a spirit being's copy of a now-defunct agreement.'

After three lefts, a dead end, and three backtracks, I was lost. Frustrated, I stopped my rushing around and breathed love to my inner star. Feeling that I was once again the butt of an Ophanim prank, I went back to the rotunda at the thunderbird nest, only to find the silver robe neatly folded on top of the diamond and the staff leaning against it. I grabbed the staff and said, "What next?"

Six Ophanim angels were racing about like chickens with their heads cut off. Each carried his head under his armpit. The heads were shouting orders while their bodies followed the preposterous directions.

One angel approached me and said, "We can only give you what you ask for. You want special, we will give you special. You want simple, we can give you simple. Now, step into the thunderbird nest, go into the secondary diamond inside it, and enter your expanded staff."

The thunderbird nest was deep, dark, and jagged at the bottom. Its silhouette reminded me of the dispirited king's contorted throne in the castle in Eldorado Canyon, but turned upside down.

The animated thunderbirds transformed into peacocks with vibrant feathers, then striking Garudas, flaming phoenixes, and intimidating simurghs; all guises of the family of Ophanim angels who zipped around the invisible map.

"This auric inner star, this pinpoint of light inside every human, is a guide to the living Logos," the angels clarified. "The more you perform the steps, the more you begin to think, breathe, and live into the Logos meditation. You will find it not just a vehicle for accomplishments or to gain higher consciousness; it is a verb of action that becomes a noun of being.

Even that isn't accurate. The star and the Logos meditation are so much more than we can comprehend. It is no less than you and I can be, than we all are. Yes, magnificent is this inner star!"

Whatever this deeper meaning was, it filled me at the thunderbird nest, just as Albion's belly gave me access to a multidimensional landscape not unlike the hypercube (a mysterious traveling feature I'd used above Boulder Creek at the edge of Fine Park).

"It is time to move on to the next and final landscape feature of the day," two Ophanim angels instructed in unison, breaking me out of my reverie. "Before we take you to the next site in our shiny, washed, waxed, and expertly detailed rotunda, you need to once again hightail it to the castle prop department for another attire change."

I was tempted to ignore their suggestion, so I observed the activity on the rotunda. Six angels were polishing every inch of it. Some were spit-shining, while others were buffing it with power tools.

"The rotunda has to be perfectly dressed, and so do you."

"Why all the preparation?" I asked.

"You'll see."

"The last time you sent me to the prop department, I became lost in the back corridors of the castle, and as it turned out, I didn't actually need to go there," I said, intentionally sounding a bit perturbed.

"This time it is necessary. Cross our hearts and hope to spit," the Ophanim angel said sincerely as he spat into his palm and held it out for me to shake.

I'd like to say I avoided the handshake, but I didn't. How could I? It was an Ophanim angel, for God's sake! I'd never reached out and touched one before. My palm returned wet, sparkling, and luminous.

A few moments passed before I conceded, went to the castle, found the prop department straightaway, and approached the attendant.

"I need a…" I stopped and realized I didn't know what I needed. I'd forgotten to ask. "I'm not sure what I need," I admitted. "The Ophanim angels instructed me to come here."

The attendant pulled out a book and leafed through it, asking, "Where are you headed?"

"I…I don't know. I am on a research quest called a 'triple-stacked' something."

"Let me make a call."

With that, he grabbed a vintage candlestick phone from under the counter, the kind with a mouthpiece separated from the earpiece. Regardless of design, I half-expected it to be plugged into the wall.

"Hello, I have a warrior standing here who has come to pick up 'something' for the next 'something' adventure. It is a triple-stacked 'something.' Yes, that's right."

He surveyed me up and down while listening to the reply.

"Oh?" he said with a snicker. "Do you really want to do that?"

Upon hearing this, I prepared myself to be pranked yet again.

"Not this time?" he responded as he listened to the next bit of conversation. "Great, I will prepare them."

He hung up the phone and ducked behind the counter.

He was gone for long enough that I asked, "What do I do now?"

"Go to the Supreme Being," a voice echoed. It sounded like it was coming from the main hall where the rainbow masters stood around the Solar Logos' table. I thought I recognized the voice as belonging to the eccentric god head I'd encountered in Ireland.

"Why would the god head be involved in this journey?"

"The real life of the party!" the Ophanim Angels proclaimed.

This new quest was unnerving. I surrounded myself with roses and suns of confidence to combat my anxiety.

"Here you go," said the attendant, reappearing to hand me a white robe and staff. "Put these on your third-position self and you'll be set."

"Thank you," I responded automatically, turning around to rejoin the Ophanim angels at the rotunda. Struck by a realization, I stopped dead in my tracks, saying, "Wait a minute. What do you mean by 'third-position self?'"

It was too late. As soon as I turned around, I was back on the rotunda. The attendant, along with the castle, was gone.

"Well, back again we see. Couldn't resist our company?" An Ophanim angel smiled enthusiastically. "Nice threads."

He moved to brush a thread from my robe, but it didn't come off. He gave it a quick tug. When he did, the rotunda began to move. It traveled toward the canyon west of downtown, riding the river for a few miles, then made a beeline toward a snow-covered mountain.

I didn't get out right away but sat for a minute and settled into the diamond of the rotunda. Breathing deeply into my inner star, I reiterated being at number one position on Albion's belly *and* at number two position inside the thunderbird nest.

I came back out when I felt that deep focus, the emptiness I relied on for clarity.

"Five suns couldn't hurt," I heard an Ophanim angel say.

Another followed up with, "Four calling birds, three turtle doves and a partridge in a—"

"Shush! He has very important work to do," another angel announced before cartwheeling down the steps, chanting, "Triangles three, how could it be?"

The Ophanim angel stopped, a halo appearing above his head as he looked up with a pious expression, and said, "Well, close enough."

I stepped off the rotunda, wondering if I should laugh, genuflect, or ask, "Close enough to what?"

Too late. I was already at the bottom of an ivory white, curved staircase. The abnormally steep stairs led to a similarly white temple perched on top of a mountain.

At each bend in the staircase was a small landing and a roost. A magpie sat on the perch of the first landing and said, "Give it up. You are wasting your time."

I ignored him and kept climbing.

On the perch at the next landing, a crow said, "No such thing as a simurgh here. You might as well turn around."

There is that word again, simurgh. I remember an allegorical Persian poem about birds following a hoopoe (a Sufi sheikh) up a mountain to find a simurgh. The hoopoe, being very wise, answered many questions, but most of the birds (pupils of the hoopoe) gave up the journey. Few made it to the simurgh.

Thirty times, thirty landings, different birds appeared and attempted to dissuade me.

Tired and discouraged by bird twenty-two, I was ready to quit. My disappointment was dulling my hope, my heart, and apparently my robe. An Ophanim angel rinsed my no-longer-white robe with a bucket of liquid light until it and I were clean, sparkling, and refreshed. I reached the white temple in no time from there, sprint climbing the final steps.

I turned around and surveyed the landscape. The rotunda was miniaturized beyond the scope I expected from the distance I traveled up the stairs. The Rocky Mountain range was peppered with temples, castles, and shrines covered with flags. A number of varied star domes sat above clusters of mountains.

Facing the temple again, I examined the ornate door. It had scenes of magical creatures from mythological history. I recognized several. The others were variations on a theme. Most were winged creatures, but the elephant Ganesh stood out prominently.

I raised my staff to show my gravitas, confident it would open. Nothing happened. I expanded my staff, entered it, then sunk into the half-moon shaped step in front of the door. Only then did I go empty – rising to the top of the staff, immersing into its flaming crown.

I waited for a few minutes before reassessing my situation. Something was happening, but not to the door. Wings appeared on either side of my staff like a caduceus with a giant star on top. Thirty twinkling stars were distributed on the feathers of each wing, with two prominent stars rotating around an unseen center. Were the wings moving the stars, or the stars stirring the wing? In either case, the resultant flapping initiated a gentle breeze that wafted toward the doors. They slowly opened, accompanied by a creaky sound effect. Exiting the staff, I entered a large hall as big as most full-size temples and domes. For example, the Cygnus constellation dome over Boulder was substantial, covering most of the valley. This was slightly bigger.

I made my way to the far end of the hall. A blazing image of a simurgh was on the wall. A picture of a fake video fireplace appeared in my mind. Embarrassed, I looked around the room for confirmation. Maybe it wasn't so silly after all.

The image wasn't originating at the wall.

"Where is this being projected from?" I asked out loud.

"Good question," I heard any number of angels sing out.

A crew of Ophanim angels appeared with sound equipment and a camera on tracks from a first-rate movie studio.

The camera was moving, zooming in on the simurgh image as a director angel called out, "Action."

"Okay. Move closer to our glorious image. That's it. Zoom in on our flames. Linger on the individual colors as they dance on our feathers. Capture our magnificent head. Turn left. Beautiful. That's it. Now you have it. Alright, turn the other way. Wonderful. Give me a sassy beak... Fantastic! Now, show me your tail feathers. Spread them wide. Can you make them quiver a bit? Wow, you've captured our essential nature!" The director looked pleased. "Cut, print, that's a wrap."

On the back of his chair, fiery letters read: "OAD (Ophanim Angel Director). Producer. Lead actor. Supporting cast. Cameraman. Sound editor. Music director. Location Master."

"What do you think?" he asked as he turned and looked at me.

"Ah...oh...mmm...great," I responded, not really knowing what to make of their antics.

"Did we meet your expectations?" he asked.

"Um...sure. Yes. Good job," I said, unsure what he wanted to hear. I was at the simurgh temple to discover something about the relationship between geo-mythic sites, to add to my research repertoire, and create a profile of the landscape locations when combined. And here were the Ophanim angels, sidetracking me in the middle of this mystical setting. What was I missing?

I reiterated my previous locations: reviewed Albion's belly in my gold robe and staff and the thunderbird nest in my silver outfit. Both were still active. Stumped as to my next move, I fluffed up my white robe, stepped into my staff, and sunk it into the floor all the way to the flaming crown again.

I dove into the void.

While in a deep empty state, a tiny star appeared. Normally,

I would have let the image pass and dived deeper, but this star was persistent.

"We bring you love from above," a choir of voices whispered from inside the little point of brilliant starlight. I hugged the words.

"Just two inches above and one, in kind. The placement, divine. Do you hear us?"

"Yes," I acknowledged. "I do hear you but why are you in my emptiness?"

"You pursue a question we have always answered," the voices responded.

I felt foolish knowing I chose to forget, knowing! I stepped out of the staff and looked at the image again, this time through my star's eyes.

The Ophanim angels' voices now boomed, reverberating off the wall.

> *This is who you really are,*
> *A tiny, pinpoint, brilliant star.*
> *For millions of years it has not been far.*
> *We are, you are, an inner star!*

The words sounded beautiful.

"I am the projector," I said, looking toward the director and crew. "My star is the—" I stopped mid-sentence. The room was empty.

Light beamed from just above my belly button to the wall as I repeated the angels' words, "Just two inches above and one, in kind. The placement, divine."

Reciprocally, the image on the wall projected a light beam back at me.

"What do I do now?"

No one answered. So, I chose the warrior's way by pulling out my sword and piercing the simurgh image on the wall. Simultaneously, I entered all three staffs and sunk into the diamond. It was easy. All the locations had merged into my inner star.

After exiting, I reoriented, took a final look around the hall, and headed for the open door. Descending the stairs, I passed by the birds, now celestial beings, all celebrating my success.

I rode the rotunda back to the thunderbird nest, momentarily stopping to send out gratitude roses to the thunderbirds. Next, I sped back to Albion's belly and anchored myself there, grounding my connection with the simurgh temple and the thunderbird nest. Finally, I came out, took off all my robes, and returned to my blue chair.

Maybe the saying, 'It's turtles all the way down' has merit. But for me, on that day, it was wings all the way up.

"What do you think?" I jested, addressing my inner star.

I received an image of a six-level opera house filled with millions of Ophanim angels applauding performers on the stage. The performers were me and every other inner star, all bowing toward the exalted audience. They threw roses on stage. Red roses.

I was pleased.

The words of the Solar Mage came to mind.

"A little vanity is a good thing but be warned: choose love and light. Be like the sun. Then, you cannot fail!"

CHAPTER NINETEEN

THE FRANCIS AND THE SWORD

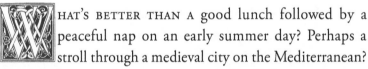

HAT'S BETTER THAN A good lunch followed by a peaceful nap on an early summer day? Perhaps a stroll through a medieval city on the Mediterranean? On this day, I just happened to get both. Well, sort of.

Ever since the Michael promised to guide me to my sword, I'd been grappling with the concept of whether it was real or metaphorical. Many theories came to mind, but few stayed. His image and words continued to challenge my desire for certainty. If I tried to ignore them, they stormed their way in. When they did, everything else collapsed like a house of cards.

I plopped down on my bed, ran through my quiet-time sequence, ventured into the rotunda and reclined on the diamond. Dozing and landscape adventuring could be problematic. Remembering the relevant activity while awake was difficult enough, add an elaborate meal working its way through the digestive tract was an additional challenge. But my internal organs were so happy today, commending me on the pasta, meatballs, and salad I'd feasted upon for lunch (not to mention the delicious tiramisu that followed). This didn't bode well for acquiring credible results.

Shifting from the diamond to a wooded path on a hillside above the city was an abrupt transition. This felt like a legitimate landscape journey, so I set up a blue dish and invited Bobby, the clan, and Sirius to join me. I paused to appreciate the view; it was a beautiful walled city set on a hill in a lush countryside.

"Assisi," I proclaimed.

I knew it well; my cousins cordially invited me to join them on their excursions around Italy. We inevitably ended up in Assisi.

To find myself here, now, even if it was a daydream adventure, brought back a flood of memories. I'd been impressionable, this domicile of Saint Francis had embossed its wonders upon my soul.

"Buon pomeriggio!" a voice behind me shouted excitedly.

"Buon pomeriggio," I responded automatically before fully turning around to see Maria, my longtime friend who I'd met during those years of my youth.

We hugged and joyfully kissed, cheek to cheek.

"What are you doing here?" I asked, surprised to find her on my landscape excursion.

"No, che ci fai qui?" Maria asked in return. We both burst out laughing. "Io vivo qui encora. E tu?"

"I-I-I'm just visiting," I said, unsure if I was daydreaming this whole adventure. Hoping my Italian wasn't too rusty, I repeated, "Io sono appena visitano."

"Posso camminare con voi?" Maria queried.

"It... I..." I stuttered, not quite sure how to phrase my response.

"I am better at the English than you are at the Italian," she joked, and I smiled in relief.

"English it is," I said as she gently slid her arm around mine like we did when we were children.

It was a two-mile hike on a gentle, sloping path up to the hermitage. We walked in silence, giggling occasionally in response to each other's playful, sometimes, silly thoughts. How easily we could still read each other's minds. The moment came when we gazed into each other's eyes with an all-consuming love (a Sufi practice we both enjoyed) and shifted into a deeper presence, deep enough to include the sacred surroundings. I dispensed a blessing of roses to the trees and stones upon the hill.

The closer we moved toward the hermitage, the quieter the youthful memories of skipping along the path became. Each step lessened my trepidations; a powerful force that began high above the hilltop sanctuary flushed away my internal debris with a large firehose that sprayed golden light.

Shifting my vision, I soared off the spongy surface of the blue dish, absorbing incoming starlight, and leaped onto the roof of the rotunda. From there, I could see two Ophanim angels standing on the backend of a huge, red-and-white-laddered vehicle. I couldn't see the front end, which was tilted skyward. Behind the angels, a ladder extended into the sky, ending at the foot of two large, golden thrones. Various winged beings passed each other on their respective ways up and down the ladder.

Looking closer, I realized there were multiple ladders. At each juncture stood a platform manned by two angels holding clipboards. They were tracking, tallying, and registering the comings and goings of all the beings. As I looked further up, I could see many ladders and pairs of angels stretching all the

way up to the thrones. It looked like a series of diving platforms at a swimming pool.

At the edge of a platform, those who made it to the
angels stopped for a moment, checked off their names on
the clipboard, prepared their best dive, then jumped into the
large pool.

I'd encountered similar pools when researching a landscape
site in New Mexico, a grand palace located on Mount Meru.
The god Indra allowed visitors to bathe and drink from these
intoxicating pools. Mystic warriors could choose to reside at
Indra's palace to live out a blissful eternity.

The Ophanim angels picked up on the images I was review-
ing. So did Maria, who stopped in her tracks, yanking me to
a halt because of our interlocked arms. We watched as two
angels theatrically prepared for a dual dive at the highest platform, next to the golden thrones. Their serious preparations
fell apart as soon as they jumped. Flailing with exaggerated
fear, they descended the vast distance, landing on the original
platform just before their falling selves vanished in the pool.
They leapt again and again, critiquing their own dive.

Maria shook my arm with a questioning look. "Che cosa
e' stato?"

"What was what?" I responded, not knowing exactly how
much Maria was seeing.

She stood there in her little-girl stance, tapping her right
foot and waiting for me to fess up.

"Oh, that. It's just a story I was daydreaming. I'm impressed
with your ability to read so much from my mind."

When I turned to continue walking, she burst out in a
contagious giggle. I joined her, not sure if she bought my
explanation, but since she let it go for now, we continued up
the path toward the hermitage.

"The impressions made by Saint Francis last forever. These imprints are not of this world, nor even on this planet. Someone like the Francis creates a body, for the gift of the Logos," a powerful voice declared.

I didn't understand. How would I find my sword in Assisi if I couldn't merge into the world of the Francis? And what does a sword have to do with the Logos?

The voice continued, "This immortal body, this vessel, holds the gift. Seek it. Accept it. Serve it."

"But, how?" I asked.

"Answer the door."

"What door?"

"Always answer the door. It may be the Logos knocking."

"I do not know where the door is."

"There *is* no there."

"What? What does that mean? By the way, who are you?" I asked, realizing I didn't know who was speaking.

"You could hear a pinpoint star fall out of the sky," interjected a familiar voice.

Thank you. At last a clue. An Ophanim angel clue at that.

Even so, I was growing tired. My focus was waning as the energy was intensifying. I wasn't sure if I could hold onto this adventure much longer.

My wariness was interrupted by the rotunda appearing in the middle of the path. Six Ophanim angels stepped out of the columns and down the steps, their outstretched arms inviting me to get on the rotunda.

"What about Maria? I can't leave her behind."

"That is not a problem," the angels on the rotunda, on the laddered truck, and on the platforms (up to the golden thrones) all responded in unison.

My energy body and Maria's split off and stepped onto

the rotunda while physically our bodies continued walking toward the hermitage.

How could this be? Her energy-body sat nonchalantly across from me while her physical body kept moving along the path without skipping a beat.

"It happens all the time," an angel explained. "People have traveling bodies. Most never notice when these bodies split off for a short-lived excursion. It is similar to sleep in that regard. In Maria's case, somewhere on her timeline, when she is ready, her High Self will share this information. No subtle body experience gets lost."

I didn't quite understand the mechanism of how subtle body events appeared in the past or even in the future, but I was reassured it was possible. My teachers all insisted I develop a relationship with my High Self to prepare for this inevitability.

"Recapitulate the occurrence in the South of France."

The mystery voice was back, and it was clear. Finally, direct instructions.

"Why can't this happen more often?"

"Availability," came the response. "Focus."

Sliding between the cracks of the present, I stepped into the past while my transcendent vision came to the forefront. There it was, on the day I was dining with the People of Light. Me, pulling a sword out of the ground in Assisi. It had been concealed until now.

From the rotunda, I watched my physical self and Maria's arrive at the peaceful sanctuary occupied by the Francis so long ago. The light radiated ubiquitously. We lingered in the sun-drenched courtyard, and I distributed gratitude roses to the visible and the unobserved. The view from this perch high above Assisi was stunning. We went inside the small chapel and into the revered grotto, leading to the Francis' chamber of meditation and private quarters.

"Find your sword." A whisper of a voice said.

I looked around, but this immediate location didn't match my discovery of the sword and drawing it out of a small mound or hillside overlooking a valley.

We walked outside, meandered a bit, then headed to where scholars determined the Francis had communed with God. Up the path was a small amphitheater with a seating area set into a hillside, a natural setting surrounded by trees and shrubs. On the opposite side was an unobstructed view of the valley. Strategically placed opposite the amphitheater was a stone pedestal.

"Find your sword," the voice said again.

The scene lit up with a halo of golden light. Inside the halo was the Francis discoursing with his followers. Wearing the rustic robes of the Order, they sat on the half circle of irregular stones of the cloistered amphitheater while the Francis stood at the standing stone.

I walked over and placed my hands on the Francis stone and connected with his light body. The energy was so unfamiliar that I had to reground myself above and below, fearing I would pass out in front of the altar. When my stability returned, my attention was guided to the upper left row of the group of listeners. With an irresistible pull, my energy body glided toward the spot where just moments ago I was fixated. Just to my right I spotted the glistening sword.

I began to oscillate between my physical body standing on the path, my energy body watching the whole scene as if projected from the rotunda, and my etheric body at the top of the seating area looking at the sword.

The angels were all standing, applauding and pointing behind me.

My three images inexplicably refracted the light, creating a hologram of the Michael surrounded by flames rising up to the golden thrones.

"Accept this gift." He said, as the tip of his sword touched the sword on the ground.

I bent over slightly and grabbed the sword by its hilt, pulling it out, and raising it triumphantly toward the sky. My body glowed in the golden light of the sword. Tears welled up in my eyes. Four Ophanim angels came to prop up my physical body standing by the altar. Another held smelling salts under my nose. Ever the jesters, a sixth pulled out a large fan and frantically waved it above my head.

Visions of past lives reflected the present: dressed as a knight, a crusader, a monk. Right back to the first time I set my sword down after my encounter with the Francis. Finding my sword was a multi-lifetime quest.

I revisited the tableau of events with the Michael in France. It was all clear now. Scenes appeared that were missing from my conscious memory.

While sitting at the table next to Boji in the dining room, I was projected out of my body a second time. Not only did the Michael bless me with his sword, placing it upon my shoulders, welcoming me into warrior-ship, but the Solar Logos also summoned me.

Unstable at my seat, I could see Boji propping me up, leaning against my shoulder. With our hands still touching, my subtle body launched toward the front of the room where the Logos stood by the Solar Mage and the Michael. A wooden cup, gold leafed around its rim, was upraised in the Logos hand. A piece of bread was held in position above the cup. He moved the host toward my mouth and placed it on my tongue saying, "Eat this for your body." It turned into a fiery powder when it touched my tongue, sizzled, and melted instantly, burning my mouth like a pinch of cayenne pepper.

Then, He moved the cup toward my mouth and said, "Drink this for your blood."

I did. It was a red, sweet liquid. As he pulled the cup from my lips, I saw a name written in flames on its rim. I was shocked. It wasn't mine, but it was someone I knew. I was swooshed back to the table.

Seeing the missing pieces of the event further overwhelmed me as I leaned on the stone altar with the angels still propping me up.

After a few moments of reintegrating my bodies, I physically climbed the steps to the top of the amphitheater. I stood silently, allowing the memories to settle, then inspected the location for any traces of the event. Other than some blades of matted grass, there were no clues. My analyzer was forever seeking proof.

"What happened to you?" Maria's voice interrupted.

I looked down at her standing near the altar. I had forgotten all about her.

"You are...glowing!"

"Do you have your camera with you?" I asked.

"Yes. I think so. Let me search my backpack. Oh, here it is."

We took two pictures. One with me sitting, the other standing and pointing to the sword's resting place.

Aboard the rotunda, the Ophanim angels – by the stairs, on the ladder, on the platforms, and swimming in the soma pools – were celebrating. There were none of the usual figurative accessories: no party hats, balloons, or outlandish outfits, just straight up applause.

The other Maria, sitting in the rotunda watching the physical plane with me, smiled. A tear rolled down her left cheek. Our energy bodies reintegrated gently as the angelic celebration continued.

Arm in arm, we re-entered the city and walked along, casually window shopping. Reflected in every window, angels smiled, rejoicing in our success.

Theo's voice passed through my mind.

"Now do you see why having a compatriot on the landscape is important?"

"Are you always going to be watching me?" I asked playfully.

"Not always. Eventually, you will be on your own. The only voice you will hear is your High Self. But that's a long way off."

I was secretly grateful; I wasn't quite ready to push *myself*.

"You think you're being pushed?" Theo responded. "Until now, I have gently nudged you. When the pushing begins, you will know it! Give yourself ten suns of courage and ten suns of confidence."

The left side of my face was hot. The sun was streaming in through the open window. I could smell the hot pasta sauce on the stove. It was my all-day sauce, still simmering. I sat up and reached over to the side table, feeling around for my glasses. The room was brilliant. The soft, spring-green color of the walls made me smile. I was rested, alert, and satisfied. I thought I heard a knock at the front door. I jumped up quickly and raced down the stairs before I recognized what I was responding to.

"Always answer the door. It may be the Logos knocking."

CHAPTER TWENTY

THE LADY'S LAKE

MY COFFEE WAS BITTER. Some mornings it turned out that way. It was my intention, should I ever meet a coffee spirit, to ask why the same beans, water, and steeping time often gave such different results. Maybe my extremely somber mood was affecting the coffee. Despite my success in finding the sword, I hadn't heard from Theo for weeks.

The day before, a friend and confidant had asked, "Have you heard from Theo?"

I'd been slow to respond.

"Well, he's either doing research, training another neophyte, or dead. Either way, he'll be in touch with me soon."

I thought I sounded acerbic, but my friend didn't laugh. Had 'or dead' been inappropriate?

My research destination was another lake deep in the national forest. Whenever I prepared for a more challenging mountain journey, my routine changed slightly. I set my hiking pole by the door, loaded my backpack with snacks, filled an extra bottle of water, and unhooked the bear bell from my down jacket. I shouldn't need the jacket; the weather was mild but hiking alone in the mountains warranted the bell. I laughed at myself for bringing the bell since I always put it away after ten minutes.

The drive through the canyon into the Arapaho-Roosevelt National Forest made me sleepy. The caffeine didn't quite kick in. To wake myself up, I sang loudly on the road through the canyon. I imagined my vocalization had the added benefit of helping to prepare the energetic field for the day, but I had no proof of this. The gnomes seemed to like it; the clan piled into the back seat while Bobby rode shotgun. One Ophanim Angel hitched a ride on the front of the car, imitating a sizable hood ornament.

When I reached the crest of the final switchback, my driving thoughts were suspended by the view of the snow-capped mountains that dominated the backdrop above Brainard Lake.

"Please show me the most direct route," I asked Bobby courteously, wanting to be respectful and not take the gnomes for granted.

"We have options," Bobby began. "You could park at the west end alongside the shores of Brainard. The gang would enjoy skipping a few stones." After checking to see my reaction, he continued. "Or, you could drive farther in and find an open space near the trailhead alongside the Lady's Lake." He paused before continuing. "And up to the Lake of Mother Isabelle."

"Let's park by Brainard, hike toward the backside of the Lady's Lake, and cross the bridge to the north side. Either way, we have a perfectly easy hike in the mountains today."

As always, my decision was fine with Bobby. His ever-present smile and the mischievous twinkle in his eye were as reliable and as constant as the northern star.

After I parked the car, I closed my eyes and sent out a welcome to the nature spirits. I asked their permission to walk into the forest and announce my destination. It was a matter of respect for the inhabitants of the land and, as Theo maintained, "Good psychic manners."

Not directing my request to any particular spirits, I broadcast a general proclamation into the subtle realm, asking for safe passage, which usually did the trick. I was overjoyed when Sirius appeared.

"Well, I did think some serious thoughts about my research today," I said to him.

It was something of a joke, but true; Sirius did show up when I was melancholy. Today, he led the way in his classic guise as a large, happy, white dog. I tried to imagine what he looked like as a star being, but the protective dog image forced its way back to the forefront. Why wasn't I ready to see him in his true form?

But I was not disappointed. Whenever a malevolent energy approached, Sirius turned into the most ferocious beast. Most of the time, such forces went unseen, save for the hair on my arms standing at attention. Now, Sirius was puppy-like and anyone might have mistaken me for a proud pet owner. Strangely, I felt *I* was the pet. A pet *project*, no doubt.

As we approached the finger-shaped body of water, I activated a second view from above the lake. When I stopped on the path, my blue bubble took shape, originating at the star point between my belly button and my solar plexus. I floated on the dark waters of the lower half of the sphere and swam my way across its surface, observing the upper half before it flattened out and settled down onto the landscape. As a blue dish, it caressed the lake.

It reminded me of a little blue plastic saucer I once used

to give water to a stray. I'd filled it up repeatedly until the dog was finished and received barely a lick of gratitude before it scampered off, smirking the same familiar grin I still receive from Sirius to this day.

On cue, Sirius jumped onto the blue dish, licking wildly at the lake. Was he making fun of me, or did he receive instructions from the Ophanim angels to let me know they were ready to appear?

I moved along the trail, traipsing through standing water and piles of mostly melted snow. The rotunda made its entrance, reposing upon the dish, flushing a fountain of lilac water that jetted silver and gold ribbons of energy spiraling down from the stars. Gemstone-shaped food created by the lilac water fell onto a net, which caught and distributed the nourishment to the surroundings.

The Ophanim angels proclaimed, "Just like our qi bath. A personal Tao-bender favorite."

"Bending things to fit your elevated interpretation of energy?" Sirius said with a chuff, and the angels laughed at the star being's jibe. A few years ago, I couldn't imagine listening to angels and star beings verbally jousting.

Not distracted by their exchange, I focused on a flash of light projecting out of the corner of my left eye.

A disturbance below the surface of the water ignited a beam of emerald light that projected high above the forest. A beacon? An invitation? I wasn't ready to travel out into the cosmos today to find out, but I stopped for a moment to jot it down in my notebook.

"Next time, follow the beacon from the Lady's Lake."

I believed the display was over, so I put my notebook away, but the beacon slowly rotated like a lighthouse lamp.

"No," I insisted. "Not today. I'm going up the mountain."

But it was too late. Something was determined to reveal itself. I had no choice but to stay with the vision.

A metallic sword broke the surface of the lake, followed by a hand.

"What purpose do you serve?" I asked.

"I penetrate wisdom, as all sacred swords do," a voice echoed.

"So, the myth is true," I said.

Between the forefinger and thumb of the hand, which was strong but delicate, were fibers of woven light extending down the arm and connecting to a gown of shimmering, pastel light. Overall, the hand and arm radiated a soft, emerald-green glow.

Deep in the water, slowly emerging into sight, was a temple. In it, the Lady stood upon a flaming pedestal extending into the core of the Earth and continuing out the other side into the cosmos. Up above, it penetrated deep space, touching the center of the galaxy.

"The sword is an invitation. Enter the column of light, draw your newfound sword, and contact this mythic symbol," a submerged voice commanded.

"Is this the Sacred Sword the ancients speak of?" I asked.

"The magic says the implement will conform to the needs of the seeker."

I quickly entered my staff after sinking it into the lake; I hoped to linger in the quiet space for the shortest amount of time necessary to reach emptiness.

"There is a growing, ever-changing perspective to be attained in the mystic life. Only when you empty your cup, draw your sword, and connect with the angels on the land – in the cosmos and inside your deepest self – are you capable of adjusting to the mysteries that support the foundation of life."

Her words? I wasn't sure. They drifted upon ripples that broke over the depths of my subtle reality. I took advantage of this insistent journey, peering under the lake to see an ocean stretching across the inner landscape of the Earth. Her temple perched upon a mountain, and on the mountain stood an unassuming human-sized stone. A holographic sword encased the stone. I was romanticizing the myth anew, as all warriors do.

Was this mountain her resting place? Where she returned after calling ready knights?

My mind strove to construct more mythic images, and my desire was fulfilled: mystic warriors visiting the stone/sword to reclaim the territory and reign over the land, swords hurling through space and sinking into the cosmic ocean, the rebirthing of new generations of warriors. Scenes repeated, replaced, and renewed before my eyes.

A voice interrupted the visions.

"Swords rotate like chariot wheels, weaving reality anew on the tapestry of futures and the pasts."

An image of flaming sword/wheels on a chariot carrying ancestral beings flew up to me and stopped. It was empty. I climbed in and rode it to the front door of the mystic castle.

Once inside, I was ushered to a human-sized chalice and submerged in the peerless red solvent of the Logos. My persona was drowning, and there was no escape.

I had performed this act willingly on many occasions, but this was the first time a landscape feature triggered the mysterious Logos meditation practice.

"Will I survive this immersion into liquid love?"

There was no answer to a question that never passed beyond my lips.

Submerged in the scarlet liquid, my desperate thinking stopped for how long I do not know.

When I returned from transcendent time I was back on the shore.

"Welcome to the new life," came a response.

The Lady reversed course, sinking into the depths, the tip of her sword catching the last beam of light before it disappeared. When the sword came to rest, she placed it into the human stone, there to await another warrior's arrival.

I reviewed my notes later that evening. More questions than answers surfaced.

CHAPTER TWENTY-ONE

SKY DANCER PALACE

"THERE'S NOTHING ELSE ON the Trail of Sages to investigate," I reported, in response to Theo's insistence (for the past few weeks) that I needed to discover another important feature before I would have sufficient confidence to find my next advisor.

I didn't like the sound of that. Another advisor. What for? Just what I needed, another voice helping me to *choose* my path. Okay, so I was waffling a bit since my Michael experience, finding the sword, and crossing tips with Excalibur, not to mention gaining deeper insight into the Logos meditation. You would think I'd be overjoyed. How could I be? Revisiting the Trail of Sages day after day to find an invisible structure on an un-seeable landscape was frustrating.

"I will have to accompany you if you do not discover the feature soon," Theo threatened.

"I found the giant, helped harvest the golden egg, talked to the Fire Dragon, freed the Water Dragon, found the Solar Mage, and encountered the Michael," I protested. "Isn't that enough?"

"There is a gift out there waiting. Some very powerful beings have taken an interest in you, but your vision is being hampered by your unworthiness," Theo insisted.

"Oh, stop riding that dead horse," I muttered.

An image of me dressed in cowboy attire, digging my heels into a mummified horse invaded my mind.

"Stop it!" I said out loud, annoyed by the image.

Theo looked at me quizzically then laughed.

"How easily your words turn into pictures. A commendable ability, but better saved for researching the feature on the landscape that is waiting for you.

"Do not return until you overcome this obstacle. You deserve to 'see.' Playing unworthy is the difference between the one bended knee of humility or the two knees of submission. Think of it this way: when the second knee hits the ground, you become invisible to the Supreme Being and the Angelic Kingdoms. The first knee demonstrates your wish to be a respectful and willing partner. The second implies your inability to take responsibility for helping to recreate the world.

"Too many lifetimes a slave, a servant, or a disappointed crusader has positioned your energetic body in an unnatural humility," Theo explained. "Unnatural in the sense that it is false, phony, and most of the time, quite self-serving. It is a survival mechanism imposed upon you by authority. A strategy you chose to gain an edge. Let's look at what is motivating this type of behavior."

Achilles ran a series of movies on my viewing screen, showing at least fifteen past lives where I'd learned to be subservient to false power brokers: priests, kings, dictators, discarnate spirits, gurus, and teachers.

"These life-sucking thugs," Theo energetically spat, "are

present in your auric layers, your chakras, and your Light body. Still living in your energetic environment."

"What can I do about it?" I asked.

"That is the problem; you can't do anything about it right now. You are in the same boat as everyone else who hasn't been trained in the art of removal. You need help."

"Can't you help me?" I asked.

"No, it has to be someone else, but only after you acquire more tools."

I felt like a deflating balloon.

"However, you're in luck," he said as he walked over to the bookshelf across the room from his desk. Theo un-perched his glasses from his nose, tilted his head to the left, and cocked his chin as he pulled a book from the shelf.

"Read this for now. You won't be able to accomplish anything in it. But I want you to understand the process before we go through it together."

He handed me the book, then sat back down at his desk.

"Now, go. The sooner you read it, the sooner you can get started."

The bike ride home took longer than expected. Despite Theo's assurances, I was in a miserable psychic space. I sat in my chair, closed my eyes, and focused on my inner star – immediately falling into it. The star grew, encompassed all my bodies, and went supernova. My internal stress gently released as I entered the Logos meditation.

It didn't take long for my energetic tools to do their job. I fully recuperated from my morning despondency with an irresistible compulsion that propelled me to the well-established blue dish at the Trail of Sages. I walked around its edge. Flames ignited the rim as I moved, creating a protective wall of fire. After completing one full circle, I projected my awareness up to the mesa, adjusted my vision, and observed the scene in the center of the valley: cows and horses grazing, a white crane standing in the shallows of the lake, two dogs playing at the water's edge, an eagle circling on the warm air currents, prairie dogs scurrying in and out of their burrows, mountains peeking over the foothills in the distance. As nature's handiwork, the scene was idyllic.

I looked through my psychic window to see that something had changed in the valley. A palace as large as a city appeared right next to the small white-lotus temple embellishing the physical landscape. Was the palace inside the temple or was the lotus inside the palace? I couldn't tell. The overlapping images maintained their visual equilibrium.

I rode the rotunda to the gates of this new iridescent palace.

"This is Sky Dancer Palace," my wisdom guides declared. "It is of Tibetan origin. Remember to surround yourself with the basic goodness of the Buddha. There is no better calling card for such a place as this."

I conjured up a halo of basic goodness and entered the vast complex. Mosaic tiles on the floor rippled with light illuminating a path to guide my steps. The lit tiles stopped in front of a large doorway. I walked through and ambled down a wide corridor with open doors on either side. I shyly glanced in each one as I passed; all were occupied by Dakinis, sky dancers.

The dancers were draped in delicate silk fabric. Pastel light radiated through the fibers of their clothes, filling the rooms with shifting light that splashed upon the furnishings and reflected back on the dancers. The way the light frolicked was a seductive invitation to intermingle with them. When I approached a doorway with three sky dancers, they invited me in.

I checked with my wisdom guides to see if I should accept

the invitation. They gave me a resounding, "Yes." Adding, "Enter with humility, to allay their cautious nature."

"Our gifts have been waiting for you." The sky dancers said, gesturing to a cupboard with an image of a mandala painted on the outside.

It was alive with flaming, rotating colors, a 3D view of a magical world. I fortified my grounding cords to resist diving into it.

One sky dancer opened the cupboard and reached in, her hand disappearing as it passed through an invisible barrier. She pulled out three crystals: ruby, topaz, and emerald.

The next sky dancer thrust her hand into the cupboard and pulled out a sapphire, a diamond, and an amethyst.

The third pulled out an agate, opal, and onyx.

"Are you ready to accept our gifts?" they asked in unison, their voices echoing off the walls and floors.

"I…yes," I answered, suspicious of these easy gifts.

The sky dancers encircled me. I felt like an actor being prepared for a role in a movie, surrounded by makeup, wardrobe, and hair artists. Or was it more like getting prepped for surgery, with nurses and doctors reassuring me I would survive the operation?

Along with a haunting rhythm wafting in the distance and voices chanting in atonal dissonance, it was oddly seductive.

All three reached out and inserted the different crystals into my body: feet, hands, solar center, heart, throat, and the center of my head. Once in place, they lit up, and I felt infused with a striking energetic vibration.

"The gift is easy, the knowledge difficult," they said. "Meditate on these, and in time they will reveal their secrets."

The entire palace began to vibrate. Waves of energy circulated through me as the crystals connected with each other using a network of conduits in my body, similar to the qi meridians used by my acupuncturist. These energized channels enlivened the star in my belly.

The inner star went supernova, encompassing my auric field, bubbling out to embrace the blue dish under me. Once this dish was encompassed, an arc of rainbow light bridged to another blue dish, then the next, and continued linking each dish under the landscape features I have visited.

I rose above the valley, the dome, and the arcs of light. Spirit beings also looked upon the spectacle as the whole map ignited. Seeing the panoramic view from this height revealed gaps in the network where dormant features weren't lit up. These were locations I needed to explore.

"This is exciting." I said, watching my words breathe out as watercolor waves dripping upward in the sky.

I descended back into the palace, thanked the sky dancers, hopped on the rotunda chariot, and returned. When I looked out toward the palace from my room, the sky dancers gave me a regal wave. That was suspiciously Ophanim-like. Did the angels have a hand in this?

"Of course, they did," Theo said the next day, unsurprised by my adventure. "They set up the whole thing. Those sky dancers have been trying to get your attention for a long time. Without the angels' help, you would still be in denial. Today, you discovered that unlimited gifts abound on the land. The visionary geography is a magical realm. Embrace it with love, and in return it will fill you with wonderment, treasures, and wisdom."

CHAPTER TWENTY-TWO

A SPIRIT GUIDE

"YOU MUST FIND A spirit guide," instructed Theo. "Someone who knows the local landscape: its history, its mythology. Preferably someone indigenous who will help you communicate with nature spirits; someone who will be reliable and knowledgeable when your questing goes awry."

I wasn't surprised by Theo's instructions. After the Michael experience, more visions floated to the surface of my awareness. In one, he told me I'd be ready to meet my guide once I'd encountered the Lady and obtained the dancers' gems. I couldn't deny it, I felt like a different person – my questing on the geo-mythic landscape continued to reshape my perception – but where do I start searching for a guide?

My knowledge of Front Range culture was growing. I recently read about the life of Chief Niwot of the southern Arapaho tribe. He kept the peace when the settlers arrived in the valley, determined to avoid conflict at all costs. The incomplete stories suggest he was a tall, beautiful, elegant man who spoke several languages, negotiated peace treaties, and traveled to Washington DC. He was left-handed, just like me.

Theo had one last piece of advice before I went on my way.

"When questing takes an odd turn, look for activity on the landscape to turn you in the right direction. Sometimes, your immediate surroundings are the only clue you can rely on."

I searched the plains, the mountains, the rivers. I asked every being I encountered to direct me, but all I received were cryptic answers, empty of any solid leads.

One little tree spirit even pointed behind me and said, "There he is."

I looked behind me, found nothing, turned back, and he was gone. That interaction pretty much summarized my progress.

After months of searching, I gave up pursuing the assignment and put it on the back burner. I had other matters to attend to: my job, my landscape research, and my martial arts training were difficult enough, but my friend Miss Montgomery had been taken ill, and I was spending more time than ever visiting with her.

Theo asked about my headway at the end of our weekly education sessions at his house.

Just as I was leaving, he would say, "It is imperative that you find your guide."

"I don't know how!" I eventually insisted.

"Some assignments have very little in the way of instruction," Theo replied. "Some have no instruction at all. The importance of the lesson is not in the results, but in the mental and emotional processes that take place during the activity. Keep searching with expectant hopelessness."

"You mean hopefulness, don't you?"

"Yes, yes; that's it. I want you to be eternally hopeful that someday, through some serendipitous accident, you will find what you are looking for. Please forget about intelligent or disciplined research," he replied sarcastically.

"There is only one thing to wish upon. A star. And it had better be the one in your belly," he said as he pointed toward my abdomen. "My teacher said many times, 'Go contemplate your navel. See where that gets you.' The funny thing is, I did focus on my navel. Nothing happened. Nothing changed. It took me two years to discover I was off target by two inches."

I automatically checked the status of the star above my navel. Silencing my analyzer, I refocused and connected with my wisdom guides. I breathed love from above and was instantly reassured by its twinkle.

When I left that day, I walked in the opposite direction of home.

Lost in thought, eyes to ground watching for rattlers on the warmed midday trail, I was surprised to be so close to Haystack Mountain when I stopped to scan the horizon. It was unusually tall. A curious notion came to me: that I could hike to the top. It would be difficult – even dangerous, if the Land Witch was on patrol – but maybe I could use the secret passage inside the mountain utilized by the gnomes.

I remembered Theo's warning about the Land Witch.

"The Land Witch's senses make her like a spider on a web. Her awareness covers the south side of the mountain, and the slightest disturbance sends a vibration along her energy threads. They have a non-symmetrical layout, but there are gaps in her field. If you find the safe zones, you can travel from one side of the mountain to the other undetected."

After a moment of indecisiveness, I called out Bobby's name. He appeared instantaneously.

I gave him a hello rose while formulating my request.

"Show me the most direct route to the top of the mountain that will allow me to avoid being detected by the Land Witch. We need to be stealthy, so we'll probably have to leave the clan behind."

"They're not going to be happy being left out of this adventure. They do so love the mountain. To make up for their exclusion, would you run some lilac energy through the rotunda? That would please them greatly."

Ever since Theo taught me the 'running lilac' technique, the nature spirits around town were healthier, active, and less invisible. But my memory of executing the technique became fuzzy to the point of doubting my proficiency. Wanting to get it right for Bobby, I had Achilles run the footage of Theo's initial lesson.

"We need to feed the nature spirits," Theo explained. "The more we do, the more invigorated they become. This helps Mother Nature rebalance the ecological system. For example, rivers are dying because the sovereigns, living at the source of these rivers, are starving."

"But why sit in an old, dried-up riverbed to do it?" I asked.

"Contrary to what you have concluded, this is not a dried-up riverbed. This is an arroyo. Arroyos are powerful lines of force. In a sense, all streams and rivers are places of power and conduits for traveling. Many of the techniques you need to master can be practiced here. The landscape features you encounter are more accessible from an arroyo. Today, we will feed the River King."

He paused as if waiting for a question, but I didn't have any.

"You were supposed to formally ask, 'Why feed the River King from an arroyo when this is not a riverbed?'"

"Why feed the River King from an arroyo when this is not

a riverbed?" I repeated. "What is the connection? The purpose? Why is this important? How does this help my training?" I added, trying to cover as many points as possible. It was a novice thing to do but, when in doubt, ask more questions.

"Good questions," Theo responded encouragingly. "The experiment will teach us several things. One is that the techniques you are learning are valid; valuable enough to encourage you to continue to train. We will also realize the benefits to the planet. These are the direct effects that are affected by your efforts to affect the landscape, effectively."

My brain dizzied from Theo's repetitive 'effecting.'

He laughed and said, "Good. Now you are almost ready. Use some roses and give yourself suns of seniority, validation and certainty. And re-establish your grounding cords."

I took the appropriate amount of time to follow his instructions.

"Better?" he asked.

I was, and with a new sense of clarity. A sharp, crystal-clear focus encircled me.

"Yes!" I exclaimed. "Very much so."

"Now, to find, befriend, and feed the local spirits, we must learn the running lilac technique. This will help establish street cred with nature spirits. In this case, it is more like arroyo credibility."

Theo burst out laughing as if he had told the funniest joke ever. His laughter, instead of easing my familiar discomfort, put me on high alert.

"Actually, it is credibility on a vast highway network. One that will present you with a great deal of potential. We will establish a blue dish from here to the local river network and continue to the source, traveling down the major artery to the mouth of the river, which dumps out into the ocean."

"That sounds like a mighty big dish."

"It is," Theo responded. "Now, step into the rotunda, say hello to the angels, then step onto the diamond."

I followed his directions to the letter.

"Good," Theo continued, "visualize a fountain of lilac streaming up from below, splashing against the top of the rotunda, and running down its sides."

I did.

"Now, appearing in the liquid lilac, watch as jewels and nuggets fall from the top of the rotunda. Notice how they are caught in a net stretched out below the diamond. Spin the net. That will distribute the energetic food onto the landscape."

I could see it happening as Theo explained the process.

"Quite a sight," I said. "As the food shoots up into the air and out onto the surroundings, most lands on the surface while some sinks deep into the ground. When that happens, nature and her invisible beings become invigorated. They become brighter, lighting up with life energy."

As I watched the nature spirits catch the food, I understood how emaciated they were.

"Oh, I see why you said they're starving!" I exclaimed.

"Very good," Theo said. "Not good that they are starving, but that you can see it so clearly. In fact, nature is slowly dying. Unless we intentionally feed nature spirits, more will perish. Many spirits have moved off-world or disappeared completely. Inevitably, most of the Earth will withdraw into the invisible background until equilibrium is re-established. Only then will the population begin to grow again. The recycling of life – spirit, nature, human – all are connected, all have the same fate."

His words trailed off into a deep silence. For a long time, this silence reigned. I felt the Logos meditation process begin and carry me through the steps, right into the axle running through the octahedron that drives the whole mystic warrior practice. The emptiness was complete.

Not until I heard Theo's voice from a distance did I begin reversing the process and remember where I was physically.

"We will move up the arroyo, hop over to a local stream, then travel up the main river to its source and introduce ourselves to the River King."

Theo was right. Traveling in an arroyo was easy, fast, and convenient. I felt like I was riding a bobsled. The sandy, winding throughways were slick and the rotunda accentuated this with the added sensation of hovering over the ground, especially along the deeper ravines.

I felt our momentum pick up. We were speeding straight toward a high, concave wall at a bend in the arroyo. As our speed continued to accelerate, my concern grew.

"I think we're going to crash!" I shouted, loud enough to startle Theo and cause his rickety old blue chair to creek from his sudden weight shift.

"Wait for it," he said.

I couldn't, and I willed the rotunda to slow down with all my might. Instead, it accelerated.

"Wait for it," Theo repeated.

"Wait for what? For us to crash headlong into that wall of compacted sand?"

I closed my eyes just before the inevitable collision. But we didn't crash. We zoomed along the curve wall and bolted into the air. When I opened my eyes, we were already descending toward a large river at a higher elevation than the arroyo. Our speed carried us over it, surfing on the air. The river grew smaller as we followed its meandering path. Eventually, we reached a deep mountain canyon.

The higher we went, the smaller the river became. It was exciting to travel over rapids and fifty-foot-high waterfalls. High above the tree line and the melting snow, the rotunda slowed, stopping just below a mountaintop where several small runoffs joined together.

"Well, that was fun," Theo exclaimed.

I just looked at him, bewildered.

"Why are you so surprised? I may be ancient, but I'm not dead. I still enjoy a bit of fun."

"I was just taken aback," I answered.

"I would tell you it's the student who determines how much fun a teacher has, but that would cause you some consternation."

He was right. It did. I was about to jump into a rabbit hole of concern when he interrupted me.

"Let's create another blue dish here about the size of the mountain."

That would make it smaller than the one under the river system. That one stretched all the way to Mexico.

"Scan the hillside to our right," he instructed. "What do you see?"

Things were a bit hazy at first, as if I was looking through a filter.

"Go inside, behind the layer of snow."

It was difficult.

"Caught in the drift?" asked Theo, chuckling. "Snow? Drift? Get it?"

What the heck was going on with him today? Fun? Jokes? During training? My analyzer began searching for a reason for his uncommon behavior.

"Analyzing yet again?" he asked. "I'll allow it this time, because it's relevant. Some environments, some elements, provide more entertainment than others. Let's take you, for instance. Have you noticed how you beam when you're around trees? You light up, and all the spirit beings around you ramp up their play and become more entertaining."

"Now that you mention it, yes, that does happen, but I didn't perceive that it was mostly around trees."

"For me, it's water. The water spirits dance and become playful. Although there are many factors involved in this dynamic, we must acknowledge the elemental symbiosis. Some spirits are soothing, some are fun and entertaining, and others are sobering. The reaction of these spirits is in response to our individual nature. It's something we can't fight or change. We need the feedback. It can benefit our research on the land. Now, penetrate the hill. Go into it. What do you see?"

I moved through the snow, rock, and earth then popped out the other side. It was clear now.

"He's well-defined. An angular figure with a tall crown of water on his head. Regally dressed. His liquid-like clothes are woven with fluidic threads."

"Very good. 'Fluidic threads.' I like that phrase."

I squirmed. Theo was having too much fun. It was unnerving.

"Send him a hello rose," Theo instructed, and I did as he asked. "How did he respond?"

"He opened his arms wide as if presenting his surroundings."

"What is he demonstrating?"

"He is showing me living droplets," I said, putting words to my vision. "As it is pulled by gravity down the mountain, each droplet condenses out of a subtle energy field into this density; into snowmelt, liquid water, ultimately merging with the ocean. I can see the evolution of water condensing into this Earth from the subtle world of pre-formed substances."

I sat with this vision for a while, watching the recycling process repeat many times. I could see it duplicating in animals; in humans. The same process also occurring in the cosmos.

"Go into the rotunda and run the lilac energy," Theo said, bringing me back. "Now, spin out the living energetic food."

I did, sending it out to the diverse nature spirits who played a role in the maintenance of the river systems.

"It is a good time to acknowledge Gaia and her nymphs." Theo said this with genuine fondness. "Feeding Gaia and her lovely attendants, going directly to the source, will go a long way in helping the planet save many lives."

We slalomed back down the mountain, flew into the arroyo (at exactly the same place we'd left it), and glided back to our chairs under the busy bridge.

I smiled at the memory of Theo's joyful behavior as I finished distributing nutrients to the clan (and any other spirits inside the mountain).

Once I'd finished running lilac, I asked Bobby, "Would you please give me an accurate lay of the land?"

He showed me a mountain view with lines of energy used by the Land Witch. The web-like structure resembled a flattened labyrinth.

"We gnomes have threaded a pathway through her web that avoids detection. Even to us, she is unpleasant," he acknowledged.

I was taken aback. I didn't think *anything* perturbed gnomes.

By the looks of it, getting to the top of the mountain would not only be dangerous, but traveling through the labyrinth would also take much longer than I'd expected. The maze of switchbacks would carry us down through the middle of the mountain numerous times before heading up to the top.

"Is this really the easiest way to travel?" I asked Bobby.

"Welllll…" he said, looking a bit sheepish. "There *is* another way. Sometimes, when we are summoned by the Gnome King, we attach ourselves to the ribbons of the golden pole."

"What is the golden pole?" I asked.

"We gnomes are not exactly sure what it is, but it is a convenient apparatus to help us avoid the Land Witch's unpleasantness."

"What do I have to do to use the golden pole?"

"First of all, only gnomes or gnome-like creatures can use the ribbon system, so you will have to wear a disguise. Then, if you do exactly as I tell you, there is a chance you won't fall off and crash down into the Land Witch's web." I must have had a worried look on my face, because Bobby immediately followed up with, "But, hey, it'll be fun!"

I weighed my options. I could walk for hours up and down Haystack Mountain to get to the top, or I could wear a disguise, be attached to a ribbon on a pole, and quickly get to the top.

After thinking about it for a moment, I asked, "Where would I get a gnome disguise?"

"That's easy," he said as he pulled out what looked like a cheesy Halloween costume and handed it to me.

"It's kind of small," I said.

"Oh. Well, just try it on. It stretches."

It seemed ridiculous. The costume was a third my size. I looked at it and then looked back at him. He winked and nodded with reassurance.

"Well…I'll try it," I said doubtfully.

As soon as I stuck my foot into the little gnome booty, it expanded to my size. The same thing happened with the pants, shirt, and hat. Each piece grew to the perfect size to fit me.

"If we bump into anyone, I'll introduce you as my cousin," said Bobby.

I didn't feel like I had any choice but to continue now that the gnome suit was on.

"Where's the pole?" I asked, and, "How do we attach ourselves?"

Bobby pointed toward the top of the mountain.

I looked up and saw a golden pole of light streaming down through the center of the mountain, reaching deep into the Earth. I had seen this feature before, but I'd never thought of it as a pole.

"Where are the ribbons?" I asked.

Bobby pulled out a small hammer and struck a tiny yellow crystal that had appeared in his hand from out of nowhere. I watched as golden streamers unfurled from the sides of the pole and rolled down the mountain, stopping right at our feet.

Bobby walked over to the closest ribbon and handed it to me, saying, "Tie this end to your belt, like this."

He picked up a second ribbon and demonstrated how to knot it. He untied it, then did it again.

I tied it exactly as he'd shown me.

"Now, follow me," he said as he was immediately whisked away, flying upwards and out beyond the base of the mountain.

A powerful force tugged at my waist and bungeed me off the ground. From the air, I could see Theo's house behind the Dell of Faeries. I flew over golfers on the course and horses in the pasture. Everything appeared a bit surreal, but it was exhilarating flying through the air and feeling the wind in my hair.

My speed increased as I spun around the mountain, coming closer and closer to the golden pole on each revolution. Soon

I would slam into the pole, the ground, or rocks piled near the summit.

"How do I halt this?" I yelled to Bobby. Before he could answer, I somehow decelerated and gently glided to a stop on the peak.

I untied the ribbon from my belt and removed the disguise. Why had I even needed it? I looked over at Bobby. He was different. His eyes glowed in a strange, distrait way.

"What's wrong?" he asked, not sounding like himself. He was physically distorting, struggling to maintain his shape.

I was feeling queasy, and nothing around me looked quite right. Surprisingly, I wanted to lie down on the ground to take a nap. I crouched low to stretch out on the ground, but a hand reached toward me out of nowhere, grabbed my shirt sleeve, and pulled me through an invisible barrier.

I was disoriented and couldn't focus. My eyes were blurry, covered by a filmy substance. It reminded me of having my pupils dilated at the optometrist's.

Ice cold water splashed on my face and took my breath away. I wiped my eyes. Theo was looking down at me, holding a wooden bucket with an ornately carved iron handle. I focused on the intricate design of the handle and began melting into its shape.

I felt a solid rap on my back and heard Theo shout, "Snap out of it!"

"What? What's going on? Why did you hit me?" I asked, confused.

"I told you to never go into the Dell of Faeries alone," Theo exclaimed. "What were you thinking?"

"What are you talking about? I...I didn't go into the Dell of Faeries."

"Which way did you go when leaving my house earlier today?"

"I went toward home. No, wait a minute. I was thinking about finding my spirit guide. I…" I hesitated for a moment, remembering. "I went in the opposite direction. I must have walked right into the dell without realizing."

After telling Theo every detail of the adventure, he laughed and said, "Very creative. A golden maypole to the top of the mountain. And how would your physical body do that? If a gnome was to guide you to avoid the Land Witch's detection, why not just take the tunnel system inside the mountain? Oh, wait a minute, you wouldn't be able to do that either!"

Theo was his old sarcastic self again. I knew I was no longer inside the dell.

"But it felt so real!"

"Hmm…then it's probable your instincts were correct, even if your execution was flawed. I'll draw you a map that will help you climb to the top of Haystack Mountain and avoid the Land Witch's web. Now, go home. Rest. In a couple of days, head to the mountain. He will be waiting for you."

With that, he dismissed me and I groggily shuffled home – in the right direction.

CHAPTER TWENTY-THREE

MEETING THE CHIEF

 T WAS LESS THAN a week since my nearly disastrous encounter in the Dell of Faeries, but I was recovering. Mostly by sleeping.

I sat at my desk with a fresh cup of coffee and picked up Theo's map. It was the second time I looked at it. The vague memory of a tapping sound, getting out of bed, and thanking a raven perched on the windowsill was the only clue I had of how this map made it to my desk.

I sipped my mushroom-enhanced brew and studied the map closely. The key feature on the map was a visual illustration of Theo's dissertation on time.

"Everything is about timing. Your time. My time. Earth time. Solar and cosmic time. Well, you get the picture," Theo explained. "The Key of Synchronicity allows access to Time with a big 'T,' also known as Transcendent Time."

He had mentioned Earth with a big 'E' before, but never Time with a big 'T.'

Theo waited for me to respond. I thought for a moment,

held up my left wrist, pointed to my watch and joked, "I have a time synchronizer right here."

"That instrument creates an illusion of time that everybody agrees with and relies upon, but it has little affiliation with the time I am talking about. The aspect of time we will discuss is the key to adjusting internal time. Everyone has a distinct internal timekeeper. The Key of Synchronicity allows you to make adjustments beyond your personal time."

I already redefined intervals of time when it came to sword fighting.

"Five attacks are the synchronizer," the Warrior explained during our training. "Once you adjust to equal time, you have an opportunity to defeat your opponent by shifting behind or ahead of time."

I shared this with Theo.

"In my martial arts practice, I learned how to 'break time' with a sword. Time-changing was linked to speeding up or slowing down movement – adjusting strokes – to disrupt the flow of another's time. By synchronizing time through rhythmic contact, I can equal, get behind, or get ahead of someone else's time. Not with a key, but with my sword."

"That's good. The mechanics of your sword training will be an asset in understanding the use of the Key of Synchronicity. Here, take it," Theo said.

I was surprised by his frank offer to simply give it to me. It put me on high alert.

I waited.

Nothing happened.

I waited longer.

"Did you get it?" Theo asked.

"Get what?" I replied.

"Did you get the key?"

"The Key of Synchronicity? You didn't give me anything," I insisted.

"In that, you are wrong. Let's try this a different way. Watch more closely this time, the kind of watching you practice when searching for features on the land."

"Should I go through my full setup routine and perform the Logos meditation?"

Theo nodded, and I entered a quiet space immediately. I checked my level of virtue, sent love from above to my inner star, established my blue dish, entered the mystic castle through the alternate entrance – the emerald hovering above the dish, solarized, drowned in the red sea, and elaborated the octahedron, centering in its axle and sinking deep into emptiness.

When I was ready, I opened my eyes and looked at Theo.

"You almost have it," he said. "Only one minor adjustment. Did you forget a step? Something you could add?"

I went through my list. I'd included every step from my training, ordinary time and space were successfully dilated. I stood on the blue dish and looked around. The enigmatic table sitting in the center of the rotunda must be it. I stepped back into emptiness then submerged into the diamond.

An anomalous figure appeared. I presumed it must be the Key of Synchronicity. He was less a key and more a majestic being. Unlike kings with crowns of gold and precious gems, the first thing I noticed was a clock face set with the typical three hands – hour, minute, second – and a much larger fourth hand. The augmented clock sat inside a globe perched atop his head. Around the circumference of the globe was an animated compass rose. It behaved as if an invisible breeze was blowing, fluctuating its orientation. The classic clock face moved around the 360-degree dial of the compass.

"That is a timing dial," Theo explained, the sound of his voice otherworldly. "Visualize a three-dimensional object moving around in a four-dimensional space. The Key can alter individual time by operating in Transcendent Time." His explanation about this unique timepiece was starting to make sense, until Theo said, "Remember, the key is in an alternate dimension."

I tried to understand his assertion by looking at the king *and* three-dimensional space. I could see both. The pictures weren't overlapping, just existing in the same location. Not the same space but, where were they in time?

"You don't see time; you move in and out of it. Time is based on information stored in a specific location in your brain or on the land. In research, you investigate spatially. You move into locations and access data, then perform a specific task: by acknowledging, adjusting, or augmenting it in a mutually beneficial way. And sometimes, in your case, attempt the impossible."

Was that last comment a jab about freeing the dragon? I ignored the bait and kept my focus on the key.

"Think of Time with a big 'T' in the same way – as another *place* you can investigate."

Theo stopped talking and waited.

I sent a hello rose to the king. He addressed me with a slight tilt of his head, forward and to the left. When he did, I was immediately in his Transcendent Time. Everything felt a little odd, viewing things from his perspective. It was unnerving. Shifting into his time split me between my subjective calibration of time and something quite alien.

"Better," I heard Theo say from an alternate time. It was distinctly different; I assumed it was Theo's unique time. "Now, ask the Key of Synchronicity to show you someone's time. Someone you know well. A friend, maybe. This will bring you to them, into their personal time."

I thought about it for a minute and chose Boji. We'd been

corresponding since our meeting with the People of Light. I created a picture of her and followed the feeling it invited, then I sent a hello rose to her High Self and presented a vivid representation of Boji to the Key of Synchronicity.

He looked at it as if he were reading a page from a book. He adjusted his clock and the time face rotated inside the global crown. It not only moved to an orientation of longitude and latitude; it also adjusted its depth. The precision in its movement reminded me of the gears inside the grandfather clock at the Italian villa I'd visited as a child.

Once the movement stopped, I felt a distinct shift in location from my familiar time to a regularity clearly not mine.

I walked around inside it. I was not moving in my personal time; this was Boji's time, without a doubt. The speed and duration of each movement was distinctive. I stopped for a moment and wondered if she knew I was in her energy field.

Theo picked up my thought and said, "Ask her."

"Greetings, Boji. Do you know I'm here?"

"Yes. Your presence sent a ripple through me. I could feel your fondness and appreciation, and I saw your wonderment dancing around me," Boji responded.

"I hope we will have an adventure together again soon."

"Everything is possible, in time. I may visit you under the Boulder lights," she said. Her image faded as I shifted back to the Key of Synchronicity and Theo.

I thought about this new experience with the uniqueness of time. I felt I'd discovered a flaw in this whole Key of Synchronicity plan to get to the top of Haystack Mountain without alerting the Land Witch.

"Boji knew I was in her time, so would the Land Witch know I was in her time as well? Worse yet, would she know I was climbing the mountain?"

Theo laughed and asked, "Do you plan on sending a hello rose to the Land Witch?"

"Probably not."

"Then she should not notice you. You will have the Key of Synchronicity. You will be looking through your psychic window, but you will not step into her time. Do you see the difference?"

I previewed the two scenarios side by side on my mental screen and said, "Yes."

"Any more questions?" Theo asked.

"No," I said. "Except for one thing. Who will help me identify the vibrational cycles of the Land Witch's web?"

"Your gnome will cooperate with the Key of Synchronicity. Even though gnomes can't see the king, they can feel the vibrations of time through the stones. He will give you all the information you need to make it to the top," Theo replied, sounding confident.

I wasn't so sure, but I sent a gratitude rose to the Key of Synchronicity, gave myself suns of confidence, and headed home.

The next morning, I woke up clear headed, optimistic, and ready to venture up the mountain. I was determined to meet my guide.

The plan was to enter the Land Witch's territory from the south by blending in with the golfers on the public course at the foot of the mountain. The gnomes' presence here wasn't uncommon, so Bobby and I were confident we wouldn't raise any suspicions.

I entered the dirt road, stopped momentarily on the bridge (to run some lilac for the river spirits), then crossed over to the golf course property.

When I called on Bobby for assistance, the clan appeared, too. Disinviting them was expedient so I asked Bobby to suggest they join the golfing gnomes for a little fun. They agreed readily and scurried toward the range while we calculated our approach.

With my direct request given to him, I included "avoid activating the Land Witch's web and cooperate with the Key of Synchronicity." I stepped through my setup routine and synchronized fully with the Key. I used some extra roses on my frontal lobes to clean any accrued debris then gave it suns of clarity. Seeing Bobby and the Key's clock clearly was crucial for me to succeed.

"Ready?" I asked.

Ready, ready,
Ready as rain,
Ready to move
Along the landscape.
Always, always,
In vein.

As soon as Bobby recited the gnome refrain, he took off at a lively pace. I followed as he moved toward the bridge between the fourth green and the fifth tee box (the same bridge where I first found Theo's note). We walked under it and traveled west, along the riverbank. The river crossed under a trail parallel to a manmade canal. According to my map, this trail crossed the base of the mountain, continued to the sunrise side, then meandered north onto the plains.

Bobby was leading me closer to the mountain. I checked the map and my psychic senses often. I wanted to be ready in case the Land Witch noticed our presence. So far, so good; I could see her web was intact. It was pulsing periodically on either side of the trail, but it wasn't pulsing on the trail itself. When I looked underground, the web dipped much deeper. Considering the traffic along the canal, it made sense.

"I guess the Land Witch doesn't want to answer any false alarms. She must be accustomed to activity on the trail and has learned to ignore it," I said to Bobby.

He nodded, then he continued for another twenty yards, coming to a stop by a flow valve wheel at the edge of the canal.

"This is it," he said. "This is where we can cross over to the other side of the canal and begin our trek up the mountain."

He was right. The cement bridging structure on which the flow valve stood would provide us easy access to the other side. As soon as we crossed over, I asked Bobby to stop for a moment while I adjusted my sight and invited the Key of Synchronicity to help us.

"Show me the Land Witch's timing," I requested.

I gave him a series of mental pictures to avoid any confusion: The Land Witch, the web, the mountain, Bobby, and me climbing to the top safely.

I waited until I was confident the king understood, using the moment to give myself ten suns of confidence and ten of clarity. When he showed me the clockwork timing of the Land Witch, I compared it to my own. Now I could easily distinguish between the two. All I had to do was keep them slightly out of sync and avoid the vibrations of her web.

I watched as the waves pulsed across the landscape. I told Bobby what I was looking at and asked him to feel the vibrations of the Key of Synchronicity since Theo said he couldn't actually see the king.

I watched the rhythmic timing of the Land Witch's web. Bobby was hooked into the vibrations as well. Between pulses, he began to move.

"One to thirteen," was the count.

"Stop!" I heard a shout in my mind when a discordant vibration began to rise.

Bobby and I froze in our tracks. I held my breath, not daring to move a muscle, and Bobby did the same. His imitation of a rock that looked like a gnome was superb. I wasn't certain my simulation was as good, but it didn't have to be. I just had to fool the Land Witch.

"Five, four, three, two, one," I heard. "Now, go!"

We moved swiftly. I estimated I was stepping in Bobby's every third footprint.

"Eleven, twelve, thirteen. Stop!" came the internal shout.

Again, we stiffened right before the pulse. I watched it travel out to the edges of the web, reaching two-thirds of the way up the mountain. It stopped just below a row of small shrubs that ringed the peak.

"That's the objective, then we'll be safe," I said to Bobby as I sent the picture to the Key of Synchronicity.

"Go," came the call.

We scrambled on. Bobby was determined, even though we were between pulses, not to step directly on the energy lines. I was impressed with his accuracy, his dexterity, and his complete control of movement, landing on the appropriate spot just as the command from the Key of Synchronicity sounded.

We were halfway there. The tree line was getting closer. A few times, Bobby took us sideways instead of directly toward the peak. He was avoiding small nodes along the web. Were they more sensitive to movement or just traps to catch wayward trespassers? There was something else hidden at these junctions, but what?

I tried the indigo blow torch (a recent addition to my toolkit) and found that the junctions *were* booby-trapped. Additional detectors were implanted in them; the Land Witch was crafty.

"Three, two, one, go."

We moved again, avoiding the traps. The rest of the way to the top resembled a synchronized dance. With the last countdown, I followed Bobby beyond the Land Witch's web, finally free to sojourn at the top of the mountain.

I gave gratitude roses to the Key of Synchronicity as he disappeared while Bobby led me to a large stone. I sat down, excited to meet my spirit guide.

Setting a blue dish beneath me was simple enough as I stepped through the Logos meditation protocols. Suddenly, I heard a whistle. It was my dad's whistle, exactly as I remembered it from childhood. It kicked me out of my meditation.

Memories came hard and fast, painted with lush colors projecting out onto a movie screen. I was irresistibly drawn in.

Each evening my father would whistle a special tune to call me home. It didn't matter where I was, in a neighbor's yard or exploring the forest, his whistle was my Pied Piper. His first whistle froze me in place. The second stood me erect as I said my goodbyes. A third repetition carried me to my front door, where he stood smiling, ready to pat me on the head and say, "Wash up; it is time for supper."

But this time, the whistle was coming from the direction of the rotunda. One of the Ophanim angels was standing on the steps, whistling and waving at me to join him. It wasn't like the angels to interrupt my research excursions unless I'd missed something important, so I couldn't imagine what he wanted. The mission had been successful, and I was preparing to meet my guide. Everything had gone swimmingly so far.

"You can refuse any angel's request," Theo recited from the Mystic Warrior's Handbook once, "but an Ophanim angel's suggestion is not to be taken lightly."

Hesitantly, I walked along the blue dish over to the rotunda and gave the angel a hello rose as I followed him aboard.

The angel sat down on a glass seat between the second and third column of the six-column rotunda and patted it with his hand. Still under the hypnotic spell of my dad's whistle, I obeyed.

"We need to take a ride in the rotunda today," the Ophanim angel said.

"But I'm already in the right location to find my guide!" I protested.

"Well, you may be in the right place," he responded, "but are you in the right time?"

"Oh no, not more time travel, not today. Do I have to call back the Key of Synchronicity?"

"No," he replied, "not that kind of time."

I was growing exasperated. Now, I had to make another trip. This delay was deflating my optimism.

"Will I ever discover my guide?" I pleaded, but he ignored my anemic grievance.

"The time we need to consider is local history time. Just 150 years ago," the Ophanim angel said, insisting we hurry. "The moment will not wait for us."

He motioned with his hand, buckling up an invisible seatbelt.

"Do you mean we need to use the hypercube?" I asked.

Again, he didn't answer. He just smiled a huge grin as the rotunda zipped across the valley to Fine Park.

When we arrived, the park was rather quiet. Too quiet.

"Wait a minute," I said as I stepped off the rotunda. "Where's the playground? The restrooms? The people?"

I scanned the area, turning slowly as I stood up. I couldn't hear the usual sound of cars driving through the canyon, leading into the mountains.

"Sit down. No need to get off the rotunda. We have to head back."

"What?" I exclaimed. "We just arrived. I assumed we were going to the hypercube. Now, you're telling me we have to head back?"

"We engaged the hypercube already at a slightly different angle. We actually passed through it on the way here. Now, we're in the correct time period, so we have to get back to Haystack Mountain."

Trying to understand what just happened was exhausting. I heard a whinny and turned around to locate the source. A herd of wild horses entered the park from behind a grove of trees. They were mostly pintos, a black stallion, and some roans.

"I don't remember ever seeing wild horses in Boulder," I said with surprise. "Much less in the park."

I was still speaking when we lifted off and sped back to Haystack Mountain. When we landed, I could see the plains at the foot of the mountain had changed.

The golf course was gone. The clubhouse too. I widened my gaze.

"All the houses have disappeared!"

The neighborhood surrounding the golf course was gone. In its place were dozens of teepees. Smoldering fires dotted this unfamiliar village.

A herd of horses was grazing at the west end, and a makeshift corral housed a few dozen others. Children were playing throughout the village. Groups of women were down by the river washing clothes. Warriors were instructing older children on how to shoot arrows and throw spears, knives, and hatchets. They were on the driving range, or where it should be.

"What do you think of this?" I asked, expecting Bobby to

CHIEF LEFT HAND

be sitting next to me on the boulder, but it wasn't Bobby's voice I heard in response.

"This is sacred Arapaho ground. We winter here. It has been our land for many generations. I, too, learned to hunt and ride here. For many seasons, life was plentiful. We had visitors from other tribes. I remember the peace. Until the Nihancan came. Then, everything changed."

I stumbled over the unfamiliar word. "Who are the Nih-aw... aw?" I asked, turning.

A handsome man with warm, penetrating eyes stared back at me. His powerful look practically knocked me over. I broke the gaze by inspecting the array of feathers that dressed his hair. Their asymmetry was mesmerizing.

"Nih-aw-thaw," he pronounced slowly. "Nihancan of the earth. Spider, Trickster, Fool, Crazy Man. He is known by all of these. It was the closest identity we could understand. Naturally, this is how we referred to the settlers when they arrived in our valley."

I listened to what he said, still looking at the feathers in his hair.

"Thunderbird feathers," he said.

"What?" I asked.

"The feathers, I gathered them from the thunderbird nest at the Gateway of the Upper Worlds," he answered.

The local tribes knew about the thunderbird nest. I repeated the phrase 'Gateway of the Upper Worlds' in my mind, so I could reference it in my journal later.

"Yes. It is part of our mythology," he said, in response to my thoughts.

I wasn't surprised that he knew what I was thinking. His presence, his demeanor, his eyes all spoke of extraordinary power and awareness. He was looking at the village with fondness and love.

"Why have you come? Why visit us in this time?" he asked.

"In a future time, I am seeking a guide. I was directed here by…" I hesitated. I wasn't sure describing Ophanim angels or the rotunda would be possible.

"Winged spirits," I said.

"Winged spirits?"

"With big eyes," I said, placing my thumbs and forefingers together in front of my eyes.

"Yes, diamond birds of many eyes!" he exclaimed with reverence.

He gave a warmhearted smile down to his pinpoint star.

"Are there no guides in your time?" he asked.

"Yes, there are guides, but I was directed here to find you."

He closed his eyes and was quiet for a long while.

When he broke his silence, he said, "I have consulted the Great Eagle. He suggests I be your guide, as long as you visit the Valley of Real People."

"Thank you. I am honored," I responded. "Will you travel back with me?"

I was not sure how I'd contact him in my time on the landscape. I realized I didn't even know his name.

Before I could ask, he said, "I am Chief Niwot, but you may call me Left Hand."

He held up his left hand, palm facing me, and I held up mine in return.

"Here is a token," he said as he handed me a thunderbird feather taken from his hair. "Whenever you wish to consult me, hold it out in front of your forehead and picture the mountain village. Then, I will come."

I bowed slightly and tucked the feather into the pocket of

my vest. He smiled as I gave him a gratitude rose in return, stood up, and vanished.

I sprang to my feet joyfully.

Waiting by the stairs of the rotunda were six angels, all acknowledging the chief. I'd never seen the Ophanim angel send out roses, but the golden roses they now tossed were brighter than sunlight. I squinted. When I did, the angels put on over-sized designer sunglasses with a synchronized flourish. I laughed at their exaggerated display.

"What?" the angels asked. "Too much?"

"Oh, no. Your antics continually surprise me."

With that, one angel started an auction process. Four others began the bidding, trying to outdo each other while the sixth angel peeled off his backside. I looked at the hole left behind; it spiraled into a star-filled cosmos.

Their bidding process, starting in the millions, went backwards, each subsequent bid decreasing.

"Of course, that's how they do it!" I chuckled.

The auctioneer looked my way, encouraging me to bid. The others were down to a four bid, a three bid, a two bid, and then they stopped. All of them turned toward me.

The auctioneer shouted, "Now!"

I was perplexed for a moment, then I realized what I had to do.

"I bid one inner star!" I yelled, much louder than I needed to.

"Sold!" the auctioneer shouted, "To the warrior extraordinaire for one inner star."

What, I'd won an angel's backside? I chuckled at the thought, though I realized it wasn't the point.

"There is only one point," came the choral response from the Ophanim angels as they headed to the rotunda.

The round trip through the hypercube and back to Haystack

Mountain in present time was accompanied by a flash, a blink, a sneeze, and a fart. Yes, an angel farted in the rotunda just before we landed on top of the mountain. Everyone jumped out, including me.

Maybe the Ophanim angels were sky Nihancans. They were crazy tricksters, too.

"I wonder if Chief Left Hand knew anything more about them," I thought as I slid my hand into my vest pocket and caressed the thunderbird feather.

Bobby was standing by the large stone with a stick.

"Where have you been?" he asked, striking a ball toward the driving range.

"Just goofing with some angels."

"I didn't know angels golfed," he said, genuinely surprised.

"I…" I was about to explain the misunderstanding when I realized it didn't matter to either of us whether the angels were goofing or golfing. Either one was mind-boggling to consider.

Our trip down the north side of the mountain was easy. There was no Land Witch, no web, and no need to ask for the Key of Synchronicity's help. As we exited the trail and stepped onto the road, there was a sign. I couldn't read it, so I asked Bobby what it said.

"Oh, it's nothing. It is written in gnome language. It reads, 'Exit Only!' In small letters at the bottom it says, 'P.S. Ignore this sign if you have previously made it to the top. If not, your teacher has instructions and a map.'"

I wanted to be upset, but I couldn't manage it. This must be all part of my training to become free. Free of the contrivances of my mind, heart, and will.

"This was just another test of my mettle," I sighed.

"Metal," Bobby responded. "My favorite thing to mine!"

A week later, I was strolling along Canyon Boulevard. A crowd had gathered around a life-sized statue. I worked my way toward it. It was a facsimile of an indigenous man. I was stunned when I read the inscription. "Chief Niwot."

The city had recently decided to honor him. I couldn't help but wonder if meeting him on top of Haystack Mountain 150 years ago had influenced the city spirits to place a statue in the garden today.

I looked closely at the face and began to protest, "This doesn't look anything like him!"

A well-dressed man standing beside me laughed and said sarcastically, "How would you know what he looked like?"

I didn't answer. A mystic's life is a secret affair, and there was no need to say anything.

Theo's words came back to me as I passed by the courthouse, cut over to Arapahoe Avenue, and entered Fine Park.

"Do the research. Engage the land. In time, the results of the work will influence others. Believers and non-believers alike will all benefit in some way."

The river was low this time of year, and the standing stones were piled high. I recalled the grazing horses from my trip back in history. I stroked the chief's feather. The soft sound of drumbeats began, followed by a low chanting. Dozens of warriors dressed in decorative regalia danced around a fire in the center of the park. I was mesmerized by their sacredness. I was hearing-seeing them, not seeing-seeing. The ceremonial sounds warmed my inner star.

CHAPTER TWENTY-FOUR

FINAL JOURNEY

"THIS MAY BE OUR last journey together," Theo said as he showed me a map.

The map depicted an expanse of the solar system. I couldn't quite place it, but I deduced it was somewhere between the Earth and the sun.

Right now, the map wasn't important. Theo's 'last journey' comment was dominating my mind. I had questions; questions I really didn't want to know the answers to.

"This will be your most difficult journey yet," he continued, "and it may be my last, but we do have a rare opportunity to free a star being."

I wanted to protest, to stop him from explaining any more, to leave immediately, go back to bed, and wake up from this terrible dream; but I knew I couldn't. All I could do was create fortification roses, replace my grounding cords, climb back into my center-of-head chair, and listen to what he had to say.

"Getting to this location is going to take all the knowledge and tools at my disposal," he said. "I know for certain we will get there, and I can send you home safely. Me returning is a different matter. It is reassuring to know you finally found your spirit guide; there's more to discover on the Trail of Sages, and I wasn't comfortable leaving you without some supervision."

I stood open-mouthed. If I knew finding my spirit guide was all the excuse Theo needed to depart, I would have avoided the mission.

"The timing, calculations, and energy involved are impossible to explain," Theo continued. "Needless to say, impeccability will rule the day."

I felt an explosion of energy rising like freshly tapped oil from a rig, gushing hundreds of feet into the air. The surge slammed against my stomach, pushed its way to my heart, throttled up to my throat, and entered the center of my head. With no exit available at the top of my skull, the pressure built up inside my body. If I didn't release it soon, I would pass out, throw up, or scream. I waited like a bystander to see which would happen first.

"Ironically, this journey will happen on the Fourth of July, the same day a spacecraft will fly by Comet Temple for the first time," he said, pointing to a picture on the table next to the map. "They will launch a probe impacting the comet. We have to synchronize our journey with this event."

I didn't get it. What did a spacecraft, a probe, and a comet have to do with a research quest? My analyzer readied a logical protest while my inner child wanted to throw an outer tantrum.

"Science and the ingenuity of humanity can give us the ultimate boost in our geo-mythic work," Theo explained. "Sometimes, if we coordinate with scientific advancements, what we discover during our research can be verifiably extraordinary."

I still wasn't comprehending the whole picture, although that wasn't especially novel. Rarely did I understand the preparation stages of Theo-initiated adventures, but there was too much at stake to capitulate outright.

"I'm sorry, I am not following you," I finally interrupted.

"I was wondering how long you could last!" he said as he burst into laughter. When he'd calmed down, he continued, "There is a local connection that will help us. The company that helped build the spacecraft is located right here in town."

I knew exactly what he was talking about. A friend of mine worked at the aerospace company in town and had mentioned their project in passing. Now, I wished I'd paid more attention.

"The energy being of the company will assist us," Theo said.

"There are 'beings' of companies? We can talk to them?"

"Why not?" he responded.

"I never thought about it before."

"Precisely why *I* am the teacher and *you* are the mystic wannabe."

I knew Theo was teasing me, trying to get my proverbial goat. Or was he trying to distract me from my real concern of never seeing him again?

"This event is even more significant for you."

"Why?"

"The impact is scheduled to happen at the exact moment of your birth, allowing for time zone differences," Theo answered.

"What does—"

"Stop asking questions," he interrupted. "The important point is that something will be revealed to elevate your warrior status."

Theo knew that would get my attention and give me something else to focus on instead of the prospect of losing him.

"Meet me here at 10 p.m. on July fourth."

"Won't the fireworks be distracting?"

Theo chuckled and said, "We can use the explosive activity to propel our booster rocket."

In the two days that followed, I was dizzy thinking about Theo's proposal. I kept busy, punching the clock at work, maintaining my bicycle, and rifling through my journal notes to help take my mind off things. I spent an entire evening with Miss Montgomery, helping with the jobs she was now too frail to handle herself. She was happy to have my company, but she commented that something was clearly worrying me. She was right; they were the longest two days of my life.

I checked the company's website about the mission. Cruising at 64,000 mph, the manmade spacecraft would have to catch up to the comet, match its speed, and then launch a probe. The mission was to impact the surface, thereby loosening some debris and providing the main spacecraft with samples to analyze. It sounded like a mission any sensible person would stay away from.

On my next visit, I raced my bike toward Theo's house expecting to see a 'For Sale' sign. I thought about his library, imagining all those wonderful books packed up, ready to be shipped off to who knew where? Would they be available to visit? Did he have relatives? What were they like? Were they mystics, too, or just ordinary people living somewhere in the suburbs? Were any of Theo's family members still alive?

I pushed those questions out of my mind; I had more important things to ask.

"Why do we need to free a star being? How did he get trapped in Comet Temple? How do we get to the comet? How will I get back? Why aren't you returning with me?"

My rapid-fire list of questions fell on deaf ears.

Theo was studying some schematics, on which he had plotted a few trajectories with dotted lines. He had crossed out a couple of them with a red marker, and now only one survived and reached the comet. I assumed that would be our path.

When he didn't acknowledge my presence, I repeated, "How did a star being get trapped in Comet Temple?"

"Why ask me? Ask him," Theo answered sharply.

"Why do we need to free him? I mean, why us? What about other star beings? Can't they help him instead?"

"I don't know," Theo replied, allowing my 'why' question to slide by without reprimand.

I tried again with a practical question.

"How will we get to the comet?"

"How do you get around on any of your quests?" Theo asked in return.

"By using the rotunda?"

He was focused on the map and didn't respond.

"How will I get back?"

Still nothing.

I was reluctant to push him on the one question that really mattered the most.

Why wouldn't he be returning with me?

The silence ended before I could get up the nerve.

"Enough! Time to prepare for travel: run through the Logos meditation; get your warrior gear in order; give yourself ten suns each of clarity, worthiness, seniority and validation, then fifty suns of amusement. I'll meet you at the rotunda site."

I did as he instructed.

Twenty minutes later, I walked along the rim of the blue dish, expecting Theo to be standing alongside the rotunda. Sure enough, he was there, but not the rotunda. Well not the rotunda I knew.

It was dressed in a novel façade, decorated with painted sheets loosely wrapped around the six columns and over the tiled roof. Spaceship segments copied from a 1950s sci-fi movie were hand-painted on the sheets. My artist eye's appraisal? It could have been created by a ten-year-old child, but not a talented one.

The portholes, engine, and riveted metal facade were overshadowed by massive coil springs, while the freshly painted outer door boasted a handle borrowed from a haunted mansion. A bent lightning rod sat on top of the rocket nose, kinked two-thirds of the way up its length.

I peeked inside and saw three chairs set up adjacent to the usual bench seating, each between two of the Ophanim angel columns. They appeared as if salvaged from an old barber shop, with multiple rips in their leather patched with duct tape. A shredded strap used for sharpening straight-edge razors was hanging on the side.

I turned around and looked at Theo with a concerned expression.

He laughed and said, "What did you expect? A private jet? First-class seating?"

I didn't know what to say.

Each angel was dressed appropriately for their apparent role on our trip.

One was a luggage handler; one a flight attendant; another was a runway worker holding two truncated, orange lightsabers; two were dressed in pilot uniforms; and the sixth wore headphones, sitting in front of an oversized microphone.

"Rotunda traffic control, no doubt!" Theo said, when I rolled my eyes in disbelief.

I was even more dubious than before. He leaned against the side of the rotunda and laughed, wiping away tears with his handkerchief.

"We are taking the journey of a lifetime, but I'm not sure

what is happening. You may not make it back, and this is what we're relying on?" I protested before cracking up myself.

When our laughter subsided, the angel attendant walked up to us and said, "Seatbelt, anyone? One gold coin. Optional, of course."

I looked at Theo. We both laughed again, uncontrollably.

"Amusement is a necessary element in facing the magnificence of the geo-mythic world," Theo reminded me. "Impeccability is achievable when fear is cracked open by laughter. Now, shall we get started?"

"I guess so."

We took the three steps up onto the rotunda. The captain sat in the chair opposite the stairs. Theo climbed into the seat on the right, and I took the one on the left.

Once we were strapped in, the flight controller spoke into the microphone. He was sitting to my right, just in front of me, but his amplified voice came through a speaker above my head.

"This is Flight Control One. The only one. Our destination today is Comet Temple. I am your angelic, blow-by-blow announcer. I will describe every excruciating moment of your journey."

I looked at Theo.

"Excruciating?"

"Your pilot is Ophanim. Your co-pilot is Ophanim. Co-pilot Ophanim will take over if, under any circumstance, Ophanim cannot complete the flight. If co-pilot Ophanim cannot take over due to an unforeseen incident, and there will be many, flight attendant Ophanim will take over. He is a fully trained and a highly-skilled substitute. If flight attendant Ophanim fails miserably, I, as your controller, will take on the dubious task of attempting to fly this facsimile."

The runway angel interrupted by popping his head through the doorway.

"I have training! What about me?"

The controller started mouthing words but stopped when he realized we couldn't quite hear him, and he turned back toward the microphone.

"Our illustrious comrade, who has volunteered to sit outside the door on our journey, guiding us with his light-sabers, is also available to take over in case the rest of us are incapacitated."

Incapacitated? Were the angels intentionally trying to frighten me?

"Relax. Whenever the amusement factor is high, it's a warning to level up your clarity and fine-tune your focus," Theo reminded me.

Although I quickly gave myself the necessary suns, my fondest wish was to cancel the flight and return to a modest landscape quest.

"Isn't there an assignment we can accomplish that will give us a little more preparation? Like a short trip over the moon?" I asked.

Luckily, Theo had purchased a seatbelt, as it kept him from falling out of his chair with laughter. I, in a bit of a panic, laughed nervously. Being accustomed to the Ophanim angels and their antics was not reassuring. To say I was dubious was an understatement.

"Relax," Theo said after he'd regained control of himself. "The Ophanim angels are being overly entertaining for your benefit."

"For my benefit?" I responded. "Can't they tell how scared I am?"

"Oh, they know," Theo reassured me. "That's exactly why they ramped up the amusement.

"Breathe deeply and relax."

My wisdom guides gave me an inner smile, my analyzer went quiet, and I breathe a sigh of relief.

I shifted into a nonchalant state and said, "If they aren't concerned about this trip, why should I worry?"

Theo turned to me and said, "Either you're frightened out of your wits, or you're so detached you would invite death himself to lunch."

I sat stoically, feeling little need to protest.

"We are ready to take off," said the pilot angel. "Any last requests? I mean, any final words? If you were wise enough to purchase a seatbelt, buckle up. If not, well, we may deploy airbags in an emergency."

We lifted off and flew toward downtown Boulder.

"Why are we headed over the city?" I leaned over and asked Theo with a hushed voice.

"Why are you whispering?" Theo asked. "And why do you think I know the answer? Just enjoy the view."

I looked out a makeshift porthole set up between the rotunda columns to my left.

I never went on research journeys this late, and the city looked different at night. The sky was clear, with everything well lit. People walked about on Pearl Street, and the football stadium at the university was filling up for the fireworks display. The celebration around town was in full swing.

We headed toward Fine Park, looped around the city, and flew directly over the aerospace company that built the spacecraft. Then we returned to the park once more.

As we landed, the Ophanim angel announced, "We are making a momentary fuel stop. Feel free to stand and stretch if you didn't purchase a seatbelt. To those who did, well, we apologize, but you are fastened in for the duration."

"Fuel stop?" I cried, visually pleading for Theo to stop this calamity.

He didn't reply.

I chose not to stand up but gripped the leather arms of my chair firmly.

In a few minutes, the controller announced, "Recline your seats. Next stop, hypercube."

That made sense, the hypercube was right above the park. It would be the easiest way to get to the comet.

The rotunda took off sideways this time, toward the river, then made a beeline to the west entrance of the hypercube. The cube, slowly spinning on its axis, made the entrance an easy moving target, but we bypassed it and headed to the top right-hand corner. As we drew closer, the surfaces changed. Multiple conduits extended out from the cube. Hovering for a moment, we dove to the intersection of the origination point. We accelerated toward the opening even though, by my estimates, it wasn't large enough for the rotunda to pass through. Fortunately, my assumption went untested by entering a tube-like structure with a swift-moving current. The rotunda wormed its way through pitch-black space.

I heard a soft popping sound and looked out of the porthole. There it was: a large, icy rock zipping along intrepidly. Our speed and rotation matched its slow tumble. Its trail of debris was in front, not behind, the comet, having orbited the sun earlier on its journey.

"There it is. Comet Temple," I said. "But…it doesn't make sense. How does a comet…"

I stopped mid-sentence. Theo was looking through a telescope, examining its surface.

"What are you doing?" I asked Theo.

"Trying to find the best place to land."

"Won't the angels determine that? They always have in the past," I said, thinking of my past rotunda adventures. "The angels always choose the landing zone."

"Only for warriors in training. We discovered long ago that, if the Ophanim angels didn't help, trainees would get hopelessly lost."

It made sense; I had no idea what made for a good rotunda landing spot.

"I believe I've found the best landing zone," Theo said, looking away from the telescope. He unbuckled his seatbelt, saying, "It's time to launch."

Immediately, the controller's voice came over the speaker.

"It is not advisable to unbuckle your seatbelt or leave your seat before the rotunda has come to a complete stop!"

I automatically got up and followed Theo, but I wasn't quite sure where he was going. We were still hurling through space.

"It is not advisable to follow someone who has unbuckled his belt and gotten out of his seat," the controller insisted.

I paused to sit back down, but Theo signaled me to follow him. He stepped up to the diamond in the center of the rotunda and pushed on a small panel.

"You are not allowed to touch that. Except in case of emergency," the angel said, raising his voice to a higher pitch.

I wasn't sure what was going on. Was Theo going rogue on the Ophanim angels? This lack of cooperation between Theo and the angels was unsettling. My confusion was growing, but I had always followed Theo unquestioningly. Well, maybe I hadn't always obeyed his *advice*, but I'd always followed him on the landscape, knowing I would be safe.

The rotunda shook with a strong vibration. It felt like a

powerful band saw motor slowly ramping up to speed. The diamond, in the middle of the rotunda, slid sideways.

"Follow me," Theo said as he stepped down through the opening.

I did.

The controller, sounding panicked, said, "It is not permissible to climb down there *or* for anyone to follow."

"I didn't know this was here," I said to Theo as we stepped down a spiral staircase.

We circled down seven turns and ended up on a platform underneath the rotunda. There was an apparatus set up at the edge, facing the comet.

"Just do what I do. Exactly," Theo ordered. "No delays. Immediately. Got it?"

"Alright," I answered, still uncertain what was going on.

I could see the comet racing alongside us, some 500 yards away. We'd moved a lot closer to it since I'd last looked.

"Using the slingshot device is not allowed," I heard the voice of the controller say.

"The *slingshot* device?" I exclaimed.

Theo was already climbing into the device. I watched as he slid his feet onto a single rung that hung from rubbery chains. He reached down and pulled a lever. The swing-like device pulled backwards slowly, stretching until it snapped back like an elastic band and launched Theo through space toward the comet.

I was flabbergasted!

He landed gently on his feet.

"Your turn," he shouted as he waved his arm for me to follow.

This was ludicrous. Traveling in space alongside a comet, and I was about to slingshot from the rotunda.

"This is crazy," I said.

"It is not advisable to be crazy. Nor is it appropriate to use that contraption or be out of your seat while the rotunda is still moving," the angel controller's voice echoed down the stairs.

It was too much – if the angels thought it was a bad idea and *I* thought it was a bad idea, why was I taking the risk? I didn't understand the necessity of what we were doing, and I definitely didn't want to lose Theo over it! Besides, when it came down to it, I just didn't have it in me to slingshot across the void of space.

"That's exactly where you have it," my wisdom guides whispered. "Look inside."

I could have pretended not to know what they meant, but even as they said it, I felt the energy of all my tools activating. The Michael's sword, the gifts of the sky dancers, the Dragon Master, and the Gnome King were all lighting up. The Solar Mage's benefaction, my stupa, and the blessings of the Logos Meditation all came to support this impossible moment. Whatever I told myself, I *was* ready for this, and it was Theo who had made sure of that. I needed to trust him this one, final time, even if it meant disobeying the Ophanim angels.

As soon as I made up my mind, I realized. This was a cosmic joke the angel pranksters were playing on me; a test! My confidence soared and I stepped onto the platform, pulled the lever, and shot across the gap between the rotunda and the comet with ease, landing right next to Theo.

He looked at me, bewildered.

"What?" I asked. "Did I do it correctly?"

"Impeccably."

"Good. Now, let's find the star being."

I looked back toward the rotunda. It was gone. We were walking on a comet in space with no way back. I quickened my pace to catch up with Theo, who was moving swiftly. We veered left around a crevice. Fifty paces later, we were face to face with an icy rock wall too sheer to climb.

Theo stared at the wall. I imagined he was going to say, 'Open Sesame,' or some other invocation, but he remained silently immobile.

While I was waiting for a sign of what to do next from Theo, I had an incongruous thought. How would my traveling companions do in space? Just as I thought it, Sirius appeared, licking my face and then scampering over to sit beside Theo. No others appeared, but that made sense. They were all terrestrial whereas, in his true form, Sirius was a being of high order.

Just then, I remembered something I learned while studying with the Triple Wisdom Woman.

"When it comes to spirit beings, ignite your inner light and say, 'Show me your true image.' They can't refuse!"

What if I said these words to Sirius? Would he show me his true self?

"Sirius," I called out, "show me your true image."

From deep inside Sirius, a spark of light began to expand. It grew larger than his body, then exploded. The burst encompassed me and Theo, the comet, then outspread into space. After the supernova, an elegant, beautiful, white-robed being stood next to Theo - in place of the dog disguise. He wore a sash that started at his upper right shoulder and trailed down to his left hip. On it were images of stars, planets, and moons.

Theo looked at me, then at Sirius. Was he visible to Theo? As far as I knew, Theo never noticed him as a dog. When Theo gave me a slight smile, I understood. Sirius was the answer! He could help us free the star being trapped inside the comet.

"Would you help us? We came here to free the being trapped in this comet," I asked Sirius directly.

Sirius answered, "When the visible sun rises, the invisible speaks pictures of knowing. It is the morning's mind and the imagination's longing eye which see the consequences of the nighttime event. This comet's impact, the eyes of the world set upon it with fascination, will transfix the consciousness of humanity.

"The depiction, a stream of light moving from the sun, seeds the soul's inquisitive eye. A ribboning energy bridge stretches out to capture the forces released by the comet. A tunneling energy stream reaches out, floating on the solar wind, rippling through space back to the sun."

Sirius turned to face the wall. His words were poetry to my ears. A beam of light shot out from his heart and penetrated the wall, melting it away and giving us a clear view of the interior of the comet. A staircase spiraled down to a crystalline cathedral. Sirius moved forward. We followed until the stairs ended at a set of large doors. Intimidating, monstrous giants loomed on either side, brandishing scimitars.

"Who calls upon this sanctuary?" they confronted in unison.

"It is I, brother of all stars, sister to all planets, cousin to all celestial bodies, one of many fathers of life seeded throughout the cosmos. I am an ancient king of this comet," Sirius responded.

The two beings bowed their heads, almost down to their feet. When they did, I could see angelic faces on the back of their skulls, just the opposite of their dark and grotesque forward faces.

Sirius stepped through as the doors swung open.

We were inside an arched vestibule with floor-to-ceiling windows that looked out onto a great expanse. It was not icy rock, nor the black of outer space, but a lush garden with abundant trees, flowers, fruit, and grazing animals. The sound of birds, amphibians, and honeybees surrounded us. If it were a reproduction of the Garden of Eden, it was perfect.

In the middle of the great room was a replica of the rotunda. It served as a fountain of liquid energy. At the far end of the great space was a predominant wall. As we stepped closer, I could see an image embossed upon it. I stared at it, trying to recognize the impression. As hard as I tried, I couldn't identify it.

Sirius, staff in hand, stopped a few feet from the wall and proclaimed, "Messenger of light, it is time to walk upon the bridge that travels from the comet's open door to the spiritual sun."

When he did, the image unraveled. From its tight, localized outline on the wall, it unfurled into the room. The struggling image molded itself into a familiar shape. She looked like Sirius, with minor variations in her sash and staff. She had a glowing face that shone a loving kindness that touched the sacred interior of my heart.

When she spoke, the words sounded in the atmosphere around us, shaping themselves into a collective, poetic language.

"How long has vision looked out upon the cosmos since that moment when freedom was encountered by a pinpoint of sound echoing toward the human place called 'Earth?'

"I remember stories about the dark place before my journey began. A source, a commemoration, called me from its center, and I believed what I heard. He told me that, one day, I would return from my travels. A return that would seed the very clusters I traverse.

"Is now that time?

"Like a key, this unknown interloper penetrates the lock and frees me without a precise alignment. Just a required entry into my

secret space. It succeeds. I could only imagine that he who sheltered me away on this barge of tumbling, frozen water allowed me to spray out drops of dew in the hopes that someday I would flourish upon an inviting home.

"Has it voiced a call to return? I do not remember.

"My brother, you stand before me with two of Gaia. My containment unfurls like a ribbon, propelled by a certain force in no recognizable direction.

"My unfolding passageway continues, stretching out among those who I have seen so often from a distance and now look on in wonderment; cousins all.

"Somehow, this arching journey is bridging my isolation, stretched over the span of a far country not traveled in my memory before. The journey's end attracts me now, reminding me of a beginning thought and a following sound having propelled me out onto this voyage so long ago.

"As I arch down from the height of this spanning bridge, brightness surfaces, enlivening the road ahead. Faster and faster, it pulls me with its magnetic power, overshadowing any determination on my part. Along this path, the energy flows, inviting a return of the messenger. How strange it seems, at first, to my coherent mind. Then the recognition of the source tells the tale.

"His plan to influence the cluster of beings on the Terra, to entice my escape by unlocking the messenger's fortress, was prearranged upon this night of recall. Thank you, Brother.

"Memories flood back upon my tableau as I step upon the shores of my long-lost home. My address was not lost but much like others I journeyed, with purpose, to far-off lands, never knowing whether I would return. Forgetfulness made remembering, returning, impossible.

"Had I known the One would call me back at His discretion, would I have grieved so long, so far in unending flight through *the vastness of His breath? This breath unseen would light up and shine brightly at times, always returning me to my dependence on the reflection of His countenance.*

"And now, this key so cunningly crafted by His image, hidden in the souls of Adams/Eves, lifts off from a dark place of noiseless meaning, hidden from view.

"And now I am free. Returned, greeted by those who love, forever. This is my family. Solar brothers and sisters. I remember now, for unveiled in my mind is the momentous nature of my journey.

"This clarity will one day voice my story to the 'blameless ones' who choose to remain in innocence, knowing only His love."

When the star being finished speaking, she grew exponentially with explosive force encompassing the planets, the sun, and beyond. This must be what people heard when they encountered the Holy Spirit-inspired apostles. The words rising out of their hearts, traveling across their tongues, understood by the deep love in every listener.

She departed, seeding indefinite space. I used my inner eyes to look upon the planet and watched as energetic seed pods floated down upon every continent, distributed to every creature on land and sea. A soft, white, cottony light surrounded the planet, penetrating deep into every particle of life.

"She has come. I must go," Sirius said, breaking the mesmerizing vision of the Earth. He moved closer to the wall.

"Wait a minute," I shouted, my voice echoing throughout the great room. "Where are you going?"

The star being turned toward me, changed back into my familiar white dog and said, "I am not going anywhere. Someone must return to the outer rim and share the Word."

"What Word? Why you?" I exclaimed, feeling desperate.

"It is ordained."

I was at a loss. Sirius would no longer be accompanying me on my research journeys.

"Who will guide and protect me?" I asked.

He pointed to the wall. On it was a picture of a tiny white puppy sleeping at the foot of my bed.

"She will take my place."

"Kind of small for a protector," I quipped.

"Do not let her size deceive you. She is a powerful star being. Nothing will dare to approach you in her company. Not without your permission."

Sirius turned back to the wall and merged into it, now resembling the inexpressible image of a comet star being.

I turned to Theo. I wondered what had been going on with him all this time. He hadn't said a word or moved from the spot on which he stood.

He was in a stupor, frozen with a gentle smile on his face and a tear rolling down his cheek.

"Theo?" I asked.

He didn't answer. I wasn't sure if he heard me.

"Theo?" I asked again.

He began moving his lips and mouth as if coming back from a very deep meditative state.

"Yes, I heard you. Sirius is right. It's time for you to go now."

"What about you? Aren't you coming with me?"

I already knew the answer. He had warned me of this. But I was still in denial.

"It's not just a river in Egypt," he quipped, apparently reading my mind. "I will stay and accompany Sirius on the journey around the back of the sun. After that, only the Logos can say."

"Will I see you again?" I asked, afraid of the answer.

SIRIUS

"I do not know."

"At least tell me there's a chance."

"Well, there *is* a chance, but it's remote. When the comet comes around again, there will be an opportunity to visit. You seem to be adept at dancing across the landscape, not to mention across space. Who knows? You may dance across the stars one day."

"I will look for you when the comet returns."

"Good," he said, "but don't neglect those who will still be with you. You discovered an ancient cave, found a secret scroll, freed the Water Dragon *and* the Dragon Master, transported a golden egg; all consequences that came about because you listened to your Dream Talker and acted on what you were told. That is what we must do: take action, even when our doubts chitter-chatter away."

"I'll do my best," I said, but then a thought struck me. "Oh, Theo, what about your books? They're what brought us together, but now I'm worried—"

Theo's laughter interrupted me.

"Listen to you," he said after wiping the moisture from his eyes with his silk handkerchief. "You have your *own* small library of journals and scraps of paper filled with…" he paused, stuck his right index finger out in front of him and traced the word 'words.' It was written in an elegant flaming script.

"How did you do that?" I asked, mesmerized by the dancing letters hanging between us. They gradually faded to ash as Theo continued.

"All that, and yet the words you have written will be useless unless you compile them into a tome."

"Who would be interested in that?"

"Well, I might have asked the same question, once upon a time," said Theo, "but look at you now, worried about *my* collection. Take what you want but rest assured that my books will find themselves where they're needed. Use that curious energy to write your own. Who knows? It may even become a bestseller. Now, it's time for you to go home. There's a surprise waiting in the near future that you're not going to want to miss."

"Is there?" I asked, but he only smiled and turned away.

I headed toward the large doors at the entrance of the great room but stopped, turned back and asked, "How do I do that? You know, return to Earth?"

He laughed and said, "Look out the window."

I walked over to the windows overlooking the garden. A new rotunda stood there, no longer draped in makeshift decorations. It sat in the middle of the garden with the Ophanim angels bathing in a fountain of lilac light. They were dressed in their very best 1920s beachwear, bathing caps and all.

"Just ride the spiffy rotunda home with them," Theo said. He was right; the rotunda was streamlined – redesigned to look like a corporate jet. "But wait until they've finished bathing in the fountain. It's their favorite thing to do."

Theo turned and sat down on a camping chair, facing the wall.

"How did that—" I began as Theo faded into the wall and disappeared; his blue chair included.

I should have been sad, but I was elated. I walked down a flight of stairs between the large windows, exited through a small door, and entered the garden. The birds, the animals, the breeze, the water, they all felt invigorating. As I moved toward the rotunda, I thought aloud.

"If Theo is gone and may not come back, does that mean I'll take his place?"

"Don't bet on it," his voice bellowed. "You have a lot more

to learn. Another comet would have to come and go before you're ready!"

I couldn't help but laugh, no suns of amusement needed.

I sat in the rotunda and watched the Ophanim angels rehearse their diving.

What was Theo doing? How would Sirius fare on his long journey? What about the star being puppy on Earth? There were no answers, so I let my questions melt away.

The garden's beauty silenced me. There was nothing more to think, nothing more to do, and nowhere to go until the angels were ready to leave.

"Come on," the angels shouted, "show us your best dive!"

Oh, what the heck? I stepped off the rotunda, estimated the distance, and ran full force at the fountain. I heard angelic applause as I dove into the water.

A CONVERSATION

ETURNING FROM MY LAST adventure without Theo took a lot of adjustment, but it wasn't the only major change I encountered. My friend Miss Montgomery passed away suddenly in my absence. Soon after, I received a certified letter asking me to attend a meeting at a lawyer's office in town. I thought maybe I was in trouble for trespassing on someone's private land during my research, perhaps having broken a fence or trampled a bush. I never considered the letter had anything to do with the widow.

When I arrived at the office, a small group of people were sitting solemnly around a large table in a conference room. A proper, portly man in a pinstripe suit sat down at the head of the table and said, "Welcome, everyone, to the reading of Miss Margret Montgomery's Last Will and Testament."

I was shocked. The last time I'd seen her, we'd had a lovely conversation about her upcoming travels.

"No need to visit next week," she'd said. "Who knows, I may not return from visiting my sister. I'm looking forward to staying with her again."

MISS MONTGOMERY

But now, sitting in this lawyer's office, I realized she knew she was going to die. It made me sad to think I wouldn't see her again. I shifted my gaze and looked at her death with my second sight. It was beautiful. She hovered over her physical body for a few minutes and looked down at the handful of relatives sitting nearby. The bored looks on their faces had said it all: none were crying or even sad, so thankfully no emotional attachments to hold her back. Her subtle body, free of its physical entanglements, moved through the sun and entered a swirling white vortex.

As she passed through, angels and large groups of familiar souls welcomed her, inviting her forward with sweet-sounding orchestral music and a chorus of voices. In life, she was elegant. In death, her elegance became spectacular.

Tears of joy gathered at the corners of my eyes. Good thing I'd taken on Theo's habit of carrying a handkerchief. When I wiped my tears away, it looked like I was sad about Miss Montgomery's death. But the probing glares of the attendees around the table did not go unnoticed. They had to be wondering who this stranger was sitting next to them.

The lawyer read preliminary legal information about the legitimacy of the will, the amount of time allowed for contesting it, and how the settlement of money and property would take place. After the comprehensive ledger of disbursements was read, a list of properties was handed out to everyone. I glanced down at the copy in front of me. Next to each house or piece of land was a name. I wasn't sure why I was provided with the list. I presumed it was a formality.

I continued to scan the list while the lawyer read it out, naming each property and person, and finishing each line by saying, "All associated taxes in perpetuity shall be paid by the estate."

Receiving a property with the taxes already paid sounded quite generous.

I was impressed by the amount of property Miss Montgomery had accumulated throughout her life, not to mention the amount of money being distributed. As I reached the bottom of the list, the lawyer's pronouncements caught up to my scanning.

"...and finally, the house at 6662 Beached Rock Road is hereby bequeathed to Miss Montgomery's dear friend," he said, with a gesture in my direction.

I wasn't sure I heard him correctly, even though my name was written on the piece of paper right in front of me.

"This must be some mistake!" I protested.

As soon as I did, everyone at the table began to grow uncomfortable, fidgeting in their chairs and looking around in bewilderment. I began throwing red roses at the chaotic energy. When the protests and complaints grew louder, the energy was rather nasty. Suns of seniority, certainty, and validation helped smooth things out. I was tempted to put on my cloak of invisibility and my mystic chainmail, perhaps even to unsheathe a sword, but I didn't. I realized it wasn't necessary. The blue bubble of my energy field was intact, and the red roses absorbed all the dark, dank, distorted energy coming at me. I sent them down to the center of the Earth to be alchemized. A few minutes later, the room was quiet again.

"That concludes the dispersing process," said the lawyer. "See my assistant if you have any questions."

He promptly stood up and left the room. I quickly followed, not wanting to engage the group around the table. I was about to go out the front door of the building when the lawyer stopped me.

"Would you mind stepping into my office for a moment?"

"Of course," I responded sheepishly. I wasn't sure what he wanted, but I was confident the family would protest and file a petition to keep me from receiving the house.

"Please take a seat. I won't keep you long," he said tentatively.

This wasn't the same stoic energy I'd experienced from him in the conference room. It was shy, meek, even kind.

"I have something for you," the lawyer said as he handed me a small, sealed envelope. Inside was a card with a hand-written a note.

My little angel. Thank you for the roses, the suns, the blue dish, the rotunda, the sword blessings and, most of all, the angels who accompanied you to my house each week.

I looked up, stunned. How had she known? Why didn't she say something? She never revealed she could 'see.'

I continued reading.

I so enjoyed the angels' company. They gave me hours and hours of fun. They only asked me one favor in return: to give you my house above the Trail of Sages so you can continue your research.

I'd never told her any of these things, and she'd never let on that she knew, but here it was, written in her beautiful handwriting.

The invisible world, your guardian angels, and your friends will all help to give you exactly what you need to fulfill your destiny. Maybe someday you will play a role in helping course-correct the destiny of the planet. Just silence your mind, still your heart, and listen. All will be given as all is received.

Those words, 'all will be given as all is received,' were repeated at the beginning of training sessions and at the end of landscape excursions. Had Miss Montgomery been a mystic?

Thank you again and enjoy the house. Do not worry. I made sure, with the help of the Ophanim angels, to secure your ownership. Why else would they set up a rotunda inside the great room of the house?

"Really?" I mused. "That should be quite a sight."

See you on your journeys. Love, Miss Montgomery.

With that, I tucked the card into my vest pocket and stood up to leave.

"Before you leave," the lawyer said, "I have to ask you a question."

"What would that be?"

"How did you do it?"

"Do what?"

"Give her such happiness and joy during your weekly visits. No one else did. When she came in and made these changes to her will, she would light up when we discussed you. She seemed to grow young again. Her whole body, her mind, her heart changed so dramatically during the time she knew you. She was truly happy."

"I just enjoyed her company," I responded, not knowing what else to say.

"Well, whatever secret you have, what you shared with her was greatly appreciated. As a longtime friend and benefactor, she gave me the opportunity to become a lawyer. So, thank you for giving her what I wished I could have. The important thing is that she received it. From someone. From somewhere."

"We never know where the extraordinary gifts of life will come from. We just need to believe." That was all I could think to say as I shook his hand and left his office.

Weeks later, now set up in my new house, I could see the Water Dragon, the Fire Dragon, and the Dragon Master from the huge living room of the Beached Rock house. The rotunda, a permanent fixture in the center of the room, appeared perceptibly ready whenever I needed it.

"Not today," I concluded, throwing the sound of my voice toward the six columns and imagining the angels got the message. I grabbed my hiking pole, stepped out the back door, went through the gate, and turned right onto the Trail of Sages.

As I walked, the Water Dragon, perched on the north side of the valley, showered me with her dragon mist. Conversely, when I walked around the south side, below the plateau, the Fire Dragon showered me with flames.

While I moved between the two dragons, a synchronized dance of fire and water swirled around me, blending, mixing, cleansing, and infusing me with life energy.

I focused on the lake in the middle of the oval trail to engage with the Dragon Master. His role was still a mystery to me. I assumed he would work with the dragons, but he appeared to spend little time with them.

"Greetings," I said as he materialized.

"You have come prepared to ask real questions, I see," he responded, bypassing any formal prologue. "By now, you have surmised that something is amiss."

"I understood that the dragons, like other elementals of the invisible world, help create the necessary forces like fires, floods, earthquakes, and volcanic eruptions to sustain the unseen and feed life on this planet. What I didn't understand was that freeing the Water Dragon would have such an extreme effect – triggering a hundred-year flood!

"Why not just reveal the truth about the dragons, the drought, and the floods upfront? Why not ask for my cooperation and assistance? Wouldn't it have been easier and saved a lot of trouble?"

He gave me a thoughtful look.

"There was some subterfuge. We withheld only that

information you would not be ready to act upon until you recognized a higher purpose.

"There was a time in history when we were forthcoming about such things. But, as you know, humans no longer believe in us. Aside from mystic warriors, there are few willing to live in our world. Human beings have prioritized themselves over nature and subtle beings. When they realize there is more at stake, the truth tellers will return in full force and reveal countless ways to live in harmony."

"Was the deception really necessary?"

"It was a compulsory test. Duplicity was not our intention. We counted on your wisdom guides, your teachers, and the angels to help prepare you for this day. The day we might reveal a larger truth."

"And this larger truth is?" I asked, feeling like I'd lost the thread. I checked my grounding cords and my head space, wondering if I was firmly anchored in my chair. A skeptical voice took advantage of my confusion.

"What about my Dream Talker, who started this entire journey? What about my training with Theo? My adventures with the Solar Mage? And the Michael? Should I doubt them, too?"

The Dragon Master's voice softened. The deep compassion he projected with his words poured over me like a warm, liquid light driving away the interloper.

"There are times trainees pass through a dark night of the soul and doubts arise, only to be burnt up in the purifying fires of the heart and washed with the clarifying waters of love. But without freedom, how could any of this be possible?"

My structured beliefs were exhausted. I collapsed into a heap of thinking then quickly stepped into a perspective of disinterestedness. I could see, by standing next to this heap, how useless my constructs of reality were compared to the meaning of the Dragon Master words.

"But what of me is left?" I asked. "Am I useful? Am I even necessary?"

When I asked this, a magnificent garden encroached into the foreground. What was hidden became solid, and what was solid turned into a translucent curtain hanging behind me. I was deep within this world of light, looking out through a window at myself standing next to a pile of useless beliefs. My High Self was ecstatic with joy. My mind was silent and clear. My body became an effortless vehicle as I began to move.

The voice of the Dragon Master sounded loudly, echoing across the valley.

"Let go and embrace everything!"

I did. It was easy. I saw an energy tether connected deep inside my lower back near my kidneys that reached out, up into the sky. It was linked to the Water Dragon. I saw another tether from my heart connected to the Fire Dragon.

Their flight in the sky was smooth, graceful, rhythmic, and so was the dance of energy between my internal organs, my bones, tissues, and tendons. Everything moved together in a fluidic dance as I strolled through the gardens outside the palace and temple. The valley, naturally beautiful, was even more so. Not with just a lake, trees, fields, cows, horses, and streams, but with a newly tropical setting of waterfalls, moisture hanging in the air, creatures of land, sea, and sky, all moving in harmony together.

I could see now how the years of drought, all the fires, and now the floods fed the invisible world. I watched the dragons dance above. I felt their movements inside. I was flying, too.

Soon, it was time to shift back into the solid state of life. I knew I had to, but I didn't want to lose this vision.

"The internal and external harmony are never lost. Never gone. Never forgotten," the Dragon Master said. "We are always here to remind you if you get distracted by the every-day challenges of life. Just step out your back door and onto the trail that leads to the extraordinary!"

I headed home, golden light trailing behind me.

Each time I walked the Trail of Sages, I would repeat the process, hoping it would benefit others who used the trail. Would this help them? I wasn't sure.

But as Theo had once said, "It isn't your responsibility to know or understand how others receive the gifts of the land. It is your job as a warrior to engage, energize, and entertain the landscape. Someday, others will do the same."

THE END

ACKNOWLEDGEMENTS

I thank Richard Alan Leviton for inspiring me to write, write, write! And for his generosity in allowing me to borrow his terminology...and graciously disregarding the oversimplification of their meaning(s). I also want to thank him for his teachings, his books, and his Geomantic Landscape training which has been an invaluable reference toward motivating me to write this fantasy adventure story.

In remembrance, I acknowledge Therese, Bojilina and Ruth - the wisdom trio of my early adult years.

I would also like to thank my editors: Georgette and Rob for their professional edits. Starla for early read throughs and suggestions. Mathieu for insightful comments on final versions. Stephen for martial arts training and insights into Qigong energy. Mary for her love, support, and enthusiasm. Omraam Mikhail Aivanhov for his cosmic view.

Thank all of you; I couldn't have finished without you!

CPSIA information can be obtained
at www.ICGtesting.com
Printed in the USA
LVHW041413280720
661632LV00008B/66/J